Trespassing

Ghost Stories From the Prairie

Barbara J. Baldwin
Jerri Garretson
Linda Madl
Sheri L. McGathy

Introduction by Troy Taylor
Founder of the American Ghost Society

Compiled and Edited
by Jerri Garretson

Ravenstone Press
Manhattan, Kansas
2005

Ravenstone Press
P. O. Box 1791
Manhattan KS 66505-1791
Tel: (785) 776-0556
raven@interkan.net

These original contributions are used with permission:
Introduction ©2005 by Troy Taylor
Beyond Imagination ©2005 by Geraldine A. Garretson
Christmas at the Gates of Hell ©2005 by Linda Madl
Dance With Me ©2005 by Geraldine A. Garretson
Déjà Vu ©2005 by Barbara J. Baldwin
Dreams of the Dead ©2005 by Barbara J. Baldwin
Fireball Faye ©2005 by Geraldine A. Garretson
Forgotten, But Not Gone ©2005 by Sheri L. McGathy
The Graveyard Dance ©2005 by Sheri L. McGathy
Griselda ©2005 by Geraldine A. Garretson
Halloween at the Gates of Hell ©2005 by Linda Madl
Lost in the Fog ©2005 by Geraldine A. Garretson
Maxie ©2005 by Sheri L. McGathy
One Night at Whistling Woman Creek ©2005 by Linda Madl
The Rose ©2005 by Barbara J. Baldwin
Trespassing Time ©2005 by Linda Madl
What's a Ghost to Do? ©2005 by Sheri L. McGathy
Whisper on the Wind ©2005 by Barbara J. Baldwin

Printed at Manhattan, Kansas by Ag Press.
ISBN 0-9659712-6-0 pbk.
Library of Congress Control Number: 2004099714
Publisher's Cataloging is available on page 239.

Trespassing Time
Ghost Stories From the Prairie

Introduction
by Troy Taylor
Founder of the American Ghost Society

American cities are filled with ghosts. Their streets are packed with spirits, wandering past derelict buildings and down misty alleyways where no man in his right mind would dare to walk. Such phantoms are of a particular sort. Theirs are the familiar faces of killers and victims, miscreants and priests, trapped in a concrete jungle for eternity. Our cities can be terrifying places; there is no question of this.

But what of the ghosts who haunt our prairies and fields? We may shiver at tales of haunted mansions, blood-soaked streets and ominous hotels that make our blood run cold, but is there really anything as eerie as the vast open fields and dark stands of woods that stretch across America's Heartland? What awaits us in this strange and unfamiliar region and what tragic ghosts still walk in the lonely places where no one can hear you when you scream?

The prairie of America can be a mysterious place and, to those who come from the more populated regions, a strangely unsettling one. Even to those of us who grew up on the prairie, it's hard to know what sometimes lurks around the next corner of the road, or around the next bend in the path.

More years ago than I would care to admit now, I happened upon an old, abandoned house in the woods. Such unusual finds were not uncommon for me. I grew up on a farm in a rural part of Illinois, and during the summer months, I would often explore the back roads, cemeteries and stretches of forest near my parents' home. This particular house turned out to be a little more unusual than most, though. In fact, it was at the moment of my discovery of this old place that I began to believe in ghosts.

The old house was located in a gloomy stretch of woods and it did not appear that anyone had lived in it for many years. There was no path left through the woods that would have provided access to the surrounding road-ways. Only a shallow track remained, long since covered with brush and decades of fallen leaves. Remarkably, the structure remained in fairly good condition. I crossed the sagging porch, pushed open the leaning front door, and entered the shadowy interior hallway behind it.

Strangely, all of the furniture had been left behind, even to the point that there were photographs still hanging on the walls and coats in a closet that had a door standing open. Yes, there was evidence of animals passing through and the weathering of years passing by, but all in all, the place had been eerily preserved.

This was all strange enough to a young boy, but it was the kitchen that would unsettle me the most. It was here that I found the last real vestiges of human occupancy in the house. There were still plates and silverware resting on the table and pots and pans still sitting on the cold, metal stove. It was as if the family that had once lived here had suddenly just gotten up and walked away one day— never to return.

What could have happened to cause someone to leave a house, and to simply leave everything they owned behind, abandoning their lives and likely disappearing without a trace?

The house has long since been destroyed, and the answer to my personal mystery has never been solved. I returned many times to that house over the next several years, until I finally grew up and moved away from home. As time has passed, though, I have never forgotten this place; and the questions that were created on the day that I first found the house remain with me even now. I searched many times for some clue as to where the former occupants had vanished, but I never found anything.

I have since come to realize that this puzzle will never be solved. And like a ghost, it has haunted me ever since. At the moment that I walked into that house, I crossed a line that I have never been able to step back across. It was at that moment that the unsolved and the unexplained became an obsession for me and it was at that moment that I truly began to believe in ghosts.

Since that time, my fascination with ghosts and ghost stories has become more than just a passion. It has become a career. Much of my own writing and research is connected to America's prairie regions, exploring the dark woods and the open fields where I grew up. This is the reason I found the stories in this book so compelling. These are not tales of ghosts that you will find in the streets or in the buildings of our cities but specters who lost their way in the graveyards, forests and the open fields. It's no surprise that one can almost feel the desperation of such wraiths as they search for redemption and peace in the loneliest places in America.

How real are such restless ghosts? Obviously, the spirits who haunt these pages are the products of the fevered imaginations of the authors; many of you reading this book believe that the ghosts of the prairie are quite tangible. Many of you may even have had your own strange experiences over the years. Like many others, you may have tried to explain them away, but cannot. Readers like you are quick to accept the possibility that ghosts exist. Not everyone is so open-minded.

Those who do not believe in ghosts say that spirits are

merely the figments of our collective imagination. Ghost stories, these readers insist, are the creations of drunkards, folklorists and fools.

If you are such a person, I hope that you will not be too quick to assume that you have all of the answers. Can you really say for sure that ghosts aren't real? Are you completely convinced that spirits do not wander the wild prairies of America? These are questions that you should ask yourself, but before you immediately reply from the comfort of your warm and brightly lit home, try answering them instead while standing alone in some prairie cemetery late one night.

Is that weeping sound you hear really just the wind whispering in your ear, or could it be the voice of a long-dead woman, crying for eternal peace?

Is that merely a patch of fog that you see moving out of the trees, or could it be the ethereal form of a forgotten pioneer, still searching for his final resting place?

Is that rustling in the leaves truly just the passing breeze, or is it the ominous sound of footsteps coming up behind you?

If you suddenly turn to look, you might realize that, despite the fact that there is no living person around you, you just may not be alone! Perhaps you are not as sure as you thought you were about the existence of ghosts. Perhaps they are not simply a part of fanciful fiction after all. Perhaps no one person among us has all of the answers...

To paraphrase the poet, there are stranger things out there than are dreamt of in our philosophies, and many of those stranger things are out there lurking, waiting for some hapless soul, among the windswept plains of the Heartland.

- Happy Hauntings! Troy Taylor

Christmas at the Gates of Hell
By Linda Madl

"You don't believe the ghost guidebook about Lutsville, do you?" asked Ashley in that way she had of making you feel like an idiot because you didn't see eye-to-eye with her. She pulled the Jeep into the gravel driveway and killed the engine.

Annoyed, Ellie said nothing. Like her roommate she peered out the windshield at a white clapboard school-house with blank windows—the Lutsville Schoolhouse. The familiar peeling paint exposed weathered wood, and the square, bell-less steeple, a remnant from a time when the prairie school had been a church, struck a sharp profile against the winter twilight. A chain and padlock secured the black double doors.

"Well, no I don't believe any of it," Ellie admitted finally, trying not to show her irritation. She'd passed the old schoolhouse on her way to school almost every day of her life until four months ago when she'd left for college. She could hardly believe the place had been written up in the ghost guidebook she held in her hands.

"Read the entry again," Ashley said, without taking her gaze from the weathered building.

"It says that 'a young woman died of cholera in the church in the 1880s,'" Ellie read. "'Since then she has been seen to materialize as a red mist hovering near the ceiling. In the spring and autumn Satanists conduct rituals in the cemetery near the creek.' That's bogus! There're no Satanists around here."

"I'm sure they don't go around heartland USA advertising they're Satanists," Ashley said with a laugh. "Read the rest?"

Ellie huffed. They'd gotten a late start on their Christmas Eve drive home because they'd had to spend three days in the dorm by special arrangement so she could work at her part-time job at the discount store. Ashley had been a good sport about the delay. They'd left town about noon. In high spirits, they'd sung and laughed as they headed west on the interstate. But as they neared Ellie's home, the differences between them—the city chick and the farm girl—began to surface.

Ashley wanted to stop at every outlet mall they passed. Ellie, who was tired, hungry, and glad to be off her feet, wanted to drive straight through. Grudgingly, Ashley had agreed until she saw the road sign to Lutsville. She'd read about the place in a ghost guide-book she'd ordered from a strange internet website. Ashley had pouted. How could Ellie refuse to stop?

So here they were. Knowing that Ashley wouldn't be satisfied until she'd heard the whole silly story again, Ellie read on, "'The building has been used as a church, a one-room school, and a township meeting hall. Strange lights are frequently seen coming from the church at night. The abandoned town site is reputedly the entrance to Hell.'"

"Eeew!" Ashley cooed with relish.

Ellie gave a snort of disgust and dropped the book into her lap. "What garbage! Lutsville is just an abandoned farm town like tons of others in the state. I can't imagine what started this gates of Hell thing. And what lights? I've never seen any lights that didn't belong here."

"Somebody did." Ashley leaned over the steering wheel to get a better look at the church steeple. "Enough people to get the story into that book."

"Ashley, I've lived within five miles of this place all my life, and I've never seen or heard anything about ghosts."

Ellie studied the cover of the idiotic book. She liked Ashley a lot. They'd hit it off the minute they'd met in the dorm even though Ashley was from Seattle. She was great-looking, funny, generous, unpretentious, sophisticated—and impulsive. She'd come to the prairie state university because it was one of the nation's top five interior design schools.

That was the other thing Ellie liked about Ashley: she had great taste. Like right now, she looked incredibly cool in a down jacket trimmed in ivory with her blonde curls tucked under a matching knit hat. Ellie grimaced at her own lank, dark hair and green, synthetic, discount store coat. She longed to be sophisticated—she wanted to have style like Ashley. That alone was enough to make her defer to her roomie. And enough to encourage her to invite Ashley home for Christmas.

Ashley's parents worked for an international organization and had to be out of the country over the holidays. So Ellie had jumped at the opportunity to ask Ashley home for Christmas. At first she had been thrilled when Ashley turned down a Vail skiing trip with friends to accept the invitation. But now she was beginning to wonder if she'd done the right thing—inviting Ashley into her world.

"Come on. Let's soak up some of these spooky vibes." Ashley opened the Jeep door.

"Vibes? It's just an old schoolhouse," Ellie said, longing to get home for the first time since Thanksgiving. "Besides, it feels like it's going to snow any minute, and Mom is expecting us for supper."

"We'll get there in time." Ashley reached across Ellie to open the glove compartment and took out a flashlight. "See? I'm prepared. You're not scared are you?"

"Nooo." Ellie opened the door and climbed out to

prove her courage. "Just hungry."

"This won't take long...unless we see a ghost." Ashley laughed.

Not funny, Ellie thought. Not that she expected to see anything except cobwebs. There was nothing of Lutsville left but the schoolhouse. The gas station and the few remaining houses had been razed years ago. The schoolhouse remained standing only because it belonged to the school district.

But Ashley seemed determined to explore the place. Ellie dutifully followed her roommate. Gravel crunched beneath their Nikes, and the icy wind tugged at the hems of their coats as they walked up the drive.

"Look, it says 1859." Ashley gestured toward the corner of the structure's stone foundation. "This place has been here a long time."

Ellie squinted in the growing darkness to make out the year carved in the cornerstone. She'd never paid much attention to the building's exterior.

Ashley bounded up the front steps and pressed her face against the window in the front door.

"See anything?" Ellie hung back at the bottom of the steps. She pulled her coat collar up around her ears against the cold

"No, just a dusty entry and the door to a cloakroom." Ashley turned around and surveyed the prairie that stretched from the schoolhouse in three directions. In the fourth direction lay a wooded creek and the cemetery where shadows gathered in the gloom.

Ellie followed her roommate's gaze. She could barely make out the headstones where she'd played as a kid.

"Boy, Christmas must have been pretty dull here," Ashley said.

"Dull?" Ellie repeated in astonishment. "Christmas is

the most exciting time of the year."

"But no lights, no music, no mall, no ice skating rink, no movie theater, no Starbucks." Ashley gave a hopeless shrug. "Just church services and prayers. No wonder the place earned such a grim reputation. I mean, where did they go shopping?"

"Shopping?" Irritation rose in Ellie again like a bad case of heartburn. But she didn't want to be rude. "In the old days, the gifts were homemade, in secret. That was the fun part. Keeping the secret. If you're expecting all that mall and shopping stuff, well, you're going to be bored to death here."

"Ellie, silly, don't go all super-sensitive on me." Ashley laughed and turned to gaze into the schoolhouse window again. "I'm just imagining what it was like in the 1880s. Do you think the place is built on ley lines or whatever they call them? You know, those magnetic lines that give a place dark power. Maybe that's why it's haunted. What stories those walls would tell if they could talk."

"There's nothing to tell, Ashley." Ellie was totally exasperated now. "My grandmother went to school here. When I was in grade school, Mom and Dad brought me here for township meetings. They were long and boring. We kids played hide and seek in the cemetery when the weather was nice. Or we colored pictures in the cloakroom when it was cold. I don't remember anybody mentioning that the place is haunted."

"Well, sure. They didn't want to scare you kids," Ashley said, still gazing into the window. "Why would they report it in that book if it wasn't so?"

Ellie frowned. Ashley had a point. Had she overheard her parents talk about ghosts but had forgotten? Maybe. But she didn't think so.

Ashley reached for the doorknob. "Too bad we can't

get in to look around."

She grabbed the chain from which the padlock hung and pulled. With a click, the padlock fell open, and the loosened chain slithered to the step. The door gave an agonized creak and swung open—just enough to be inviting.

Astonished, the girls stared at the blackness within.

Ashley gave a nervous laugh. "The padlock wasn't fastened."

"That's weird," Ellie said, becoming uneasy. It wasn't like a caretaker around here to be careless in locking up.

"And so the gates of Hell open." Ashley laughed again, her nervousness obviously dismissed already. "Come on, Ellie. Show me the place since you know so much about it."

"Wait," Ellie called. "What if somebody is in there?"

Too late. Ashley had already disappeared inside. There was nothing to do but follow her.

The air inside was stale and musty. But after the icy wind the darkness was warm. Ellie pulled her collar away from her face and glanced around. Enough twilight fell through the long windows to illuminate the room. Ashley, who was only a few feet ahead of her, hadn't bothered to turn on the flashlight.

The place was deserted and just as Ellie remembered— one large room with a dais at the far end, narrow clear glass windows along both sides, and the cloakroom flanking the entrance. Great cobwebs draped like netting from the ceiling to the light fixtures overhead. The pews and the altar and the school desks had been removed long before Ellie and her parents had attended township meetings here.

"Sure doesn't look like a church inside," Ashley observed.

"I think the congregation built a new church in town a long time ago," Ellie said. "But this used to be a busy place. Something was going on here at least once a week. That's why that ghost story sounds so stupid to me."

They walked around the room, eventually drifting to the wall to examine the old black-and-white photos of past classes. Ellie had forgotten about them. They'd hung on the walls between the windows as long as she could remember, those rows of little pale forgotten faces. A caption read "Class of 1898" and another was labeled "Grades 1 through 12, 1904." In several of the 1900s photos there appeared a teacher, an older dark-haired, grim-faced woman cinched up in the long-skirted, hour-glass fashion of the times. Ellie leaned closer to read the name: "Class of 1909 and Miss Margery Warren." She didn't recall having heard the name before.

"Didn't anybody smile in those days?" Ashley asked. "They look almost pained."

"I guess they wanted to be dignified for the occasion," Ellie said, thinking Miss Warren might have been pretty if she smiled.

Suddenly Ashley put her finger to her lips to silence Ellie.

"Hear that?" Ashley clutched at her sleeve.

In the quiet Ellie heard a soft scratching from high above at the far end of the room. She glanced upward, recalling the ghost guide's mention of a red cloud materializing near the ceiling. All she saw was a water stain. The place probably needed a new roof.

"What was that?" Ashley squeezed Ellie's arm.

Her eyes had grown so wide Ellie could see the whites glittering in the twilight. She almost laughed.

"I doubt it's the gates of Hell opening, if that's what's bothering you," she said. "It's field mice."

"No, not that sound," Ashley whispered. "I heard voices singing."

"It was probably the wind whipping around the eaves," Ellie said, then fell silent to listen again. All she heard was the scratching of mice.

"Do mice make that much noise?"

"Of course they do," Ellie said, taking pleasure in Ashley's sudden cowardice. It was just like her roomie, all gung-ho one moment then can't-split-fast-enough the next. "There's probably a whole extended family living in the ceiling. Mom, Dad, Sis, and Bro with Granny and Grandpa. Uncles and aunts. Dozens of cousins. Little god mice—"

"Oh, shut up. Let's go," Ashley said, with disgust. Casting a wary glance over her shoulder, she started toward the door. "I could have sworn I heard music."

"You're not scared are you?" Ellie couldn't resist the dig as she followed her roommate toward the door.

Outside the ground was already covered in snow, robbing the countryside of its darkness and shadows. Wasting no time, Ashley gingerly made her way down the steps and across the drive toward the Jeep.

Ellie looked for the chain and padlock but apparently the snow had covered them already. Her dad would know who to call about locking up. By the time she climbed into the vehicle, Ashley had turned on the headlights and was attempting the start the engine. It turned over, and then died.

Glad to be on the way home at last and thrilled with the first snowfall of the season, Ellie rolled down the power window and stuck her arm out. She smiled as huge snowflakes revealed their lacy texture on the green sleeve of her coat. "This is great. We're going to have a white Christmas."

Ashley cursed under her breath and turned the key in the ignition again. Once more the engine died. She tried a third time. The starter whirred and the engine almost caught. The Jeep shuddered. The engine sputtered and died. Then the headlights and dashlights flickered and went dark.

"I don't believe this," Ashley muttered. "What do we do now?"

Suddenly chilled, Ellie pushed the power button to roll up the window against the cold. Nothing happened. "Dead battery?"

"Duh." Ashley glared at her and cursed again in the scatological vocabulary of the dorm that Ellie admired and had begun to use herself. "Now, we can't even close the window, and it's freezing in here," Ashley finished.

"No biggy," Ellie replied, unwilling to apologize. She dug into her pocket for her cell phone. "I'll call my folks. Dad will come and get us."

The cell phone screen indicated a low charge. Cold foreboding trickled down her back like a melting snowflake. Now it was her turn to curse.

Ashley already had her phone in hand. "Mine says no signal. What now?"

"We walk," Ellie offered, careful not to let her dread show. The prairie in a snowstorm was not a good place to be.

"Walk five miles!"

"We'll pass Cathart's place first," Ellie said. "That's about two miles from here. They'll let us use their phone, if they're home."

"Wait, wait," Ashley said, still clutching her cell phone. "I'm getting a signal. Here, call your parents!"

Ashley shoved the phone toward Ellie. She dialed her parents' number. The machine answered. Feeling frustrated and abandoned, she left a message.

"They must be out checking on the livestock before the storm really sets in," she muttered as she ended the call. "My dad will be here the minute they get the message."

"We can't stay in the car with an open window."

"We could go back inside to stay warm," Ellie said.

They turned to look at the haunted schoolhouse. Against the whitening countryside it loomed bleak and unwelcoming.

"You know that was only mice that we heard in the ceiling."

"Yeah." Ashley frowned as she appeared to be thinking over their options. "We'll stand right in the entry by the door where we can watch for your dad."

"Right," Ellie agreed. To tell the truth, she hadn't liked the feel of the deserted schoolhouse either, but what choice did they have? "Let's go."

Once inside, safe from the cold, they faced each other from either side of the window.

They stood silent at first, but never one to hold back Ashley began to vent before long. "Why on earth did you roll down the window in a snowstorm anyway? It was a dumb thing to do!"

"I like to look at the snowflakes on my sleeve," Ellie replied, feeling safe enough now to be indignant. "How was I to know the Jeep battery was going to die? While we're throwing the blame around, why in heaven's name did you bring along that ridiculous ghost book?"

"Because I like ghost stories," Ashley snapped.

"I don't." Ellie glanced toward the door into the big room. Beyond the entry lay inky blackness. She turned her back on the darkness, wanting to forget it. "I think you brought that book along because you thought it was going to be boring here," she added. "I bet you wish you'd gone to Vail to ski. You can say it. I don't care," she lied.

"Only an imbecile would want to be in a cold, dark, deserted building on Christmas Eve," Ashley quipped.

If Ellie hadn't been so irritated, she would have laughed at the contradiction in Ashley's response. She could point out this had been Ashley's idea in the first place. But she held her tongue. Instead, both folded their arms across their chests, avoided looking at each other, and stared out the window of the door.

Ellie hardly saw the curtain of snowflakes falling. All she could think of was that she and Ashley were going to be stuck together for two weeks, trapped in the same house, in the same bedroom, hating every minute of it. Smiling tight smiles at each other, trying to make her parents believe everything was all right. All the while they would hardly have a civil word for each other.

The entry that had seemed warm and sheltered only a moment before became frosty. The silence that loomed between them was unfamiliar. Until now they had always found plenty to talk about—despite their differences. That was one of the things that Ellie liked about Ashley. She could always hit on the fun things they had in common, the classes and instructors, the anal dorm rules, the buff guys. But now the stupid ghost book had ruined everything.

Across the window Ashley stood in silence, no doubt thinking the same thing.

Without warning a soundless blinding flash burst from behind them. Their faces were instantly mirrored on the windowpane.

"What was that?" Ashley whirled around.

Ellie turned, too. The door into the larger room was as dark as it had been an instant earlier. Her heart pounded in her chest, but she managed to remain calm. "I don't know. Headlights from the road maybe?"

"From behind us?" Ashley switched on the flashlight and cast the beam through the doorway into the darkness beyond. Nothing. But neither of them made a move to enter.

"Lightning, maybe," Ellie offered, though she didn't believe that explanation either. "It happens sometimes in snowstorms."

"That was probably it." Ashley switched off the flashlight and pulled her phone from her pocket. "Sure wish your dad would hurry. Should we call again? No, my phone says no signal now."

"It won't be long," Ellie assured her, but her heart was still pounding so hard that she felt she needed to speak up to be heard over the noise.

"Good, because I don't think I want to stay here much longer."

Freaked now, they stood tense and stiff at the window, companions in fear—if nothing more.

Suddenly Ashley grabbed Ellie's arm. "There it is again. Music. I hear music. People singing. Hear it?"

Ellie listened, but heard nothing. They both turned to stare into the dark room. Another blinding flash flooded through the door, illuminating the dais. They clung to each other and blinked against the brightness. A faint golden glow grew over the far end of the room. Ashley's grip on Ellie became painful. The swelling brilliance brightened the walls and reflected off the window glass, revealing the emptiness. Then the silent radiance vanished.

The faintest whisper of song teased at Ellie's ears. Goosebumps prickled down her arms. Against the vanishing brightness she thought she'd seen a silhouette of the backs of heads, like a row of children seated at old-fashioned school desks.

Then the smell of something burning reached her.

"Smell that!" Ashley cried. "But I don't see any fire."

"Let's get out of here." Ellie reached for the door.

"Wait!" Ashley put a hand out to stop her. "I hear the singing again."

"I'm not staying to listen."

"But you heard it, too. I could see it on your face. Do ghosts sing?"

"You're the ghost expert," Ellie quipped, impatience momentarily overriding fear.

"Didn't the book talk about strange lights?" Ashley pressed. "Not singing. Let's look."

Ellie stared at her roommate in disbelief. This was a lousy time for Ashley's bravado to return. But Ashley had already headed toward the darkened room.

"Are you crazy?" Ellie demanded, but she practically trod on Ashley's heels to avoid being left in the dark entry alone.

Scouring the floor with her flashlight beam, Ashley walked straight to the dais. Ellie scurried along behind, dismayed by the great motes of darkness hovering in the lofty corners.

"Do ghosts make as much light as we saw?" Ashley asked. "Do you think that glowing thing will come back?"

"Not while we're here, I hope." Ellie stood as close to Ashley as she dared. She could hear the singing again. It wasn't the sound of wind whipping around the eaves. It was like piano music—the plinky sound of an out-of-tune upright instrument.

"Listen. They're singing a hymn of some kind," Ashley whispered, as if she was afraid of disturbing the singers. "Do Satanists sing hymns?"

"I don't know. The light is back." Ellie reached for Ashley's arm and backed toward the door. The light on the dais had returned—and was growing again. It seemed stronger now; the brilliance more vivid, churning, smoldering, promising to fill the room with an unearthly incandescence. "Let's go."

Both bolted. They reached the front door at the same time. Their shoulders collided. Bouncing off each other, their extended hands missed the doorknob.

Ashley recovered first, her fingers closing around the knob. She twisted it and lunged against the door with all her might. It held fast. She blurted another curse.

"Let me." Ellie shoved her roommate aside. She grabbed the doorknob and thrust her shoulder against the wood. The door held.

Ashley pushed against the door, too. Unspeakable terror of some unknown thing filled them. Frantic, they struggled with the knob. It remained stuck.

The light brightened, defining their shadows against the wood.

Ellie caught her breath. Ashley whimpered.

The singing was plain now, as loud as a CD at full volume, childish voices raised in song. The tune was familiar to her, but not clear enough for her to place it.

"Get us out of here!" Ashley gasped as if this was somehow Ellie's fault.

"How?" Ellie asked, but she was already forming an action plan. "Remember the campus self-defense class?"

Ashley nodded, her eyes wide with desperation.

"When it grabs us, you hit it in the groin. I'll go for its eyes."

"Groin?" Ashley hissed. "Does a ghost have a groin?"

The light increased, washing out the details of the entry hall. The music grew louder, too.

Oddly, with the mounting sound a seductive peace stole over them. Their hands fell away from the doorknob. The air grew warmer. Their fear eased. But they remained with their backs toward the door into the schoolroom.

The music had grown recognizable at last.

"O Come All Ye Faithful," Ellie whispered.

Ashley smiled. "My favorite Christmas carol."

They could hear the voices of children singing with all their hearts.

"Ellie, we've got to look."

Ellie wanted to escape. What if this seductive feeling was just a ruse to get them back into the room? But she was curious now—more curious than cautious. Curious enough to make her trembling legs work the way she wanted them to work. She and Ashley turned around. Hand in hand they crept to the doorway and peered in.

To their surprise they saw the backs of dozens of children dressed in old-fashioned clothes. The girls and boys were facing the dais as they sang. Silhouetted on the dais was an hour-glass shaped figure with her back to them.

The golden glow swirled around the room. The breeze it created ruffled the girls' hair. It coalesced over the dais into a sparkling core that began to stretch downward, widening like a skirt. Then it surged, spiraling upward toward the ceiling before the dark figure. The magnificence of the sight brought a gasp from the girls.

With a magic more masterful than a movie's special effects, the form morphed into a towering Christmas tree. The tang of cedar and the scent of candle wax reached them—the burning smell they'd sniffed earlier.

The girls could only stare.

A silvery star crowned the top. Red and white garlands

of popcorn and berries draped over the boughs. Tinsel sparkled. Colorful ornaments made of cutouts, tinsel and cotton adorned the branches. Shimmering golden points of candlelight clung to the boughs. The glowing tree pulsed with life as real and as inspiring as a mirage can be.

The music wavered, growing louder, then softer like an unsteady radio signal. The images of the children wavered, too.

Open-mouthed, Ellie and Ashley basked in the presence of good will and joy. The scent of oranges and cloves tickled Ellie's nose and the caroling was sweet to her ears. It all seemed so familiar and perfect—so I've-been-here-before—and completely unfrightening.

"It's beautiful," Ashley whispered in awe. "And exciting!"

Ellie could only nod. Then she observed the silhouetted image of the woman in the cinched-up skirt and wide-sleeved blouse. Miss Warren? The apparition was almost as clear as a real live person. Was this the ghost then?

"Do you see her?" Ellie asked under breath.

Ashley gave a nod.

The presence began to turn, slowly. Ellie sucked in a breath and squeezed Ashley's hand. What would they see when she faced them? A skeleton's face or a Jason's mask?

She turned and grinned at them.

"See, the school teacher is pretty when she smiles," Ashley said in a voice full of wonder.

Miss Warren was lovely. As if she'd just seen the girls standing in the doorway, she raised a hand and beckoned them to come in.

"She's inviting us to sing with them," Ashley said.

"I know. Why not?"

The urge to join in was irresistible. Ellie took up the

verse. Ashley began to lip the words, too.

* * *

Jim Stead pulled in behind the Jeep parked in front of the old Lutsville schoolhouse. He'd driven over as soon as he'd gotten his daughter's phone message. The footprints in the snow leading up to the building sent a sense of relief through him. He'd seen a flash of light across the windows as he turned the corner. So the girls were inside with their flashlight, safe, if a little cold. This was bad weather for car trouble.

As he walked up to the schoolhouse through the snowfall, he saw that the front door was ajar, its padlock and chain missing. Odd. Carl Cathart usually kept the place locked up tight against vandals and curiosity seekers.

Security hadn't been a big issue around Lutsville until some fool had started spreading stories about the place being haunted. Since then there'd been no end of trouble with gawkers driving by, squinting into digital cameras and video cams, looking for ghosts, witches, and such.

When he reached the front door he heard voices raised in song. It was the girls singing "O Come All Ye Faithful" at the top of their lungs. He smiled to himself. Singing to keep their courage up.

"Ellie?" He walked through the entry and into the schoolroom.

The two girls were sitting in the middle of the floor with the flashlight aimed at the ceiling and their backs to him. They seemed to be watching something on the dais. They continued to sing verse two.

"Ellie?" he repeated, louder this time. Why hadn't they heard him? "You two all right?"

Ellie started, turning toward him at last. Bewilderment crossed her face. Then she looked around as if something had gone missing.

"Dad. Isn't this a wonderful old place?"

"Yeah, lot's of history here." Jim stared at his daughter, trying to imagine what had put such a rapt glow on her face. She'd never liked coming to Lutsville when she was a kid. She'd thought it was boring.

The girl at Ellie's side, the invited roommate he assumed, looked up at him and smiled, too. "They celebrate Christmas here."

"Who?" Jim asked, looking around at the cobwebs and dust.

Ellie climbed to her feet and touched his arm. "The vibes are still here, Dad. That's what Ashley means. The good will and the joy of the season. It's still here."

"Well, I wouldn't be surprised if it was." He chuckled. "Did you know your Great Uncle Louis used to put on the Santa suit and hand out the gifts from under the tree? Many a Christmas was celebrated within these walls."

"Really?" Ellie exclaimed. "I didn't know that about Uncle Louis."

"Look!" Ashley cried, holding out her hand. "I found this in my pocket!"

On her palm lay a homemade Christmas tree ornament fashioned of a colored cutout from an old-fashioned magazine and pasted with tinsel and red yarn—a rosy-cheeked, bewinged cherub—ready to hang from a cedar bough.

"It's just like the old ones Grandma had, Dad," Ellie said.

Ashley offered it to Ellie. "Here, a gift for you, roomie."

Ellie smiled and held out her hand. She started at the sight of a similar homemade cutout ornament—an apple-cheeked Santa carrying a puppy—trimmed in tinsel in her hand. "Where'd that come from?"

The girls laughed and threw an arm across each other's shoulders as if they'd been separated for years.

"The spirit of Christmas is here." Ashley smiled at Ellie. "A good ghost. I'm so glad you invited me to come home with you to see a prairie Christmas."

"Yeah, me too." Ellie smiled at Ashley, and then they admired the ornaments in their hands.

"Good, that's settled," Jim said. He'd never completely understood girls, though he'd raised three daughters. He was just glad that his youngest was home safe with her friend. "Let's jump-start that Jeep and get you guys home. Your mother has a hot meal waiting for us."

"Hey, Dad," Ellie began, as they walked out of the schoolhouse. "Did anyone ever die here?"

"Let's see," Jim said, thinking back on what he knew about the old schoolhouse. "I believe one of the school teachers had a heart attack here. Miss Warson or something like that. She was a spinster lady and taught here for years and years. Loved the place. Everybody liked her."

"Not cholera?" Ellie asked.

"Cholera? Oh, no. The cholera epidemic was long before Miss What's-her-name's time. Why?"

"No reason," Ellie said, glancing at her roommate, who said nothing.

Outside, Ashley made one last attempt to start her vehicle before they hooked up the cables. The Jeep rumbled to life without hesitation. The girls looked at each other, astonished, and then giggled.

Jim shook his head. Who knew what automotive glitch had kept the Jeep from starting? He'd have a look under the hood tomorrow. All was well for now. He was just thankful the girls were safely home.

"This is going to be the bestest old-fashioned

Christmas ever," Ellie said, hugging Ashley again.

Ashley laughed. "I think so, too. Boy, did that ghost guidebook have it wrong. Just throw it in the back."

"Yeah, the ghost guidebook had it wrong but I don't think I want to visit here on Halloween," said Ellie, tossing the book into the back seat. They laughed and drove off, full of the Christmas spirit.

- The End -

Dance With Me
By Jerri Garretson

Geneva stood at the top of the attic stairs and stared. It was going to take a small army to clear out this mass of stuff. Either that or she and Palmer would be working here for the next six months, which wouldn't be so bad, spending all that time alone together instead of in separate offices at the museum. Two lovebirds exploring a mysterious old estate. She held out her hand and admired her engagement ring for a moment.

The Randall family must have been stashing things up here for generations. It looked as if they had started at the far side of the room and filled it to the rafters, all the way to the door, and then shut it and gone downstairs, never to return. There were only tiny paths through the piles. It would be a challenge just to maneuver.

Was any of it worth much? She was inclined to think there were some gems hidden up here. Going through it could be exciting but the thought of having to catalog all of it for sale was daunting, not to mention packing it up to ship to the auction site. Luckily, this attic had a sturdy floor, a couple of windows and real stairs.

She climbed over a small leather-bound trunk and inched past an ornate cradle. That would bring a hefty price, if the museum didn't decide to keep it. Reclusive Amelia Randall had willed her entire estate to the county historical museum, except for a few things that were to be given to her nieces and nephews. The museum couldn't possibly keep everything. The board had voted to open the house as a museum, keep the main furnishings and the best pieces, plus any historical documents they found, and auction the rest. Geneva laughed. They had no idea just how much there was to auction!

The house would be a beautiful museum, though. The Kansas cattle baron who built it in the 1880s wanted a castle for his bride, and he built one. There were many fine old limestone houses in Kansas but few were built with towers and crenelated parapets like this one. It was truly a prairie original, constructed with fine craftsmanship by immigrant German stone masons. Back then, it would have stood alone on the gently rolling hills with not even a tree for shade. Now it was surrounded by towering old oaks and elms, luxuriant lilac and forsythia bushes, and a mammoth hedge. The city had grown in a hundred-and-twenty-some years and the family had gradually sold off parcels of the ranch to developers. Amelia's house was flanked by expensive newer homes. No matter how extravagant they were, they paled beside this grand dame.

Geneva opened a mirrored walnut wardrobe. It was filled with fancy silk dresses that must have been as old as the house, probably very fragile now. She fingered a gorgeous gown trimmed with yellowed French lace and examined a little girl's sky-blue dress. She wondered if the pale green one would fit her. She'd love to own it. Maybe she could bid on it.

Her eyes were drawn to something behind the cabinet. A huge ornate frame, taller than she was, had been turned to face the wall. It was heavy but she was able to slide it out a few inches. Touching it, she was seized by a feeling of urgency that she had to see what it was. She drew her hand back in surprise. What was so important about an old framed canvas? She reached out again, and was immediately flooded with a desire to see it. She tried to push aside some of the boxes and furniture and tugged on the frame. Damn, she couldn't get it all the way out.

As she yanked on it again, viselike fingers grasped her wrist.

Frightened, she tore her hand away and tried to escape from the attic, but her feet felt like lead. She took a deep breath, bit her lip, and with great effort, inched away from the wardrobe and sat on the trunk. Her heart was pounding and her wrist hurt. Seeing no one in the attic, she closed her eyes, counted ten deep breaths and forced herself to calm down, but she couldn't shake the feeling that there was a presence in the attic with her.

There was a tiny hint of sound, like a soft breath, someone quietly breathing near her, behind her. The hairs on the back of her neck rose. She swung around on the trunk. Nothing. Nothing visible, but the breathing had not stopped. Her skin prickled with a kind of super-awareness. She thought she heard a man's voice, so faint it almost wasn't there, saying, "At last." It paused, then continued, "Lovely."

Geneva almost didn't make out the words, almost convinced herself she hadn't even heard them, but the voice, low as it was, sounded silky and seductive. While her body registered fear, stiffening and preparing to jump over the trunk and run down the stairs, she couldn't stop herself from responding to the voice. One part of her mind screamed "danger," but the other craved to hear more. She sat paralyzed.

"Look at me," the voice whispered, husky, inviting. "Dance with me."

The voice grew stronger, more musical. The breathing drew away, toward the painting. Geneva, mesmerized by the voice, was pulled along with it, caressed by it. She tried to hang onto her own sensibility, to reason. This couldn't be happening. Was she hallucinating? She forced herself to breathe evenly and look around the room, stood and willed herself to leave. She climbed over the trunk and managed one more step toward the stairs, but before she could reach the door, it swung silently shut and she heard the key click in the lock, saw it turn.

The key was there, right in front of her where she could reach it, but she couldn't muster the strength to touch it. She felt a finger, light as a feather, trace a path down her bare arm and encircle her wrist again. A sensual touch this time, ever so slight, but sapping her will with its powerful energy.

"Come," the voice said. She seemed to float over the trunk and back to face the wardrobe. Her hand reached out for the frame. As soon as she touched it, she felt a desperate hunger coming from the painting. It wanted her. She couldn't withdraw her hand.

Deep within herself Geneva was conscious of losing her will to a menacing force she could not see, but the voice was so compelling and pleasing that she wanted to let go. She wanted to be with the source of the longing, know it, be absorbed by it. She forced herself to close her eyes and strained to concentrate on moving away. She nearly fainted and fell across the trunk. Half conscious, she lay there, eyes shut, blindly waiting, too weak to move.

Her skin could now sense the presence around her even without hearing or seeing anything. She knew it was behind her, at the painting. Watching. Longing. Still there, but lacking the intensity she felt when she touched the painting or the presence touched her.

"You will come to me," the voice whispered, husky, low. "You will fight, but you will still come."

Geneva screamed. She pounded her fists on the trunk. The action and noise brought her out of her trance. She scrambled clumsily over the trunk and to the door.

Just as she was desperately rattling the key in the lock, working against the unseen force, she heard heavy footsteps charging up the attic steps. She flung the door open and fell into Palmer's arms, nearly knocking him down the stairs.

"My God, Geneva, what's wrong?" He struggled to keep his balance while holding her tight.

"Get me out of here," she gasped.

Palmer wrapped his arm around her waist and guided her down the stairs. She was weak and her balance was off, but she made it. At the second floor landing, she pulled free of his arm and headed for the bedroom on the left where she sat heavily on the edge of the bed, breathing hard. Palmer followed, pulled up a chair, and grabbed her wrist to take her pulse. When he touched her, she flinched.

"What happened up there? Your heart's pounding and you look like someone drained the blood out of you."

Geneva lay back on the bed, exhausted, staring at the ceiling. She didn't feel strong enough to talk and none of it seemed real now. Nothing, that is, except the painting. What was it? Anyone hearing her story would think she was a mental case. She had doubts about her sanity herself at this point.

She looked at Palmer. Why hadn't she sent him to the attic and spent her time poking around in the closets down here? Would he have noticed anything odd up there? He held her hand and fingered the engagement ring as though she should have trusted him more.

"I'll be all right," she said shakily. "Would you get me a drink of water, please?" She was thirsty, powerfully so, and waiting for a drink would buy her a little time to decide what to say, even if the thought of being alone terrified her.

Palmer gave her a dubious look but headed down the

stairs to the kitchen. Geneva sat up slowly. She had a slight headache and felt groggy but her racing heart was slowing down and she was feeling more in control. What the hell had happened to her? What was she going to tell Palmer? She made up her mind fast, hearing him coming up the stairs.

He handed her the glass of water, clearly checking to see what shape she was in. She hoped she was doing a good job of appearing normal.

"Okay, shoot," he said. "What happened? I've never seen you terrified like that."

She gave him a sheepish smile. "It was so quiet up there, and the place is just crammed with stuff. It's going to take more than the two of us to catalog, pack and move it out of there. I was completely startled by a sudden noise, like something scrambling around up there, coming toward me. I just got spooked. Maybe squirrels have gotten into the attic."

Palmer eyed her, obviously doubting her story. He took both her hands in his. "Squirrels could make you that panicked? Did you see one?"

"Check it out yourself," she countered. If he came back down without mentioning anything odd up there, would she feel reassured, or just wonder why it only happened to her?

"All right," he said. "I will. I don't think you ought to work up there until we're sure you're not going to die of fright. Want to go home for the rest of the afternoon?"

"Of course not," she snapped. She would have loved to go home and spend the rest of the afternoon curled up under an afghan with a cup of tea and a good book, anything to distract her from remembering the attic, but she didn't want Palmer to know that.

"Well, if you're going to stay here, did you notice the

big oak desk and filing cabinets in the library? The old lady may have inherited a house crammed full of stuff but she apparently kept her papers in order. If you feel up to it, you could take a look at them. You might find some instructions that didn't come with the will."

Geneva nodded. "I'm fine now." She got to her feet, hoping she didn't look as shaky as she felt, and walked carefully down the stairs, hanging onto the carved oak banister to keep her balance.

Palmer was right. She had only glanced into the library before and mostly focused on the elegant paneling and the rich Oriental rugs. On the ornate walnut desk, she saw three neat stacks of papers, each with a sheet on top that provided a label in an old-fashioned, graceful script. This organization seemed such an opposite of the jam-packed attic and cellar. Did the old lady just inherit the mess and leave it that way while living her own life in quiet, methodical order?

She glanced over the piles. It looked as though Amelia Randall had been preparing to leave her estate for a long time. Going through these papers would probably be tedious enough to calm her down and get her mind off the attic. She sat in the big leather chair and pulled the nearest stack toward her. The graceful script on the top sheet said, "Of first concern." Geneva turned it over and looked at the next sheet. It read,

"It is my fervent hope that whomever enters my home to dispose of the contents will read these pages before proceeding. I have not been reclusive all these years because I am antisocial. I have been trying to protect the community from a menace within these walls. I dared not reveal it while I was alive. Before going any further, insure that no woman enters the attic, and no woman comes into contact with the large *portrait of my uncle, Adam Randall. Have several mature men who do not live in this community remove that painting, encase it in cement and bury it as far from habitation as possible."*

A little too late, thought Geneva. I've already done both. Her hands trembled, shaking the paper. A menace. Adam Randall. Was that the presence who so thirsted for her? The spirit, or whatever it was, that locked her in the attic?

"Under no circumstances are any of my relatives to be allowed into this house as long as the painting remains here. None of them know the truth about Adam, and they would be tempted to keep or sell the painting, unleashing a horror no one will know how to contain. In the bottom drawer of my file cabinet, you will find a journal that I started when I was eighteen. It will tell you all you need to know about Adam Randall. It will be difficult to believe. Trust me. It is the truth. I go to my grave defending the women of this town. —Amelia Randall."

Geneva sat, silently mulling this over. Was anyone going to believe it? Would the historical society actually spend part of Amelia's estate to get rid of an old portrait in such a strange manner? She supposed they would have to if it were a legal condition of the bequest, but since there had been no mention of it in Amelia's will, maybe it wasn't enforceable. Couldn't she reveal her secret even to her attorney?

Despite her fright in the attic, Geneva's curiosity was aroused. How could a painting possibly be so dangerous that old Amelia would go to such lengths? Why hadn't she just destroyed it years ago? She looked around at the calm, orderly library, a place Amelia could have spent many cozy evenings reading, writing, or maybe crocheting some of the fancy doilies and antimacassars that graced the room. Were there more clues in her neatly piled papers?

Geneva glanced quickly through the rest of the documents on the desk. Descriptions of furnishings and lists of things to be given to Amelia's nieces and nephews, particularly her jewelry, some family silver. Papers about the house. The deed, along with an insurance policy. She would turn them over to the society's lawyer. They didn't interest her. The diary did.

The filing cabinet drawer was heavy and Geneva had to wrestle it out. Inside, she found stacks of old yellowed letters, and a packet of sepia photos on tattered cardboard mountings. The letters and photos could wait. The diary could not. She had to find it. Nearly the entire drawer was emptied before she found a book wrapped in a blue silk scarf and tied with a faded black ribbon. She drew it out and unwrapped it. Sitting on the floor, she began to read.

"April 20, 1928. I shot Adam today. My grandfather managed to cover it up and make people think Adam shot himself by accident. No one would think his sweet little eighteen-year-old niece would do it. I still see him coming toward me as I pulled the trigger. I wasn't going to end up like the others. Someone had to stop him. I don't regret killing him. I just wish he had dropped dead immediately instead of screaming that he would haunt me all my life and bleeding all over the carpet until my father and brother came and took him away. I hated him, and I still do. Daddy called him an evil seed and I hope he rots in Hell for what he did to all those girls. At least he didn't do it to me."

"*April 23, 1928. Adam's funeral was today. So many people came, you'd have thought the whole town loved him. Many people did. To them he was the good-looking jeweler, the charming bon vivant, the catch of the town. He had them all fooled. They didn't know what he could be like, what he could do to women with his seductive good looks, that chocolaty voice and all that money.*

"*The jewelry store will go to Daddy, I guess, since Adam was never married. It must have been hard for my grandfather, having to bury his son, but he never said anything hurtful to me about killing him. All he said was, 'Amelia, you did right to defend yourself.'*

"*After the funeral, they all came over to our house. All those funeral guests. I had to stand there trying to look appropriately downcast, like I was sorry my uncle was dead. There was that damned painting of Adam with that smoldering smile, still gazing down upon the crowd from the parlor wall. I hated it almost as much as I hated Adam. I begged Daddy to burn it but it was so well-known that people would ask where it went and wonder why we took it down when he died. We had to leave it up for awhile.*

"*I could feel those eyes following me as though Adam were still there, watching me the way he had for the past year, until he finally grabbed me and pulled me into his room and tried to tear off my dress. He didn't know I'd started carrying a pistol in my pocket. I could see how he looked at me. I wasn't going to be helpless if he attacked me. I wasn't going to end up like the other girls Adam seduced or forced himself on, the ones that were in some other town, and that my grandfather had to support after they were disgraced. Grandfather tried. He really tried to make Adam stop, but Adam wouldn't listen to anybody. He swaggered around town, that gorgeous eligible bachelor with the fancy jewelry shop,* and no one in town knew what a monster he really was. No one but us."

"April 24, 1928. Adam is back, returned from the grave. He was in the parlor last night, swearing that he would haunt me and this house forever. He swore that if I ever married, he would kill my husband and children. He said I couldn't stop him. I thought I would go mad listening to him, but finally I told myself that he hadn't gotten the best of me when he was alive and he wasn't going to do it as a ghost. I told Daddy and Grandfather about Adam's ghost. I thought they wouldn't believe me, but they'd heard him, too. 'It's the painting,' my grandfather said. 'Somehow he found a way into it. It's as though the thing is alive.'

"I asked him again to burn it, and he shook his head. 'That will bring doom on our house. He needs the painting. It's his existence now, if you can call it that. He'll kill anyone who tries to destroy it.' I don't know how he knew that Adam could carry out those threats, but he was sure Adam would. 'I regret the day he was born,' he added. 'I should have killed him with my own hands instead of covering up his crimes. Until the day he attacked you, I kept hoping he would change.'"

"April 30, 1928. We have to be on our guard all the time. Now that Adam is a ghostly presence inhabiting that painting, he watches everything we do in sight of the parlor. I don't know if he can get more than a few feet from the painting, but he seems to get stronger as the days go by. He hasn't tried to touch me. Grandfather thinks he can't, because I'm the one who killed him. I hope that's true."

Geneva looked up from the diary. It was hard to believe such a creepy story but her experience in the attic certainly fit with what she was reading. Could Adam really have been that handsome? That cruel? The story was compelling. She had to know more.

"*June 19, 1928. Today my friend Annabelle came to visit. It's been two months since I killed Adam and I've avoided seeing people as much as I could, but Annabelle kept sending me notes about how she missed my friendship. I should have met her somewhere else, but I invited her for tea. We were sitting in the parlor chatting and having petit fours when I saw it. Adam staring down at Annabelle. I nearly dropped my cup and saucer. Annabelle stared back at him. She rose and walked slowly toward the painting, like she was in a trance. 'What are you doing?' I demanded.*

"*'Whatever do you mean?' she asked, turning to me, puzzled. 'I was just looking at the painting of that handsome uncle of yours. Such a tragedy that he died so young.'*

"*I couldn't think what to say. I couldn't tell her that I shot him when he tried to force himself on me. I should have told her about all the other girls but she wouldn't have believed me. She was all dreamy-eyed, as though she'd fallen in love with a painting, and I guess she had. She'd seen it many times, but that was before Adam had taken up residence in it. Now his magnetic eyes were caressing her as though they were alive. It was horrible! I made up an excuse about not feeling well and got her out of the house. It was then I knew that I didn't dare allow women into our home ever again, at least not if they could see that painting.*

"*I told Daddy about Annabelle and the painting after she left. He looked grim and horrified. I was grateful that he believed me, but*

39

what are we going to do if we can't destroy it?"

"June 22, 1928. Daddy and Grandfather got a ladder and took Adam's portrait down. They hauled it up to the attic and told me never to go up there. It's better having it out of the parlor, but I can't help feeling that as long as it is in our house, evil things will happen. Grandfather is sure we will all die if we try to destroy it, and he says that taking it somewhere else will only unleash Adam's horror there. We don't talk about it with anyone. What would they think?"

"June 24, 1928. This is the saddest day of my life. I wasn't sad the day I killed Adam, but today I hate him more than ever, and I don't think I will ever be happy again. Annabelle came while no one was home. We were all down at the jewelry store deciding what to do with things. I'm good with figures, so I was helping with the inventory. Adam knew we were going to be gone today and he must have put it into her head the day Annabelle was here for tea, coaxed her to come back. She got in through the kitchen door. We never locked it. We will now.

"As near as we could tell, she was drawn right to the painting. How else would she have known to go to the attic? Only God knows for sure what Adam did to her, but she must have jumped out the attic window to her death. We found her on the drive, crumpled and bleeding, her lovely lavender frock torn from her throat and ripped down to her waist. There was a jagged slash across her cheek, as though she had been hit with something like a ring. Her eyes were wide open, staring up at us with cold terror frozen in her dead gaze."

"June 27, 1928. I went to Annabelle's funeral today. God,

how I wished that I had never invited her to tea, that I could bring her back to life. I miss her so! I didn't want to hear the gossip around town about how she died. It's a good thing there were other people who knew where my grandfather and Daddy were when she died, because there were some who wanted to accuse them of attacking her and pushing her to her death. She was my best friend, the one I could always talk to, ever since we were only six years old. I wish my mother or grandmother were still alive so I could talk to them. Their deaths were supposed to be accidents, but now I wonder. Could Adam have caused them, too? And if he did, did anyone ever know?"

Geneva's hands trembled. What if she had stayed in the attic this afternoon? What kind of a monster was this Adam?

"June 30, 1928. Grandfather told me he managed to turn Adam's painting to the wall and slide it behind a big old wardrobe. He won't let anyone go to the attic, and he hopes that if anyone does, if Adam can't see them, he won't have that kind of power over them."

Grandfather got it wrong, Geneva thought. Except that Adam's power would probably be far greater when the painting faced someone with those painted eyes and his victim could see him. Victim. She'd almost become one. Was Palmer safe up there?

A muffled scream came from the attic, followed by a thump that Geneva heard clearly all the way down in the first floor library. Instant dread washed over her. "Palmer," she called, "are you all right?"

There was no answer.

Then another scream, louder this time. "Geneva, help me." Palmer's voice sounded strangled.

Geneva grabbed the phone and called 911. Her heart was pounding so loud she could scarcely hear her own voice as she gave the address and said they were being attacked. The dispatcher wanted her to stay on the phone but Geneva let the receiver drop when she heard Palmer calling again. She picked up the nearest heavy thing she could find, a silver candelabra, and ran up the stairs.

When she reached the attic, she found Palmer bound to the trunk, bleeding from the head where he'd been bashed with a metal box that lay on the floor near him. He was moaning. She dropped the candelabra and tried frantically to untie him, but powerful, invisible hands pulled her away. Clasped her. Embraced her.

"Dance with me," the smooth, throaty voice whispered near her ear. Intimate. Yearning. "I've been waiting so long. I don't want to be alone for eternity."

Geneva caught a glimpse of the painting of Adam Randall, which Palmer must have pulled the rest of the way out from behind the wardrobe and turned around. She caught her breath. He was the handsomest man she'd ever seen. She thought she would melt into those riveting eyes, swoon into his arms, even as she fought to look away, to wrench herself from his grasp, to reach for the candelabra. If she could just reach it…

"One dance, Geneva, just one," breathed the voice, softly, on the back of her neck. "Forever." Adam whirled her around and gripped her tightly.

"Palmer," she screamed. She felt herself being drawn, danced, toward the painting.

* * *

Palmer struggled against the ropes binding him to the trunk. He couldn't save her. He watched in horror as the unseen force pulled Geneva, sobbing in terror, toward the portrait. She melted into it and disappeared. There, in the painting, he saw the faint, ghostly image of his fiancée, superimposed on the eighty-year-old portrait of an incredibly handsome, smiling man.

The police arrived quickly and called an ambulance. Palmer's incoherent story about being attacked by an invisible force, tied up and used as bait to bring Geneva to the attic was dismissed. If he hadn't been lashed to the trunk, Palmer was certain they would have suspected him of foul play.

They never found any clues about his attacker. Except Amelia's diary, with its preposterous story about Adam Randall. Palmer was the only one who believed it.

They never found Geneva but he knew exactly where she was—dancing with Adam. Forever.

- The End -

Griselda

By Jerri Garretson

Ryan carried her over the threshold, just as though they were really married, laughing as he strode through the archway into the living room. He plunked her unceremoniously onto the sofa and plopped down beside her.

"There. What do you think?"

Amy took a long look around the room, eyes shining. Ryan was so excited when he found the house and asked her to move in with him. Was she taking a foolish chance? She'd only known him a month, but he was so positive it was the right thing, the best thing to do, and so insistent …they could save money living together, and besides, they were so much in love.

The house was small and already furnished, the type of place that was difficult to find. The couch was old, but in mint condition, and a rather pleasant shade of maroon. A matching easy chair sat on the other side of the room. A fake Oriental carpet matched nicely, and there were even end tables with lamps and a glass-topped cherry coffee table.

"It's great, Ryan," she said. "But how can we afford it?"

"The rent's cheap," he said.

"Why?" she asked, suspicious.

"Don't know for sure," he said, jumping up and pulling her with him. "Something about having a hard time keeping it rented, so they were going to try lowering the rent for awhile. Come and see the rest of the house. Look, isn't this a great kitchen?"

It was. Light green and white, with a big window

over the sink and a cupboard with etched glass doors. An oak dining table with four chairs. Amy ran her fingers over the countertop, smooth marbled green Formica. It was certainly a big step up from her two room apartment with the fold-down bed, two-burner cooktop and no oven. A real home.

But, said the nagging voice at the back of her mind, why did they have trouble keeping a cute little place like this rented? It wasn't so far out in the country that people couldn't drive in to work.

"You've got to see the bedroom." Ryan pointed through another doorway. "Your favorite colors."

He was right. It was as though someone had planned it for her. Light blue walls and fluffy white curtains. There was a quilt in patterns of blue on the double bed. Handmade hooked rugs in shades of blue dotted the floor. Why would anyone rent a place with a handmade quilt and rugs like that? It was more like renting a house-sized bed and breakfast accommodation. Quaint and charming. Cozy.

Ryan had already put his two favorite photos of her on the nightstand on his side of the bed. She smiled. Just like him. He was always taking pictures of her.

She glimpsed the door to another bedroom down the hall. "Can we use that room for a study?" she asked. "For our computers and books and things? But we'd have to remove the bedroom furniture."

"No problem. There's a basement, so we have some storage space." He pointed at a door next to the bathroom.

"What's down there?" she asked.

"Not much. Just an old cellar."

"Let's take a look," she said, flipping on the light and starting down the stairs.

"Hey, where are you going?" Teasingly, Ryan pulled her back to him and planted a kiss on her mouth. "The basement can wait. We have things to bring in."

"I want to see it," she said. Maybe it had something intriguing in it. Or maybe not. Whoever owned the house had probably cleaned it out. Just like her to want to snoop. But was it really snooping if she lived there?

"It'll wait. Come on. You bring in the groceries and I'll get the luggage. We'll go back to our old places for the rest of our stuff after we have some lunch." He headed for the car.

Amy lingered in the doorway, looking out at the surroundings. It was so peaceful and green. Huge oak and cottonwood trees towered over the house. The shade was deep and cool. From the line of trees that ran along the south side a ways from the house, she could tell there must be a river or stream nearby. There were tall, old lilac bushes blooming lavender and white, like a mammoth hedge. She took a deep breath of the fragrant air. A storybook house.

Ryan gave her a playful shove as he edged past her with the suitcases. "Come on, Amy. I'm doing all the work."

"Okay, I'm going," she said.

Halfway to the car she turned back to see the house in its perfect setting. She gasped. At the edge of the picture window, a faint shadow moved between the living room drapes and windowpane. For an instant, she saw two eyes peering from it. Then it was gone.

Amy took a deep breath and closed her eyes. She looked back at the window. Nothing was there. She hoisted two sacks of groceries and headed for the house.

It should have been homey to put away groceries in a real house, make lunch together, eat at the round oak table. Ordinary, but special, their first meal in the house. Ryan munched on a crust of French bread and leered at her. She gave him a slow, tentative smile. She knew where his mind was, but hers was still on the eyes at the window.

"Penny for your thoughts," he said, cupping her chin in his right hand.

"Promise not to laugh?"

"Sure," he said. "What's up?"

She took a deep breath. "I was wondering," she began, then hesitated. Out of the corner of her eye, she saw a small, faint shadow move past the kitchen doorway. Something was in this house, watching them.

"Are you sure you don't know why they can't keep renters?"

Ryan frowned. This obviously wasn't the mood he expected on their first afternoon together in the house. "They didn't really tell me much. The woman who rents it said the owner moved away about five years ago. She was told to keep the furnishings in it and rent it out. The owner hasn't decided whether to come back to live here or sell it. She thinks people don't like living this far out of town."

"How many renters have they had?" Amy asked.

"I didn't ask, but what difference does that make?"

"The distance might have been more than some people liked, after they tried living here, but I don't believe that's the real reason. I saw something. There's something in this house."

"Oh, for heaven's sake, Amy, that's ridiculous. What did you see, a mouse?"

"No, a small shadow with eyes. I've seen it twice."

He stared at her, silent, for several seconds. She could see how reluctant he was to continue the conversation.

Finally he said, "Some people are superstitious and have overactive imaginations. I hope you're not one of them."

"Are you sure that woman didn't say anything about renters being frightened away?"

Ryan didn't answer. He got up from the table and went outside.

Bewildered, Amy watched him from the kitchen window. Ryan had never treated her like that before. He paced back and forth across the yard. It wasn't the way she had pictured their first afternoon together in their new home, either.

He brought the last things in from the car and told her to leave the dishes and come along to get another load of things from their apartments.

She grabbed her sweater on the way out the door, and then, on an impulse, she turned and whispered into the house, "I saw you."

That evening, when they had put away the most important things and stashed boxes along the walls to work on later, Ryan placed a vase of lilacs on the coffee table and seated Amy on the couch. He poured a glass of wine for each of them.

"To our new life," he said, lifting his glass in a toast. He smiled his warm, infectious smile. "And another surprise." He pulled a small box out of his pocket and opened it. "Will you marry me?"

Both Amy's hands went to her mouth. She took a deep breath. The ring was exquisite, probably a family heirloom. Ornate gold filigree held a deep blue sapphire surrounded by a graceful curl of diamonds.

Ryan didn't wait for an answer. He took her left hand and slipped the ring on her finger. "Now you're truly mine," he said.

Amy couldn't say anything. It was too soon. She

wasn't ready. She searched for words to tell him.

Ryan pulled her close, his arm around her shoulders. "I know it's only been a month, Amy, but I don't need more time to know when I've found my bride. You're here with me, in our own home. That says more than words."

Does it? Amy fumbled with the ring, turning it on her finger. Who else had worn it? Why wasn't she thrilled? Had she somehow promised too much by moving out here with him?

"It's beautiful, Ryan, but..."

"Drink your wine, Amy. We're going to have a beautiful life together. You'll see."

Again, his melting smile and warm kisses drove away her doubts. Ryan knew what he wanted. She was so tired, almost numb now, too tired to make a decision about the rest of her life. She would sleep on it. Things would be clearer in the morning.

* * *

When she awoke, the first thing she noticed was that Ryan wasn't beside her. Her eyes were bleary and her body was heavy and clumsy, but she dragged herself out of bed to find him.

The clock said 11:37. She stared. How could that be? She always set her alarm for 6:30. How could she over-sleep five hours? She'd never been late to work in her life, and it was almost noon.

Forcing herself to focus, she tried to remember where she'd put her purse. She had to call in sick. She was nauseated and she could hardly walk straight.

Ryan was nowhere in the house and the car was gone. She couldn't find her purse.

Amy searched the house for a phone. There was none. Without her purse, she had no cell phone, either.

Her sluggish brain tried to comprehend. She took a shower and made a pot of coffee. Gradually, her mind cleared.

How far was the nearest neighbor? She hadn't paid much attention to that when they drove out yesterday, but surely she could walk there and use their phone. That's when she discovered that both front and back doors were locked. Ryan had given her no keys. She should have been able to open the doors from the inside but she found it wasn't the normal bolt lock that was keeping the door securely closed. Fear streamed through her as she rattled the doorknob. She was a prisoner.

Scrambling now, she tried the windows. None would open more than four inches, too small a space for her to crawl through. She could break one, throw a box or a chair through it, but now as she sat down in the bedroom, breathing hard, she contemplated the consequences. For whatever reason, Ryan had deliberately taken her only means of communication, locked her in, and left in his car. Why? Was he just afraid she'd leave him?

If she managed to get out, without any idea how far it was to another house, or whether anyone would be home when she got there, what was she going to do? Hide out in the bushes? From what? From Ryan? The idea seemed ludicrous, but so did being locked in the house. What could he possibly be up to? What would he say when he came back? What would she say? She turned it over in her mind, trying to put a positive face on it, trying not to believe the worst. Had he drugged her wine last night?

The house was silent, but it felt as though something was there with her. She looked up and caught a fleeting glimpse of the small shadow. It passed right through the door to the basement. For the second time, it seemed to be leading her to the cellar. She tiptoed to the stairs and opened the door, flipped on the dim light and started down, slowly, quietly, pausing on each step. Was she a fool to follow it? Had Ryan deliberately left her with some otherworldly thing?

She saw nothing until she reached the bottom of the stairs and turned to look at the far wall. Perched in the shadows on the top of an old bookcase was a Siamese cat. The bookcase stood in front of a large built-in cabinet that ran the full length of one wall. The cat's image seemed to waver slightly, but the blue eyes examined her with intelligence and looked from her to the cabinet and back. It pawed at the cabinet door.

Amy licked her lips. Just as she decided the cat wanted her to open the cabinet, she heard a car pull up outside. Relief flooded through her. Someone would open the door, or Ryan would be there with an explanation. She wasn't going to get caught in the cellar and find herself locked down there. She raced up the stairs and shut the basement door just in time to hear the front door click shut and a key turn in the lock. Ryan headed toward her with his arms full of clothes on hangers.

"Hi, Amy," he said. "You're finally awake. I got the last load of clothes from my apartment. Have you had lunch?"

She couldn't believe he acted so casual. "Where have you been? Why did you lock me in? Why did you take my purse? What am I supposed to do about missing work?"

He laughed. "One thing at a time. Wait until I get these clothes in the closet."

She followed him to the bedroom.

"Would you get me a cup of coffee, please, Amy?" he asked, his voice easy and pleasant, as though she had merely asked him if he'd had a nice day.

She stared at him, anger building. Had he expected her to still be asleep when he came?

"Go on, be a sweetie," he said. "We'll talk all about it in a minute."

She went to the kitchen, poured the coffee and banged the mug down on the table.

When he sauntered in and sat down a few minutes later, his wide gray eyes appraised her with just a hint of amusement. He took a sip of coffee.

"Now, what's all this about?"

"What the hell do you think you're doing, leaving me here and locking me in?" she demanded.

He smiled at her. "Amy, you were so sound asleep that I couldn't wake you. Your alarm went off, but you didn't hear it. I thought you weren't feeling up to par, so I just let you sleep and went to work. I got off early so I could come check on you." His explanation was disarmingly plausible.

"Where's my purse?" she asked. "I couldn't find my phone to call in or call you."

"Are you accusing me of taking it?" Ryan looked shocked and hurt. "Amy, why would I do that? We brought in all those boxes yesterday; heaven knows where it is. I'll help you look for it. But don't worry about work. I called in for you." He got up and stroked her back.

At first she stiffened against his touch, but it was gentle and warm, as always, and she began to relax. "What about the doors? Why did you lock me in?" She was beginning to melt.

"I only wanted you to be safe out here, Amy."

"Wouldn't I be safer if I could leave in a fire?"

"There won't be any fires, Amy. Let's go find your purse."

A few minutes of hunting produced her purse from behind a stack of boxes. Amy was sure she had left it on the kitchen counter, that she would never put it in such a place, but there it was. It would do no good to accuse Ryan of hiding it there. She hunted in it for her cell phone.

"My phone is gone, Ryan."

"I'm sorry you lost it," he said, "but you won't be needing it, dear."

"Just why is that?"

"Because you're here with me," he said. "We don't need anyone else. It's just us now. I'll take care of you."

The panic was returning. "But I have to go to work, Ryan."

"No. You don't," he said. "Just be here for me, always."

Knowing the front door wouldn't open, she ran for the living room. She picked up the heavy vase of lilacs and drew back her arm to throw it at the picture window, but Ryan caught her wrist, grabbed the vase from her hand and dashed it to the floor.

"I wouldn't try that if I were you," he said, the honey now gone from his voice.

She struggled against his grip. "Why, Ryan? Why?"

"I thought you were different," he said. "You told me you would love living in the country, just you and me."

"But not as a prisoner," she said.

"I prefer to think of you as an honored guest."

"It's not my home if I'm a guest," she said. "It's not my home if I can't leave."

He shoved her onto the couch. "I should have waited. It was too soon, last night, but once we're married, you'll see."

Amy didn't say what she was thinking, that she

would never marry him, never wanted to see him again once she escaped. Did she dare give back the ring? Or would that provoke him even more?

A shadow crept past the archway. Now she could make out that it was a cat, the Siamese cat from the cellar, only curiously, it was faint. Transparent, like a ghost. Again, she had the odd sensation that it was trying to lead her somewhere. She got up to follow it.

"Where do you think you're going?" Ryan's voice was harsh, a voice she had never heard before.

"If you don't mind, I have to go to the bathroom." At least that would allow her to see where the cat went. She followed it down the hall. Just as she reached the bathroom, the cat looked at her expectantly and then disappeared through the door to the cellar again.

Amy closed the bathroom door, hoping for a short time to herself to think. She didn't dare go down there now, with Ryan waiting for her in the living room. She might not ever get back out. She flushed the toilet and washed her hands, prolonging the moment when she had to face him again. Was there any way to reason with him? She picked up a nail file and put it in her pocket.

She stood in the living room archway. "I'm sorry, Ryan. I panicked when I found myself locked in and couldn't find my phone. It's beautiful out here." She waited.

"What I want," he said, "is just what I said. The two of us living out here, you always here for me. No one else ruining our lives, no interfering. I'll take care of you.

"But I can't trust you now, can I? I'll have to keep you locked up until I'm sure you won't try to run away. Don't think I couldn't find you and bring you back if you did."

"Please, Ryan," she said. "I'll stay here with you. Just don't lock me in. Let me have my phone." She knew it was a risk, asking for anything. Her heart was pounding, but she was trying her best to look eager to be there with him, trying to hold back the tears.

He didn't answer, just stared at her, stony-eyed.

Hope drained away.

Suddenly, he got up from the couch and pulled a pair of handcuffs from his pocket. She tried to run, but didn't get three steps down the hall before he caught her and snapped a cuff on her wrist, yanked her arms behind her and cuffed them together. Then he dragged her into the bedroom and tossed her on the bed.

"Don't try anything stupid," he said.

He went to the other bedroom and dragged the mattress to the cellar door, pushed it through and let it fall thumping down the stairs. He grabbed an armload of bedding, sheets, a pillow and a blanket, and threw them down the stairs after it. Next came a box of her clothes.

"There, you're so damned curious about the basement, that's where you'll stay." He pulled her off the bed and shoved her to the top of the steps. "Go make your bed."

"With handcuffs on?"

He unlocked them and shut the door between them. "You try anything and you'll be handcuffed to the pipes down there."

Tears welled up and spilled down her cheeks. "Let me out!" She banged on the door.

There was no answer.

She sank down on the small landing beside the door, listening, trying to figure out what Ryan was doing, hoping he would change his mind and let her out. After an hour or so, she thought she heard him leave.

It was no use just sitting there. She dragged the mattress into a corner and piled the bedding on it.

There wasn't much in the cellar, just the old bookcase in front of the long knotty pine cabinet, a beat-up old recliner and a floor lamp with no shade. In one corner, there was a makeshift bathroom. It wasn't enclosed, but at least there was a toilet next to a utility sink. There were some tiny windows high up on the wall but she didn't think she could get through them.

She was sitting on the edge of the recliner, trying to think of a way out when something soft and light landed in her lap. She felt a hint of sleek fur and saw the barely perceptible shape of the Siamese cat. If she touched it very softly, her hand did not pass through it. She could find its contours. If she sat very still, she could hear a soft purring and feel a cold nose lightly nuzzling her. The faint but alert blue eyes turned up to her, searching her face. Amy held her breath. Was she petting a ghost? Clearly it meant her no harm. Instead of frightening her, the cat's soft presence and purring calmed her racing heart.

After a few moments, the cat jumped off her lap and onto the bookcase. Again, it pawed at the cabinet door.

Amy inched the bookcase away from the door and managed to pry the cabinet open. As soon as she did so, the cat jumped inside and disappeared in the gloom to the right. The cabinet appeared to be empty and there were no shelves on the side where Amy had opened the door, though she could see shelves behind the door to the left. Had the cat gone through the wall? She could feel the wooden interior wall on the right side of the cabinet, but there was no sign of the cat.

Hoping the old floor lamp still worked, Amy dragged it over to the cabinet and looked for an outlet. The nearest one didn't allow her to put the lamp right in front of the open door where she wanted it, but she could lean it on the bookcase. That was close enough to get some light into the space. The cupboard was so large that she could easily climb into it, which she did with a bit of dread, imagining that Ryan might come down the stairs and lock her in. She hadn't heard him come back into the house, though.

The cat was definitely not in the cupboard. Where did it go? It seemed so deliberate about showing this to her. She angled her body around so that more light fell on the right side where the cat had disappeared and felt around the edges of the paneling. To her surprise, there were metal hinges on one edge. It must be a door, but there was no knob or latch that she could find. She pushed it, but it didn't give.

She ran her hands slowly up and down the right side of the door, opposite the hinges, and then moved in bit by bit from the edge. Her fingers curled into an indentation that seemed to serve as a handle. Amy braced herself and pulled.

To her surprise, the door creaked open and she was staring into a dim space surrounded by old stone foundation walls, except to the left, where a faint light glowed. She stepped down from the cabinet into the square space. It was tall enough for her to stand. When she faced the left, light filtered around the edges of another door, which she found she could open in the same way.

What she saw in the long, narrow room behind the cabinet made her gasp in horror. A shaft of afternoon light pouring between the dark curtains on a small window fell directly on a life-sized photo of a young woman. A young woman who looked like—her. My God, who was she?

Amy crept closer, eyes wide. It wasn't just that the portrait looked like her that made her heart pound. It was because in the picture, the woman was clutching a knife that was thrust into her breast. The resemblance was strong, but it was someone else who had the same shoulder-length red hair, though Amy's was curlier; the same honey-colored eyes, though Amy's had flecks of green; the same full mouth. Her look-alike was thinner and taller, and her nose was narrower. She was sagging, with blood dripping down her pale green satin nightgown. Her eyes were pleading, her mouth opened to beg for life. Whoever took that photo wasn't going to let her live.

She was wearing the sapphire and diamond ring.

Amy twisted the ring on her finger, desperately trying to pull it off. Why would Ryan give her that ring?

Breathing hard, Amy steadied herself against a desk that stood beneath the portrait. Her hand brushed a smaller picture frame sitting on the desk and knocked it over. She drew her hand away quickly, frightened at what she might find, but forced herself to search the long, narrow room for a better source of light.

Fingers trembling, she switched on a lamp. The room was papered with photos of the same woman, but in many of them she was with Ryan. He hadn't spoken of any past relationships. Fear crawled down her spine. She was frantic to find out who the red-haired woman was, what had happened to her. She picked up the picture she had knocked over and let out a soft moan. In the engraved silver frame was a wedding photo. Ryan and Julie Lockwood, it said.

She sank to the floor.

Amy had forgotten about the cat until it jumped into her lap, frightening her so badly that she dropped the photo. That brought her to her senses again. Why had Ryan lied to her? Was there really anyone who rented out this house, or had he just kept the house he had lived in with Julie until he found another woman to snare? Had Julie loved him? Did he love her?

She looked at the portrait again, the blood so real, Julie's face so beseeching, that Amy felt sick. Where was Julie now? She didn't want to admit it to herself, didn't want to allow a suspicion to rise in her mind, but she couldn't stop it. She had to find out all she could before Ryan came home, and she prayed that she wouldn't still be in that room when he came back, prayed that she'd find some way to escape.

She slid the bottom drawer of the desk open and found a photo album. It offered more photos of Julie, of Julie and Ryan together. Julie and a Siamese cat. Someone had written in "Griselda" beneath the photo.

The album wasn't full. The photos just stopped. Shaking, Amy brushed the ghostly cat off her lap, pulled herself to her feet and yanked open the top desk drawer. There was a folder tied with a green satin ribbon—was it the one from Julie's hair in the portrait?

Inside were newspaper articles about the disappearance of Julie Lockwood in May 2000. Ryan had come home after work and his wife was missing. He had called the police immediately, terrified that she had been abducted but there were no signs of foul play. Nothing had been disturbed, nothing taken, except her purse and her passport. There had been a $5,000 withdrawal from their savings account that day. The police concluded she had run away.

Ryan had been the frantic husband of a missing, pregnant wife, crazy with worry. There was no note; she was never found. Amy dared to hope that Julie had escaped, that the portrait of her dying of a knife wound was Ryan's sick idea of revenge, produced with a computer, perhaps.

Until she reached into the desk drawer again and found the purse. With the passport.

And Ryan's notes detailing everything he had done after he found out Julie had betrayed him by getting pregnant. He wasn't going to share Julie with anyone, certainly not with some sniveling, crying infant! The damned cat was bad enough.

Julie had begged to leave, to go home to her parents and have her baby, begged for a divorce, begged for her child. She was only nineteen.

Amy shivered. It was as if her world had turned to ice. Tears streamed down her cheeks, partly for Julie, partly for herself. What had he done with her body?

The Siamese cat nuzzled her softly. Griselda. How did she become a ghost?

Defending Julie, the notes said. Ryan had slit her throat.

Griselda jumped lightly onto the desk and then up and through the curtained window. Amy pulled the desk chair under the window and stood on it, trying to see where the cat went. She could barely make out Griselda's faint shadow running across the side yard to the lilacs. There, she lay down and put her head on her paws.

Julie's grave. It had to be.

Amy quivered and rubbed her arms. She dropped the curtain closed, put everything back the way she had found it, and searched for a way to escape. There was a curtain over a door that probably led to one of those outside basement entries that were under trap doors, the kind you see on farm houses. She tried the knob. Nothing. This door, too, was locked.

She couldn't bear staying in the narrow room that reeked of jealousy and death any longer and retreated to the main cellar. Sitting on the battered recliner, she tried to clear her mind. Without a plan she was doomed. Would she join Julie among the lilacs? What would it take for Ryan to kill again? Why had he kept all that evidence?

The answer seemed to scream at her from the portrait. He wanted to remember Julie and what he had done to her, and he was sure it would never be found. Except for Griselda, he was right. No one coming down to the cellar through the house would ever suspect there was anything behind the wall with the built-in cabinet, and there would be no reason to enter from the storm cellar doors if you were sure you'd seen everything. Why would he worry now? He'd been free of suspicion for five years!

Now he even had a replacement for Julie. No wonder he had never introduced Amy to his friends or family, or anyone else.

She rubbed her wrists where the handcuffs had been too tight and looked up at the locked cellar door. All she had to work with was a nail file and the ghost of a cat. Unless there was something else in that awful room.

She was working up her courage to go back when she heard a car drive up. Griselda shot out through the cabinet doors. Amy hastily closed them, shoved the bookcase back in place and dragged the lamp over to the recliner. She started putting the bedding on the mattress. How was she ever going to face Ryan as though she knew nothing of his past?

He walked around overhead, in the kitchen. She heard water running, the chirp-chirp-chirp of the microwave, and then a knock on the cellar door. She wasn't getting any closer to him than she had to. She walked to the foot of the stairs and in a steady, controlled voice she said, "Come in." What a ridiculous game to play! Why was he even knocking?

The door opened and Ryan put down a tray of food.

"We can't have you starving, now, can we?" he said. "You can leave the tray by the door when you're finished."

He shut the door and locked it.

Amy retrieved the tray of food. How did she know it wasn't poisoned? She hoped that he was still fantasizing about keeping her and hadn't made up his mind to kill her.

It was warmed-up pizza. No plate. No knife or fork. Trust him to think of that. Nothing to use for a weapon or a tool. She ate and did as she was told.

The light outside was growing dim. She could hear Ryan overhead shoving boxes around and unpacking things. He got the boom box going, playing "Moon River," her favorite song. Loud. He played it over and over again until she wanted to scream. The sound reverberated through the small house. She remembered how romantic she thought he was, dancing with her to that song in her tiny apartment.

She didn't want to risk sleep but she was exhausted. Rummaging through the box Ryan had pitched down the stairs, she found some old jeans, a t-shirt and sneakers to sleep in. She wasn't going barefoot, in case she had to run. She lay on the mattress and stared at the ceiling.

Griselda jumped up on her chest. The ghost cat settled down, light as a feather, and began to purr. The sound soothed her and gave her courage.

Finally the house was quiet. By the time her watch said 11:00 p.m., Amy hadn't heard anything upstairs for an hour. Unless he was reading or just waiting to see what she would do, Ryan was probably asleep. Did she dare sneak back into the hidden room while he was in the house?

As if Griselda had read her thoughts, the cat jumped to the bookcase again and pawed the cabinet door. Amy wasted no time. She dragged the bookcase away from the cabinet, careful to make no sound, and slipped in through the hidden door with Griselda.

Ryan had been there. She was sure of it. He must have come in through the trap door while the stereo was so loud. She couldn't quite figure out how she knew he had been there. Nothing seemed changed…No, the photo on the desk had been moved. She tried the top desk drawer. It was locked. Panic washed over her. Did he know she had been in here? Surely not. If he had, why wouldn't he have done something by now?

She tried the other desk drawers. All locked. What else could be in them? Something worse than she had already found?

Griselda wound between her legs and rubbed against the desk. She reached up both front paws and put them on the left middle drawer, looking up at Amy with her transparent blue eyes. "Here," they seemed to say.

Amy slid the nail file across the top of the drawer between it and the desk frame and felt it stop against the metal locking tab that prevented the drawer from opening. If she could figure out which way it turned, maybe she could push it down. She worked at it furiously, first from one side and then the other, frightened of what she might find, terrified of being discovered, but desperate for answers.

Her thumb and forefinger were blistered, but the lock wouldn't budge. There had to be a way to get it open! She brushed her hair back and felt the barrette. She pulled it from her hair and opened the wire ends. She worked one around in the lock, twisting it over and over.

Suddenly, it gave. She yanked the drawer open and almost let out a scream. In a clear plastic box was a large carving knife. The knife in the painting. There were specks of dried brown blood on it.

Amy recoiled. She knew whose blood she was looking at. Waves of revulsion rolled through her. She thought she would faint. Time seemed to stand still.

It was Griselda rubbing softly around her ankles that brought Amy back from the brink of paralysis. She snatched the plastic box, glad for a weapon, even one that had killed Julie Lockwood. Heart pounding, she climbed back through the cabinet and lay down in the dark, the knife tucked under the mattress, waiting.

Hours passed. Amy's terror subsided. Maybe he wasn't going to come after her. Maybe he didn't know she had been in the secret room. The exhaustion she felt earlier returned and she drifted off to sleep, Griselda by her feet.

* * *

How long had she been asleep when the barest tapping of a ghostly paw on her eyelid awakened her? She opened her eyes a slit to see moonlight streaming in through the far window and the silhouette of a large man standing over her. Ryan!

Did he know she was awake? That she had seen him? Had he seen the knife?

Apparently not. He began to reach down as though he were going to embrace her.

Amy rolled off the other side of the mattress and stood up, snatching the knife up behind her back.

"What do you want, Ryan?" she asked, keeping her voice level and cool, trying not to shake. Trying not to let him see her fear. Determined not to let on what she knew.

His voice was back to the silky, romantic tones he had used in the past month, the voice that had seduced her into believing he was the one. "What I always want, Amy," he coaxed. "The two of us, together. Just like before."

"It's not like before, Ryan. I'm locked up now. I can't love someone who holds me prisoner."

"You'll get used to it. You'll come around."

"No, Ryan," she said. "I won't."

He took a step to come around the side of the mattress toward her. Just as he did so, Griselda jumped at him and clawed at his face. Amy was surprised to see long red scratches appear.

"That damned cat," Ryan bellowed, rubbing the wounds and looking around to find her. She had disappeared.

"You know about her?" asked Amy, astonished.

"Of course I know about her," Ryan growled.

"You told me I was superstitious or had an overactive imagination."

"I know what I said."

"I thought you just found this place," said Amy. "When did you see the cat?"

Ryan didn't answer right away. He sighed heavily.

"You're too damned curious for your own good," he said. "You and that blasted cat. If I can't trust you…" His voice trailed off.

"Trust me?" she asked. "What can I do locked up in the cellar?"

For answer, he lunged at her, reaching out to grab her by the hair. She flinched away from him in time, but he caught sight of the knife as in glinted in the moonlight.

"You'll never live to tell about it," he threatened, coming for her.

But she was faster.

She didn't know where the strength came from, or what helped her to move so swiftly. Just as he charged toward her, she turned back and held steady. The knife plunged deep into his chest, forced in by his own momentum. He fell forward on her. She felt herself buckle under his weight and cried out in pain as they hit the floor, the handle of the knife jamming into her stomach.

He rolled off her gasping and flailing, then tried to extract the long blade from his chest. A dark stain was spreading across his shirt.

Amy crawled free of him and ran blindly up the stairs. He struggled to his feet and lumbered after her.

The door was locked. She couldn't open it.

"You'll never live," he choked out.

He pressed her against the cellar door, his blood smearing her. She nearly threw up.

She grabbed the doorknob for support and kneed him in the groin. As he doubled over in pain, she used all her remaining strength to push him down the stairs.

He crashed in a heap at the bottom and lay still.

She crumpled on the landing and wept in the dark.

When Ryan didn't move and the minutes ticked past, she wondered whether she would still die in the cellar. No one knew where she was and she had no way of getting out.

But Ryan must have the key.

It was a sliver of hope, but it meant she had to search him.

Weak and spent, she didn't even trust herself to walk down the stairs. She slid down one step at a time until she reached the bottom. For long moments she listened to him draw rattling, sick breaths as the pool of blood spread across the floor. Would he come after her again?

Once she was satisfied he was unconscious, she forced herself to reach into his pockets, heart pounding.

She had the key, but just that one.

She climbed the steps and unlocked the cellar door. The house looked peaceful and homey in the moonlight.

She flipped on a light switch and began to search.

Before she found his keys, she found Ryan's cell phone. She called 911.

* * *

They found her sitting in the living room softly petting something they could not see.

"He's in the cellar," she said. "Julie is under the lilacs."

- The End -

Déjà Vu

By Barbara J. Baldwin

MORETOWN, OK—A bus carrying five preschool children slid on an icy road and careened over an embankment early today. The driver and three children escaped with minor injuries. Two children remain hospitalized in critical condition.

They rose quietly and flew out the window without a sound. The curtains waved slightly as though a breeze had passed, yet the windows were closed tight against the cold, snowy night. Because they were young and had been told by their parents countless times not to stray, they remained in the small town but their curiosity took them beyond the bounds of the building. They didn't feel the freezing temperatures and the falling snow didn't penetrate their light clothing. The pain of their injuries disappeared and they delighted in their newfound freedom.

"To the park," Billy said, squeezing his friend's hand and urging her onward.

"I can't do it," Sally said when they got to the swings. "I haven't learned how."

Billy pumped higher and higher until the swing flew completely around the bar at the top. "Yes, you can. We can do anything." The swing spun over and over, wrapping the chains tighter until Billy sat very high in the air.

"I'm dizzy!" He let go of the chains to hold his head and promptly fell towards the ground. He landed with a soft 'poof' on the snow. He looked down. The cowboys and horses on the blue background of his pajamas were covered with snow. He brushed it off, but never felt the cold wetness.

"Push me," Sally said, wiggling her bare feet in the air a foot above the ground. Her flowered, yellow night-gown fluttered in the night.

Billy complied, but soon wasn't having any fun. "Let's go to the slide." He left her behind as he zipped over the playground and raced up the slide instead of taking the steps. Turning over and lying on his belly, he let go of the sides and slid quickly to the bottom, plopping into the snow. He rolled over and looked up through the drifts. He could see through the snow. He looked down. It almost looked like he could see the snow through him.

Through the rest of winter, Billy and Sally continued their escapades in town. They never ate, seldom rested, and as the time went by stayed away longer and longer with their amusements.

"I miss my mommy," Sally said late one night.

Billy, being two years older, came up with a plan. That night they zipped high in the air above Sally's house and sat on the telephone wires. Almost immediately Sally heard her mommy's voice and then the voice of her Grandma Jones. She couldn't understand what they were saying, but her mother's voice sounded so sad it made Sally cry and she didn't know why.

Billy hugged her and told her it would be all right.

"I miss my friends," Sally cried another night.

The very next day, Billy held her hand as they found their way to the preschool. They saw their pictures on the bulletin board that was always decorated for what their teacher called "the seasons." Their faces smiled out of the center of two flowers.

"Why are we the only ones on the flowers?" Sally asked out loud, but the teacher didn't answer.

She and Billy stood in the middle of the bright red

and blue carpet that covered the floor as the children held hands and sang "Ring Around the Rosy."

"I'm it." Sally clapped her hands, laughing happily at being the first in the middle of the circle. But then Bonnie skipped into the center and the children gleefully called Bonnie's name.

"I'm first," Sally said, pushing at Bonnie. The little girl turned around to face her, pausing for just a second with her eyes wide. But she didn't speak and when the children called her name again, she began playing the game as though Sally weren't there.

Sally started to cry. "I want to go home," she told Billy.

Billy curled her hand in his and together they walked past the little desks and out into the bright sunshine. Billy was sad, too, because he missed playing baseball with his Dad and chasing his dog around the yard. They had gone to see Zero one night but he had growled at them and wouldn't play. Now, Billy didn't know what to tell Sally.

Billy took her back to the swings at the park. He wanted to push her to make her feel better, but she just sat there. Her small shoulders bowed; her head hung down. He looked around and spied some flowers that had been planted under a tree. He pulled up two small daisies and took them to Sally.

"Here." He held out his chubby hand, the daisy bent in half because he had broken the stem. She lifted her head and smiled, but it was a very sad smile and it made Billy's stomach hurt. Still, she took the daisy and tucked it behind her ear. Billy took the other one and stuffed the stem into the buttonhole of his pajamas. He was concentrating so hard on that small task that at first he didn't hear it.

When the sound came again, his head jerked up.

"They're calling us back," he said excitedly. "Come

on, let's go." He grabbed Sally's smaller hand and they quickly raced back to the building. But when they arrived at the place where they had first left, Sally tugged him to a stop.

"I can't go with you," she said sadly. Her pale green eyes shimmered with tears.

"But you have to. You're my best friend." Billy's brow furrowed. "They're calling again, stronger this time. I have to go."

"I know," Sally said, "but I can't." And she watched, heartbroken, as Billy disappeared back into the building where she couldn't go, his wilted daisy floating to the ground next to the wall.

Inside the hospital ward, Billy's mom and Sally's mom sat side by side at the small beds where their children lay in comas.

"Do you think they will ever wake up?" Billy's mom asked.

"I don't know," Sally's mom answered, tears clogging her throat. "Sometimes I swear I hear Sally's voice. Just the other day when I was talking to her Grandma Jones, the line was so full of static I could hardly make out a word Grandma said. But clear as a bell, I thought I heard Sally call me."

Billy's mom nodded. "Mrs. West at the preschool says the children miss them so much. She told me that Bonnie even thinks she's seen Sally when they play 'Ring Around the Rosy.'"

Sally's mom started crying again. "That's her favorite game."

"Mommy?" A reedy voice immediately stopped the conversation. Both mothers jumped up from their chairs and bent over the sides of the small beds.

As one child spoke again, the monitor on the other

stopped clicking its steady rhythm and gave off a long eerie alarm. One mother cried in joy as the other cried in heartbreak.

* * *

Bill first noticed her in the park one summer when he was fifteen. He and his friends were playing football and even though he jumped high, the ball sailed over his head. He chased after it as it rolled to a stop at the swing set. He grabbed the ball and stood, coming face to face with bright green eyes and pale blonde hair as the girl dragged her toes to bring the swing to a stop so she wouldn't hit him. Something about her gaze tugged at his consciousness and a fleeting image raced across his mind so fast he couldn't catch it.

"Bill, come on," his friends called. He just stood there, wondering what it was about her that pulled at him.

The girl gave him a shy smile. "Hi," she said.

"Hi," he replied. His friends yelled at him again and he turned and raced back towards the game. When he looked over his shoulder at the swings, the girl was walking away.

* * *

Bill got a job at the local Dairy Queen the minute he turned sixteen. He wanted enough money to buy a car. His mom didn't want him to have one because they lived in the country and she was afraid for him to drive in the winter. She told him he had been in an accident when he was only five, but he really didn't remember it. All he knew was that his friends had cars and it was important because he didn't want his dad driving him to school dances when he had a date.

The girl came in for ice cream after softball practice and Bill realized she was on the same team as his little sister. She had grown taller since he last saw her, but her green eyes still looked at him with a sense of awareness, as though she knew him. Bill's stomach dropped to his toes when she came up to his counter to order.

"Hi," she said, giving him that same, shy smile. It was the middle of summer but Bill could swear he saw snow swirling around her head and white flakes landing on her lashes. He blinked and shook his head because for just a moment, he thought her yellow jersey had a ruffle around the neck and tiny flowers on it, just like a little girl's nightgown.

"Hello," she said again to get his attention.

"Sorry," he apologized. "Do I know you?"

She shrugged. "I come out and listen to CDs with Beth sometimes," she answered. Beth was his sister. "My name is Daisy."

Daisy. Electricity sparked between them. A sense of dizziness swept through Bill, as though he had been spinning in circles for a long time. It was the same kind of feeling he had as a kid when he and his friends tried to get his tree swing to go high enough to loop over the branch.

That summer, he helped Daisy with her pitching and batting whenever he wasn't working. Beth tagged along when they rode their bikes down the dirt road to the river. If his friends knew he was hanging out with his eleven-year-old sister and her friend, he would never hear the end of it. After all, he was going to be a junior this year.

Whenever they were together, Bill always had a sense of déjà vu. It was like he knew her but he didn't. There was this sense of something just out of reach, but the feeling was fleeting and always disappeared before he could latch on to it.

He liked Daisy as a friend, and if he were truthful,

he and Beth got along just fine, unlike most brothers and sisters. He had always been protective of her because she was five years younger than he was. His dad told him that little girls were precious and should be taken care of and not bullied about. His mother reminded him about their neighbor, Mrs. Jones, who had lost her little girl, Sally, in the same accident he had been in, and even though she had more children, they were all boys. In fact, some had been Bill's friends most of his life. Funny that he didn't remember Sally, but then he didn't remember the accident either.

Since Bill had been held back a year in school because of the accident, he was a senior when Daisy and Beth started high school. Daisy's parents wouldn't allow her to go out on real dates, but Bill could pick her up and take her and his sister to the school dances. He didn't mind because he liked being with her. Before long, they were inseparable. Bill helped her with her algebra and biology and she tutored him in French, which he had to have to graduate. She cheered for him at the football games and he went to all of her volleyball and basketball games.

When spring came, Bill took Daisy to the city park. He wanted to ask her to prom and didn't want his younger sister around this time. They walked over to the swings and she sat down on one of the seats.

"Do you ever get a feeling of déjà vu?" she asked as she pushed back and put the swing in motion. "Sometimes I think I have been here before—in this exact spot with the exact same person."

Bill looked at her from the next swing as he kicked back and forth, trying to get the swing to go high enough to be parallel with the top bar. He remembered trying it with his friends, but not with Daisy.

Daisy. He dragged his feet on the ground, skidding to

a stop as his heart pounded faster than it ever had during sports. He looked over at her to see snowflakes drifting softly down all around her. He glanced up to realize it was only the old cottonwood tree that stood near the swing set, but he couldn't shake the feeling that she was right. They had been here before.

His gaze followed the cottonwood fluffs down to the ground, where bright colored flowers were planted around the base of the tree. In a trance, almost as though he watched his own body do it, he walked over to the tree and picked two daisies. One of the stems broke as he pulled it from the ground, so it drooped to the side when he held it out to Daisy.

She tucked the flower behind her ear. He looked down, trying to find a hole to put his own daisy in, seeing cowboys and horses on a blue background instead of the bright red football jersey he knew he had put on that morning. In his mind, the years dropped away and he was five again, swinging with Sally. But Sally had died in that long ago accident.

His gaze met Daisy's.

She smiled at him, her bright green eyes glittering, and suddenly he knew.

"You've always been my best friend," he said softly.

- The End -

Forgotten, But Not Gone
By Sheri L. McGathy

"Wait." Chloe pulled on her boyfriend, Matt's, arm, wishing now they hadn't left the high school campus for lunch. "Can't we go around?"

"What's the matter? Afraid of a few ghosts?" Lonny Blakeman's laugh was a bit too high-pitched as he strolled up beside them.

"No, I'm not afraid." Chloe slapped Lonny playfully on the back. "I don't believe in ghosts." Turning to Matt, she added, "I just don't understand why we have to cut through the old cemetery."

"Because," Matt said, as he stepped behind her and wrapped his arms around her waist, "It'll take too long to walk around. If I'm late for history class one more time, old man Seymore will ban me from prom." He leaned his chin on her shoulder and said, "You do want to go to your Senior Prom, don't you? It's the Bicentennial, and I plan to wear my flag suspenders."

Chloe laughed. "Who says I'll miss prom?"

"Ha, ha." Matt poked her in the ribs. "Come on. If we hurry, we can just make it by the final bell."

Chloe shrugged and followed Matt and Lonny through the open gates and along the footpath that led away from the limestone wall encircling the cemetery. Near the back, the waist-high wall separated the local high school from the old prairie cemetery—separated the living from the dead. The thought sent shivers up Chloe's spine.

The cemetery overlooked the small community of Prairie Pride. Many of the graves nearest the high school were unmarked, the remains within nothing more than nameless souls. Her grandfather said the graves were from travelers who'd died along the Oregon Trail. None of that mattered to Chloe. She didn't care. She hated the place. Hated the whine of the wind as it swept past the headstones, some so weathered you could no longer make out the names etched upon them. Yet, most of all, she hated the loneliness that haunted the place and the constant reminder that no matter what you did in life, eventually you were lost to time. Death was final and that frightened her.

The grass felt spongy beneath her feet. She frowned as brown, muddy water oozed up and soaked through her tennis shoes. Last night's storm had been less than kind to the old cemetery, evidenced by the broken tree limbs littering the ground and the flattened, mud-soaked grass.

Chloe noticed many of the graves close to the wall had suffered the worst of the rain. Layers of topsoil had washed away, taking with it large patches of grass and leaving behind deep rectangular depressions that pocked the earth.

A sparrow splashed in the dirty water at the edge of one of the washed-out graves, its head bobbing up and down as it pecked at something buried in the mud. Its constant chirping reminded Chloe of laughter. She paused to watch, unable to keep from smiling at the bird's animated antics.

A small, pale object broke free of the mud and dangled over the water's surface, yet before the sparrow could claim his prize, it flew away, leaving its treasure behind.

Chloe started toward it.

"Chloe, what are you doing?" Matt called after her. "We'll be late."

She ignored him as she squatted beside the grave. The topsoil here had sunk a good foot. Rainwater pooled at the base and trickled out in a slow, brown stream. A small bunch of wood sorrel clung to a large dirt clod at the edge of the grave. The pale purple blooms were speckled with mud, the petals wilted and sagging toward the ground. Tangled within the plant's roots was a tarnished chain with miniature charms dangling from several of the fine links. Chloe prodded one of the charms with her finger and smiled as the image of a small child swung free of the mud. It appeared to be carved from ivory. To either side of the charm was a delicate silver heart. She plucked the chain off the sorrel bulbs. In all, the chain held seven tiny hearts and six ivory charms, each the image of a child, yet no image appeared to be the same.

Lonny whistled. "Would you look at that? Where do you suppose it came from?"

Chloe nodded toward the grave.

"What?" Matt asked as he approached.

As Chloe held the bracelet up for him to see, a shrill ringing rent the air.

Matt grabbed her wrist and hauled her to her feet. "That's the period bell. We've gotta go now. In five minutes, we're officially late."

Lonny waved them on. "Go on. I've got study hall this period. Nobody cares if I'm late."

Stuffing the bracelet in her jeans pocket, Chloe started running.

She and Matt took their seats just as the final warning bell rang.

Mr. Seymore glanced over the rim of his glasses and said, "Miss Brown, Mr. Cooper. So glad you could join us."

"Oh, so are we, sir." Matt sounded so sincere.

Chloe turned toward the window to hide her laughter. Her giggles stopped as soon as she saw the woman standing on the other side of the limestone wall. Mud streaked her plain black dress and stained her once-white apron. Her brown hair hung in matted disarray down her back and stood in sharp contrast to a face with skin as pale as moonlight. Chloe wondered where the woman had come from and what she'd been doing to look the way she did.

Somewhere in the distance, Chloe heard Mr. Seymore's nasal voice say, "Class, turn to page 251…." as she watched the woman take a step closer to the wall. Her dark eyes seemed to bore holes in Chloe's skin when she held out her hand toward the school.

"Matt." Chloe squeezed his arm and whispered, "Look out the window. Who's that woman?"

"What woman?"

"Right there," Chloe said louder than she intended.

"Miss Brown, have you something to share with the rest of the class?"

Chloe glanced out the window. The woman was gone. "N-No, Mr. Seymore. Nothing."

* * *

Chloe moaned and buried her head under her pillow. The tapping continued…slow and rhythmic…the sound working its way beneath the layers of down.

She sat up and frowned. What was making that sound? She threw back her covers and started to reach for the light switch above her headboard when a muffled moan joined the tapping to resound throughout a room gone suddenly cold, changing the once familiar darkness into a presence that felt both alien and menacing.

Laughter echoed from the deep shadows that draped the room.

The hair along Chloe's arms bristled and a tingle raced up her spine. "Who's there?" she whispered.

She was answered with more laughter, followed by the soft patter of footsteps on the wooden bedroom floor.

Something scraped against the window screen.

Clutching her pillow to her chest, Chloe slowly turned toward the window, toward the strange tapping that refused to cease. The woman from the cemetery was standing on the other side of the screen.

Chloe screamed.

She was still screaming when the bedroom light snapped on overhead and her mother shook her shoulders.

"Chloe! Wake up. You're dreaming."

"No, it was real." Chloe shook her head and pointed toward the window. "There was someone there, I saw her. She was standing on the roof."

Her mom glanced around the room. "Dave?"

"Now, Flo," her dad said, even as he pulled back the drapes and peered out the window. "There's no way a person can get up this high without a ladder."

"Dave." Her mom narrowed her eyes and jerked her head toward the door.

Just then, Chloe's older brother, Brad, stumbled into the room. "What's going on?"

"You've perfect timing, son." Her dad patted Brad on the shoulder. "Come on, let's take a look outside."

Brad moaned and followed his dad down the hall.

"Now, back to sleep," her mom whispered against her cheek before snapping off the light. She closed the door behind her as she left the room.

Chloe looked at her alarm clock. It flashed 12:00.

* * *

Chloe sat up and rubbed the heels of her palms against her eyes. Yawning, she dangled her legs over the side of the bed and gave the room a quick glance. Early morning sunlight streamed in through the window, sweeping away the night's shadows along with the lingering dredges of her dream.

"Dream," she mumbled as she slipped on her jeans. "More like a nightmare."

"Chloe, are you awake yet?" Her mom's voice floated up the stairs.

"Yes, Mom," Chloe yelled back as she tossed off her T-shirt and pulled a clean one from the dresser. Still yanking the shirt over her head, she started toward the door and stepped on something sharp.

"Ow!" She stumbled forward and barely avoided hitting the wall. "What in the…" She stared down at the charm bracelet lying on the floor. Chloe glanced toward her nightstand. She could have sworn she'd left the bracelet there next to the alarm clock. She retrieved the bracelet and spread the tarnished chain with its dingy-white charms flat upon her palm. As she flipped over one of the ivory charms, she thought she heard tapping from the hallway, but when she turned to see, there was no one there.

Goose bumps raced along her arms as her dream came back to her with vivid clarity. She recalled laughter, the sound of footsteps, and the woman outside her window, tapping on the screen, a screen that was two stories off the ground.

The thought made her shiver.

"Don't even go there, Chloe girl," she immediately scolded herself. "You don't believe in ghosts!"

She frowned down at the six tiny charms and seven tarnished hearts. Clamping her hand over the bracelet, she mumbled, "And this needs cleaned."

She stuffed the bracelet in her jeans pocket and left the room.

* * *

"Give me a minute, Chloe," Mr. Noel said without looking up from the small square of blue velvet. "I need to finish this appraisal for Mrs. Jackson and then I'll get your bracelet for you."

Chloe nodded, though she was sure he didn't see her.

While she waited, she strolled along side the counter-top, running her fingers across the smooth glass as she admired the fine jewelry nestled upon yards of blue and red velvet.

A bell chimed, the cheery jingle announcing another visitor to the store.

"Not again." Mr. Noel's voice held more than a hint of irritation.

Chloe looked up from an array of glittering silver and gold chains just as the jeweler pushed the front door closed. As he returned to the counter, he nudged his glasses back in place, then nodded toward the door. "That bell's been ringing all day, but nine times out of ten there's no one there." He rubbed a hand over his balding scalp, then sighed. "I guess I'll have it looked at before it drives me crazy."

Chloe glanced at the plain glass door with its faded yellow shade and black and white WELCOME sign posted in the lower right corner. As she watched, a hazy grayness seeped under the threshold and spread outward at the base. It hovered over the tiled floor for the briefest moment before slithering back beneath the door.

Suddenly, the store felt anything but welcoming to her.

"Chloe?"

"Yes?" She barely managed to keep her voice level.

Mr. Noel crooked a finger at her, then bent down and pulled a small box from a shelf beneath the counter. He looked up as she approached. Lifting the cardboard lid, he said, "This is an interesting piece of jewelry. I don't think I've ever seen anything exactly like it."

He spread another blue cloth out on the glass display

case and carefully arranged the bracelet so the polished charms pointed away from the now shiny chain. "Look at this." He pointed down to one of the hearts.

Chloe could see the word "boy" etched into the smooth silver followed by the letters "JT."

"Six of the seven hearts have something similar. Four say "boy", two say "girl." The seventh heart simply has four numbers imprinted on it: 1876. And see here?" Mr. Noel flipped one of the carved charms over. "Each scrimshaw piece has a set of letters that match the letters etched into one of the six hearts."

Chloe's head came up. "Scrimshaw?"

"Whalebone." Mr. Noel carefully placed the bracelet back in the box, then slipped the box into a shiny tan bag with the words "Noel's Jewelry Store" printed in the middle. "Looks like you found yourself someone's idea of a mother's ring." He handed her the bag. "Maybe even a hundred year-old one. Interested in selling it? The craftsmanship isn't especially fine, but it might be worth something since it's so unusual."

Chloe paid him for the cleaning. "I think I'll hang on to it for now."

"Suit yourself." Mr. Noel nodded toward the bag. "But if you change your mind, give me a call."

"I will." She waved as she walked away. As she reached for the door handle, the bell rang and the door swung open, banging against her arm. She dropped the bag. When she bent to retrieve it, she noticed a muddy footprint staining the tile floor. Pale purple petals from a sorrel bloom clung to the wet outline of a bare foot.

Her heart raced in her chest. A part of her didn't want to look up even as she glanced over the top of the welcome sign. The woman from the cemetery was there, standing on the other side of the road with both hands outstretched, her dark, unblinking eyes staring toward the store.

* * *

Chloe kept her steps small and quick as she hurried away from the store. When she reached the end of the block, she paused and glanced behind her. The woman was gone. Chloe slowly released her breath. She hadn't realized she'd been holding it.

As she pressed the crosswalk button, a cool breeze wafted over her arm. On its breath rode the hint of laughter. Her world seemed to pause, then fade away as the hesitant touch of tiny fingertips trailed across her waist. She saw the shadowy shapes of children skipping around her, heard their footsteps on the smooth sidewalk as they sang, "Ashes, ashes..." before they sank to the ground, their laughter begging her to join them if she dared.

She wanted to. She smiled, imagining herself singing and dancing while her laughter trailed out behind her. She took a step forward.

"Chloe, look out!" Matt grabbed her arm and yanked her back to the curb.

The blare of a car horn rushed in to fill the void left behind when the sweet call of laughter faded.

"What were you thinking? Why would you step into the traffic like that?" Matt entwined his fingers through hers and pulled her a few more steps away from the curb. "You could have been killed."

"I..." Chloe shook her head. She glanced toward the curb. What had she been thinking? She shrugged as she met Matt's concerned gaze. "I must have been daydreaming."

Waves of soft brown hair fell forward to tickle her cheeks as Matt pressed his forehead against hers.

"About me?"

Chloe laughed. "You wish."

"A guy can dream." Matt flashed her a toothy grin. "Come on. I finally got the beast running again." He patted the hood of his '72 Duster. "Let's go for a drive."

He held open the driver's side door and waited for Chloe to slide in before he climbed in and started the car. As he pulled away from the curb, he nodded toward the bag in her lap. "What'cha buy from old man Noel?"

"It's the bracelet I found at the old cemetery." She shrugged. "I had it cleaned."

Matt eased the car over the railroad tracks that marked the edge of town. As soon as they were beyond the tracks, he punched the accelerator. The car immediately responded, zipping past the Farmer's Market as it raced down the highway.

Chloe snapped on the radio and leaned back. She sighed as the wind tossed her hair from her face. It felt good to do nothing.

Matt draped an arm over the back of the seat. "So. How's the bracelet look without all the dirt?"

"It looks good." Chloe pulled the bracelet from its packaging and slipped it on. She held her wrist out for him to see. She smiled as the small charms twirled and swayed in the breeze from the open window. "Mr. Noel thought it might be worth something. He wanted to buy it."

Matt glanced at the bracelet as he offered her a sip of his limeade. "Are you gonna sell the thing?"

"I don't think so. I really like it." Chloe glanced out the window as they neared the abandoned stone house that marked the turnoff to the river road. She swore she'd seen someone standing beneath the cottonwood tree near the side of the house. Yet, as they drove past, all she saw was the tree's shadowy silhouette against the crumbling limestone wall. She kept her gaze locked to that shadow as Matt made the turn onto the dirt road. Dust immediately invaded the car. Chloe leaned over and rolled up the window on the passenger door. As she sat back, she glanced into the rearview mirror.

A scream built low in her throat and threatened to choke her as she gazed into the black, soulless eyes reflected in the silvery glass. She couldn't look away, though she wanted nothing more than to close her eyes to the nightmare she found herself within. She was caught between the sane and the insane. She wanted to both laugh and cry, but was unable to do either as she stared at the woman sitting in the back seat.

The woman's silence invaded the car, and in that strange void where nothing existed but her and the woman in the back seat, Chloe heard one word drift out from the static-filled radio: mine.

And then the woman was gone.

"What the..." Matt yelled as limeade splashed against the dash.

Chloe stared down at the crushed paper cup clutched in her hand and the cubes of yellow-green ice scattered across her lap.

Matt pulled the car to the side of the road and slammed it into park. "What's wrong with you lately?" He didn't wait for her answer. Instead, he reached into the back and grabbed a rag off the seat. Chloe remained silent as he mopped up the limeade and brushed the ice from her lap. She didn't move as he took the crushed cup from her hand and tossed it out the window.

Dropping the rag to the floorboard, he leaned back and ran his hands through his hair. "What's going on?"

"Nothing," she lied. What could she say? That she

feared she was slowly losing her mind because a woman only she could see was following her.

"Damn it, Chloe!" Matt slammed the heel of his palm against the steering wheel. "Why won't you talk to me?" He glared at the bracelet. "You've been acting weird since you found that thing."

Tears blurred her vision as Chloe fumbled with the bracelet latch. "Nothing's wrong with me." The clasp wouldn't open. "Nothing!" she shouted. "I'm not crazy!" She buried her face in her hands and began to cry in earnest. "I'm not...crazy."

"I never said you were." Matt pulled her against his chest and stroked her back.

She felt safe in his arms.

When her tears eased, she sat up and wiped the moisture from her face. "I'm sorry." She shook her head and gave a halfhearted laugh. "I have been acting like an idiot. But I'm okay now. Promise." She ran her hands through her hair and sighed. "And as much as I'd rather stay here with you, I need to go home."

Matt nodded. He didn't say another word until he'd pulled up to the curb in front of Chloe's house and stepped out of the car. He held open the door for her. As she ducked under his arm, he caught her wrist, his fingers pressing the tiny charms into her skin. "Are we okay?"

She brushed an errant curl from his forehead. "Yeah, we're cool."

The tension between them evaporated the moment Matt smiled. "Lonny and I are going to hang out tonight, play some pool. You wanna tag along?"

"I can't. My parents are taking a weekend getaway, and Brad and I are supposed to use the time to bond." Chloe rolled her eyes before adding, "If we don't kill each other first."

"How 'bout I stop by later and save you?" Matt said as he got back into the car.

She offered him a hint of a smile. "That might be nice."

"Then it's a date." Matt waved as he drove away.

As the car disappeared around the corner, Chloe looked down at her wrist and frowned. A ring of tiny blisters marred her skin. Six blisters in all, one for each carved charm.

* * *

Chloe wasn't sure whether it was the insistent drone from the TV that woke her, or the fact that the house seemed strangely still, as if it held its breath in anticipation.

She stared at the OFF THE AIR logo glowing on the TV screen and the white sheet of paper taped at its center that read, "You fell asleep, so I left. Brad."

Chloe pulled the note off the screen and tossed it on the coffee table. "So much for bonding." She sighed. It was late. Matt must not have been able to get away.

"He's probably out with Brad," she mumbled.

Switching off the TV, she started for the staircase. She hadn't taken three steps when she heard an audible click echo into the silent room and saw a pale glow creep across the floor.

"What is going..."

She turned and found herself face-to-face with the woman from the cemetery, the woman she knew was dead, even though the shrinking realm of sanity within her mind argued it was impossible.

Chloe clung to that sanity as the woman passed her hand through Chloe's arm, leaving behind icy numbness where her fingers met Chloe's flesh. Chloe willed her feet to move, willed her eyes to look away from the woman's lifeless stare, but fear held her frozen. When the woman jabbed a finger toward the TV, the bracelet on Chloe's wrist began to shake, making the tiny charms rattle. The sound filled her with dread.

The TV screen flickered and the speakers crackled in response. The OFF THE AIR logo disappeared in a wave of rolling lines and white static, replaced by the wavering image of a shadow-draped barn, its weather-worn boards warped and rough where the paint had peeled away. The barn sat silhouetted against a night sky riddled with the sharp flashes of lightning. Wind sucked at its closed doors. Chloe heard the rattle of the old hinges.

The woman nodded at the bracelet on Chloe's wrist, then lifted her chin toward the TV. The blue-gray glow of the screen now showed the gloomy interior of the barn. A single lantern hung from a rusty nail over a stall near the back of the room, its light shining upon the heads of six tawny-haired children: four boys and two girls. They were laughing.

"Mine…" the wind wailed as its breath blew the barn doors wide and knocked the lantern from the nail. Flames leapt high; the laughter turned to screams.

Chloe gasped and turned away, only to find she still faced the TV. She spun about again, yet the TV continued to stand before her. Chloe's knees went weak. As she watched, a new scene flashed across the screen. Six tiny coffins lay on a straw-strewn floor, the lids pried open, the nails still protruding from the bowed wooden planks.

The image of the woman who now stood beside Chloe appeared on the screen, sitting at a table with the remains of what looked to be either leg or arm bones scattered about her. Each bone had an end sawed off, each end gathered close to the woman as she hunched forward and carefully tapped a small pointed awl against the severed pieces. When she finally lifted her head, six tiny charms had taken the place of the bone shards.

The woman pointed a pale finger at Chloe's wrist as the TV speaker crackled, "Mine...mine...mine."

"Oh my God," Chloe managed to gasp between dry lips. She was wearing the bones of six dead children, and their dead mother wanted them back.

Chloe backed away from the ghost even as she fumbled with the clasp that held the bracelet secure. It refused to open under her shaking fingers.

The ghost floated forward, her dark stare never leaving Chloe's face.

Chloe fell back against the stairs.

The radio by the staircase snapped on. "Mine," a static-filled voice screamed from its speakers.

"Here." Chloe held her trembling arm out even as she scooted backward up the steps. "T-Take it."

The ghost had disappeared.

"Mine," the speaker hissed again, then fell silent. The TV snapped off, shrouding the room in suffocating silence. Chloe peered wide-eyed into the darkness. Where had the woman gone?

Chloe eased off the stairs and crept forward, her fingers gliding along the wall in search of a light switch. Before she could find the switch, the front door blew open and banged against the far wall.

She gasped and pressed deeper into the shadows. A chill wind swept past her and knocked the TV to the floor. The screen shattered, sending bits of glass and blue-orange sparks across the carpet. The sparks leapt to life. As the flames grew, haunting laughter merged with the very real stench of smoke.

Outside, lightning crisscrossed the night sky. The sharp flashes illuminated the woman framed in the door-way. The flickering glow of fire danced in her dark eyes as flames raced across the floor and crawled up the wall. Bits of liquid fire dripped from the ceiling, blocking Chloe's path to the door.

She screamed.

"Chloe!" Matt appeared in the doorway where the woman had been only moments before. He reached through the fire licking at the door frame and clutched Chloe's wrist, dragging her from the house. Cold rain stung her face as they bounded down the porch steps and collapsed in the grass near the street.

Matt knelt beside her. "Are you okay?" Before she could answer, he stood and said, "Come on, we've got to call the fire department." He took her hand and pulled her to her feet.

The sound of laughter made them pivot toward the house. Matt took a step forward, then halted. "What the…?"

Chloe stared at the house. No light reflected in the windows, no smoke rolled from the roof, no flame roared from the open doorway.

"How can a fire just disappear? I saw it…" Raindrops slid down Matt's face and dripped from the end of his nose. He frowned. "Come on." He threaded his fingers through hers. "Let's look inside."

Chloe pulled back. "No, wait. It's a warning." Her voice sounded foreign in her ears.

"A warning? From who?"

"From her."

The woman glided forward, her feet never touching the ground, her stare never wavering from Chloe's wrist. Lightning flashed overhead in rapid succession, each flash bringing the woman closer.

Matt eased them backward toward his car and fumbled for the door latch. Lightning flashed across the sky, followed quickly by the boom of thunder high above. He yanked the car door open. "Get in!"

Chloe jumped in and scrambled out of the way as Matt dove in behind her. He slammed the door and hit the lock.

He pressed his forehead against the window, his breath fogging the glass. "I can't see anything. Where'd she go?"

Lightning flashed again, revealing the woman's face outside the window, staring back. By the next flash, she was gone.

Matt yelled and half crawled, half jumped over Chloe to the other side of the car. His fingers shook so badly he could barely turn the key in the ignition. When the engine roared to life, he slipped the car in gear and hit the gas pedal.

The continuous swish whomp, swish whomp of the wiper blades echoed throughout the car. Chloe thought it sounded like the beat of a heart.

Matt stared straight ahead, his knuckles white where he griped the steering wheel. Finally, he said, without looking at her, "Who—what was that?"

"A ghost."

Matt slammed on the brakes, throwing them both forward. "A ghost?"

Chloe stared down at the bracelet. "I understand now what she wants. I have to return it. I have to go there."

"Go where?" Matt turned to face her.

"I have to go there," Chloe repeated, her voice rising to a high pitch. She dug her fingers deep into his arm. "It's not mine. I have to give it back."

"What are you talking about?" Matt rubbed his temple and frowned. "Give what back?"

"The bracelet."

His eyes grew wide. "You mean the cemetery?" When Chloe nodded, Matt stuttered, "N-No. N-No. If that thing wants her bracelet back, then we'll toss it out the window and she can damn well come get it." He grabbed Chloe's wrist and fumbled with the clasp.

Chloe smelled the smoke just before Matt yanked his hand away.

He stared down at his fingers. "It burned me."

"You saw her, Matt," Chloe whispered. "She's real. She's getting stronger. This time, it was a warning. Next time, it might not be." Chloe stared down at her clasped hands. "I can't just throw the bracelet away. I don't understand why I know this, but I have to put it back where I found it. I have to return it to the grave or she'll never stop haunting me."

Matt rubbed the flat of his hands down his face and groaned before leaning his forehead against the steering wheel. The patter of rain on the roof only served to intensify the silence between them. Finally, he mumbled, "Okay."

He straightened up and eased the car forward. "Okay, I'll take you."

* * *

The rain had turned to little more than a fine mist by the time Matt pulled the car to a halt in the back lot of the high school.

"Wait here." He left the door ajar, walked to the back and popped the trunk. "Take this," he said when he returned, handing Chloe a flashlight. He clicked on the one he carried.

Chloe climbed out of the car and passed the flashlight's beam across the limestone wall. The pale glow disappeared into the haze beyond.

"Do you remember where the grave was?"

Chloe shook her head. "Only that it was close to Mr. Seymore's class." She shrugged. "Not too far from the wall."

"Come on." Matt placed his hand on the small of Chloe's back and nudged her forward. "We can climb over the wall near the east steps. That'll put us close."

The sound of their footsteps seemed magnified as they walked along the edge of the parking lot. Once they were over the wall, Matt swept his flashlight in a wide arc, allowing the beam to pan slowly over the ground.

Everything seemed out of place from the daylight world Chloe knew. Tree limbs sagged forward, their heavy branches brushing against headstones that appeared strangely animated in the flash of lightning overhead. A hush lingered over the place, disturbed only by the soft cadence of fine rain hitting the leaves. It was as if the dead waited to see what would happen next.

"I think it was that way." Chloe's breath escaped her in small white puffs.

Matt nodded.

They'd gone only a few steps when laughter drifted out of the darkness. Matt's flashlight beam caught the faint form of a small boy weaving in and out of the headstones before he disappeared into the mist. From somewhere off to their right, a child's voice called out, "John Thomas, come play." It was followed by more laughter, then silence.

The beam from Matt's flashlight trembled in the darkness as he whispered, "Hurry."

When the windows of Mr. Seymore's class came into view, they eased away from the wall and swept their flashlights in wide arcs. The graves here bore no markers. In the dark, they all looked the same.

Chloe shook her head. "I don't know—"

"Ashes, ashes..."

She snapped the beam up. The weak light shown upon the blurry shapes of six small children outlined against the curtain of mist. With their hands joined, they skipped in a tight circle before falling to the ground in a flurry of laughter. As one, they faded into the haze.

The bracelet tugged against Chloe's wrist. The six bone charms strained against the chain. She knew what they were trying to show her. She pointed the flashlight to where the children had disappeared. "The grave is over there."

Matt's voice quivered when he said, "Let's go."

They made their way to the place where they thought the children had vanished. Matt spotlighted the sunken grave. The beam reflected off the black water pooled within. "Throw the bracelet in and let's get out of here."

Chloe tucked her flashlight beneath her arm and fumbled with the bracelet's clasp. As she did, lightning flashed overhead, revealing the woman rising from the grave directly in front of them.

Chloe screamed and fell backward. Her flashlight hit the ground with a loud splat, its beam illuminating the woman's dark, lifeless eyes. She grabbed Chloe's leg. "Mine, mine, mine," she moaned and slowly started to sink back into the grave, dragging Chloe down with her.

"Matt! The bracelet! Get it off me!"

"Oh God, oh God, oh God," Matt shrieked and dropped to his knees. He grabbed Chloe's wrist and tried to pull her free.

Chloe clung to Matt's arm like a lifeline while the mud oozed up around her waist. Her legs had gone numb. "I'm sorry," she cried out as the mud inched close to her chest. "I didn't mean to steal it. I didn't know it belonged to anyone."

The bracelet slipped from her wrist.

"I got it! I got it!" Matt screamed, scooping the bracelet out of the grass and flinging it into the grave.

A skeletal hand rose from the mud and caught the bracelet before it could hit the water. "Mine," the wind sighed as the hand sank back into the ground, the bracelet wrapped around its bony fingers.

Matt dragged Chloe from the grave. "Let's get out of here!" He took her hand and started running toward the wall.

"Ashes, ashes…"

Chloe spun about. Six globes of light emerged from the hazy mist and threaded their way with slow, graceful ease through the sagging tree limbs and solemn headstones. When they reached the woman's grave, they paused; then, one by one, the globes floated downward to disappear into the earth, trailing laughter behind them.

The faint flash of lightning glowed off to the east, and the thunder was now little more than a distant rumble that barely disturbed the quiet hush clinging to the old cemetery. Chloe clutched Matt's hand as they walked toward the school. As she climbed over the wall, she paused and looked toward the monuments that stood as silent testament to lives lived and lost.

"Forgotten, but not gone," Chloe whispered.

"What?" Matt's eyes were wide as he glanced back toward the grave.

She wrapped an arm about his waist. "It's over."

As they made their way across the parking lot, Chloe glanced back at the old prairie cemetery and whispered, "Gone, but not forgotten."

- The End -

Maxie
By Sheri L. McGathy

I never thought I'd want a dog. In fact, I never imagined myself a dog kind of guy. But when I held Maxie for the first time and she nuzzled that fluffy little black face with the big white patch over the left eye against my cheek, I knew I was in love. Funny thing, getting a dog was my girlfriend's idea. The girlfriend lasted about a month; Maxie stayed around for twelve years.

On the day Maxie died, I was with her, holding her head in my lap and stroking her brow. I didn't want her to go, but I knew she had to. *Please understand,* her brown eyes seemed to say, *I love you, but I'm old and I'm tired. I want to go.* Then she licked my hand and simply passed away.

I kissed her forehead and whispered, "Don't you worry, girl. You'll always be with me."

I had her cremated and brought her ashes home, where she belonged. As I placed her urn on the bookshelf in my living room, the wind kicked up and blew my front door open. A cool breeze swept through the room and circled about my legs to send a shiver up my spine. I went to shut the door and paused with my hand on the handle. The leaves in the trees hung still, and the tall shafts of wheat in the field across the road stood calm. There was no breeze.

I pushed the door shut. The room smelled like Maxie. I hung my head and cried.

That night I dreamt of her. In my dream, I walked through my front door to find her there, wagging her long, bushy tail in greeting as she always did. I was so happy to see her. I knelt down to scratch her behind one floppy ear, only to have her prance away and run into the living room. I laughed. This was a game we played when she had something she wanted to show me.

I followed her. As I rounded the corner, I gasped and took a step back. There, in my living room, were ten other dogs. Near the couch, a pair of black Labs lay with their heads nestled against their paws while a third Lab, his yellow coat shaved along his left hind leg, stood with his tongue hanging out. Two golden retrievers sat to either side of the recliner, their tails wagging against the carpet, while two basset hound puppies with the saddest eyes I'd ever seen lay on their backs in my recliner, their droopy ears dangling over the seat.

A well-manicured, white poodle, every bit as tall as the yellow Lab, stood at the far end of the room, his dark eyes focused on me. The heads of a border collie and a very black German shepherd peered at me from around the kitchen doorway. Maxie lifted her eyes to mine and I swore I heard her say, *"We'll be here to watch over you, always."*

I woke up bathed in my own sweat. I snapped on the light by the bed and stared at the ceiling. When I sat up, I noticed a slight impression in the covers on the left side of the bed. The same spot Maxie used to sleep in. I traced my fingers over the spot, somehow not surprised to discover it warm. God, I missed Maxie. I could understand why I would dream of her, but why all these other dogs I didn't know?

This went on for well over a week. Each night, I found my dreams filled with visions of Maxie. Sometimes she was alone. Sometimes, she greeted me with the other dogs at her side. I always woke to find the covers mussed and the spot warm where she used to lie. In a way, it was comforting to dream of her. I looked forward to it. I even began to like the idea of the other dogs hanging around.

One day, I told my friend, Gail, about my odd dreams.

She shrugged. "Rob, did you request Maxie be cremated alone?"

"What? No. Why?"

Gail raised a brow. "Because if you don't ask, they'll cremate your pet with any others waiting that day."

I shook my head. "But they sent me her ashes."

"Sure they did. But how many others did you get, too?"

I called the vet that afternoon and was told Maxie had been one of eleven dogs they'd cremated together that day.

Eleven dogs. Exactly the number I saw in my dream.

As I hung up the phone, I whispered, "Don't you worry, girl. You and your friends are home."

- The End -

The Graveyard Dance
By Sheri L. McGathy

Will drove slowly past the vacant buildings. He hadn't been back to New Hope in over seventy years, and by the looks of the place, neither had anyone else. The town was a shell of its former self, now nothing more than a few decaying buildings caught in the shadows of a dying day.

"Nothing here but the ghosts of faded dreams." He sighed. Over the years, he'd developed a habit of talking to himself. It made him feel less alone.

When he reached the edge of town, he turned left. Everything about the area had changed or been remade by time. He feared his memory could no longer be counted upon to recall correctly. He took the first dirt road he came to and inched the car forward, hoping to see anything that looked familiar.

He glanced at his watch. "Sun won't set for a few more hours. There's time. The old cemetery has to be around here somewhere." He tightened his swollen fingers on the steering wheel, ignoring the pain. *It just had to be here.*

To his left, he could see a field that had once been bordered by a limestone wall, but now all that remained were a few rock piles half buried in weeds. He pulled to the side of the road and shut off the ignition. Something about this place drew him.

He got out of the car and stared beyond the field to a line of cottonwood trees. His heart fluttered in his old chest. Could it be? Had he found it again after all these years?

The prairie grass rustled against his pants legs as he made his way through the field. A hot, humid breeze pushed against his back, but it offered no relief from the heat. Soon, he was panting.

He stopped and mopped the sweat from his brow with a handkerchief, then continued. When he reached the trees, he paused to bask in their cool shade. He'd forgotten how hot Kansas could be in early June.

Beyond the trees lay another field of tall grass rippling in the late day breeze, but no sign of what he hoped to find.

His old joints popped in protest as he eased his body down to the ground and leaned back against one of the trees. "All this way." His voice seemed out of place in the solitude surrounding him. "Only to discover I really can't go home again. No matter how much I long for it, or how hard I try."

He closed his eyes. "Home," he whispered and let his memories take him where his feeble body could not....

... "William Joseph McNae," Aunt Ruth bellowed out the back door.

Will had to cover his mouth to keep from laughing out loud as his friend, Tommy O'Shea, shook a finger in the air much like Will imagined Aunt Ruth would surely do if she caught him.

"William!" Aunt Ruth's voice was getting closer.

At eleven, Tommy was older than Will by a year, making him the leader by default. When he hitched a thumb over his shoulder, Will nodded. Fishing poles in hand, they ducked under Mrs. Meloan's freshly laundered sheets and ran around the side of her house to reach Main Street. Then, they sprinted past the general store where Mr. Harrison stood, like he did every evening at closing time, broom in hand, sweeping the stoop. Will waved as he and Tommy sailed by.

When they neared the Meeting Hall, Old Man McGregor looked up from the checkerboard and wagged a crooked finger eastward where an impatient moon already claimed the horizon. "Full moon's good for fishing. You boys catch me a big, fat catfish for breakfast. Hear?"

"Will do," Will called out without slowing.

At the edge of town, they turned left and took the old settlement road. Once well traveled, the road was now little more than a dirt trail, winding a solitary path through fields of wild grass and little else, but it was the quickest route to the river.

The mournful creak of the old cemetery gate haunted the breeze long before the cemetery itself came into view. Beyond the gate, nearly reclaimed by the prairie, lay the remains of the original New Hope settlers.

Will paused, taking in the crumbling rock wall and the lopsided black-iron gate hanging by a single pin. Headstones stood in disarray, leaning forward at odd angles, the names carved upon them long since weathered away. Other markers lay face down on the ground, forlorn and forgotten. Long shadows from a stand of cottonwoods ghosted across the ground as the sun slipped below the western horizon.

"Let's go," Tommy said, pulling on Will's arm. "It's spooky here."

Will nodded. As he turned to leave, his foot caught on the discarded crosspiece that used to straddle the top of the cemetery gate. He didn't have to look at it to know what it said: "New Hope never forgets its own." It was their town's motto.

He had a hard time believing those words as he glanced at the neglected cemetery.

Just as they started down the slope toward the river, a flash of white lit the sky, followed by the distant rumble of thunder.

Will looked skyward. "Not supposed to—"

The snap of a whip echoed high above them, chased quickly by a high-pitched screech and a fast rat-a-tat-tat.

"What was that?" Tommy spun around and stared back at the old cemetery.

"Tommy, look." The hair on Will's arms stood up as he pointed to the rising moon and the dark silhouette of a phantom coach illuminated against its pale face. Two black horses strained against their leather harnesses as they tugged the coach earthward. Each thrust of their hooves lit the sky with rippling bolts of lightning, while each downward stroke of their legs produced the boom of thunder.

The earth shook beneath Will's feet when the coach's spinning wheels met solid ground and surged forward without slowing. The whip snapped again, and sparks flew from flashing hooves as the horses veered toward the old cemetery.

Will watched the coach race across the field. He couldn't move, even though some still-sane part of his mind urged him to run.

As the coach drew up alongside the cemetery gate, Tommy slipped a shaking hand in Will's and stuttered, "Th-the driver. He h-has no h-h-head."

Will gulped.

The coachman tipped his stump their way while he pulled up on the reins. The wheels had barely stopped spinning when the coach door creaked open to reveal its occupants.

Tommy gasped. "It's the Ferguson family." His voice sounded distant. "But they left town...Ma said there was an accident, that they were..."

Will gripped Tommy's arm. "Dead."

They stared with their mouths hanging open as Mr.

Ferguson stepped from the coach and helped his wife, Molly, down. Then, with his arm draped across her shoulder, he strolled them beyond the old cemetery gate. Mrs. Ferguson, in life a stern woman and rarely without a scowl, smiled as she hugged her husband's waist.

Ten-year-old Sara Ferguson stepped down from the coach and skipped past.

"Sara," Will whispered. She'd been his friend.

She paused near the old crosspiece half hidden in the tall grass. Bending down, she traced her fingers along its faded words, then smiled at Will before running to catch up with her parents.

As soon as she passed the gate, the horses lunged against their harnesses, lurching the coach forward to disappear into the deeper shadows of the night.

A light fog rolled in from the river and flowed into the cemetery in slow, shimmering waves. It surged to the edge of the gate, then ebbed back, easing over the headstones to blanket the graves in an eerie whiteness. The Fergusons smiled as the fine wisps floated about their feet and coiled around their legs. Their bodies began to glow and their eyes took on a silvery hue.

"Will, let's get—" Tommy snapped his mouth shut as the mournful wail of a bagpipe drifted on the night breeze.

The haunting notes wafted across the field while the fog mingled with wispy shapes oozing from the graves. Merged, they drifted upward in slow lazy turns, each spin revealing first a head, then shoulders, followed by arms that reached skyward while legs stepped free of the ground.

Will sank to his knees, pulling Tommy down with him.

Joining hands, the spirits gathered about the Ferguson family and began to dance. Round and round they went, gliding beneath a canopy of pale moonlight while fog swirled like soft clouds about their legs.

Will didn't know how long he and Tommy knelt there, watching the spirits dance beneath the cottonwood trees. He couldn't recall when the music faded or when the spirits returned to the grave. Yet, he swore he'd never forget the smile on Sara Ferguson's face as she joined the dance. At that moment, he knew, she'd come home.

As the sun eased up over the eastern end of the field, Tommy turned his wide-eyed stare to Will and extended his pinky finger. "Swear you'll never tell anyone."

Will hooked his finger in Tommy's and nodded. "I swear...."

"...And I never did say a word." Will shook his head. "Who'd have believed me, anyway?"

He sighed. Tommy would have believed him, but Tommy disappeared somewhere over France during WWII.

"He never came home." Will blinked back the tears forming in his eyes.

Soft, snow-like fluff rained down upon him as a sudden cool breeze whipped across the field and shook the cottonwoods overhead. The rumble of thunder jerked his thoughts from the past and back to the present.

He got to his feet and squinted toward the eastern horizon as he searched the darkening sky. Could it be? Was it possible? He dared to hope. Then, he saw it outlined against the gray, cloud-filled skyline.

The coach was coming.

Will's hands shook. Maybe he could follow it; maybe he'd find the cemetery after all. Maybe...

The coach veered from the road and headed straight toward the tree line. As it came to a halt before him, the headless driver tipped a shoulder toward the coach. When the door swung open, Will heard a familiar voice say, "Hello, Will."

Tears sprang to Will's eyes. "Tommy, you've come home."

His old friend offered him a lopsided grin. "I was only waiting for you." He held his hand out. "Come on, Will. It's time for us to go."

As Will stepped into the coach and took a seat across from Tommy, he looked back to his old body slumped against the cottonwood tree and smiled. "New Hope never forgets its own."

- The End -

The Rose

By Barbara J. Baldwin

ive years ago in May, Dad bought a rose bush and planted it out in the front yard. Even though my mom's favorite color was red, the cardboard tag proclaimed the blossoms would be "princess pink." The tag guaranteed the bush would have beautiful pink roses after becoming acclimated. When it didn't bloom—not a single blossom—Dad just figured it hadn't gotten used to its new home.

For the next three springs, he trimmed the bush back to the wood, getting rid of the dead canes and leaves. As the weather warmed, long stems with plenty of thorns and green shiny leaves flourished, making it look full and thriving. But not once in all those years did a single pink blossom greet him when he walked out the front door each morning. Though he pruned and fertilized and watered whenever the hot Kansas wind dried the soil, it never bloomed. It only continued to prick him with its thorns every time he tried to trim it or make it grow up the trellis he had put in the ground right beside it.

Finally he was ready to pull the rose bush out of the ground and toss it in the dumpster, but Mom said no. The rose bush would grow and bloom when it was ready.

Two years ago in early spring, Dad died. The neglected rose bush stood tall and scraggly next to the house. Every time I visited Mom, it reminded me sadly of my dad, and my eyes misted as I remembered how hard he had worked to make that bush blossom. With a deep sigh, I knew I should take time to cut it back as Dad had done to stimulate its growth. But first, I went inside to see how Mom was doing.

At the end of our visit, I dug through the tool shed for Dad's pruning shears. When I couldn't find them, I asked Mom, but she hadn't had the heart or energy to do any yard work. I told her I would bring some clippers over later, gave her a kiss goodbye and walked out the door. As I got into my car, out of the corner of my eye I thought I saw someone kneeling by the rosebush. I turned quickly, but no one was there.

I got out of the car, going to stand directly over the bush. The canes had been neatly cut back to the wood, leaving healthy six-to-ten inch green stems. I walked around the house looking for a neighbor who might have come over and pruned, but no one was visible. When I came again to the rose bush, I saw the shears, sharp tips stuck down in the dirt just like Dad always left them so the kids wouldn't hurt themselves.

My cell phone rang before I could question Mom about the strange occurrence. One of the kids had let the dog out and now he was lost. I snapped the phone shut and climbed into the car to go chase the dog down, thinking I would have to remember to ask Mom the next time I visited.

On the first anniversary of Dad's death, new canes on the rose bush mysteriously began stretching up the trellis where they had never gone before. The leaves were full and green and there were prickly thorns in abundance. One solitary rose bloomed that year.

Just one, white rose.

The bush had been planted years before, but I seemed to remember the roses should be pink. I asked Mom about it.

She just shrugged and said, "It has a beautiful rose on it. That's all that matters." Mom spent a lot of time on the porch that summer, studying the rose bush. Maybe she was trying to figure out its secrets. Maybe she just missed Dad.

We had a gentle fall, but winter appeared overnight with freezing temperatures and an eight-inch snowfall. Mom called when I got home from work to thank me for covering the rose bush before the storm. I opened my mouth to tell her it wasn't me, but hesitated. Maybe the boys had done it after they got home from school. But then, I had never known my boys to go to Grandma's house without begging cookies and milk from her, and she hadn't said anything about that.

I smiled. I'll be the first to admit I don't have a very religious background. I don't believe in all that super-natural stuff, but somehow I felt my dad was still around, keeping an eye on things—specifically my mom and his rose bush.

This is the second year that Dad's been gone. Mom has moved slowly on with her life and has even accepted a date now and again from a nice widower in her neighbor-hood. When I stopped by the house the other day, Mom was standing in the yard, watering the grass and the rose bush.

"I never pruned that rose bush," I blurted out when I came to stand beside her. "Not once in the past two years. Did you?"

She smiled and shook her head. "I know you didn't."

"Well then, who?"

Mom whispered and I strained to hear her words. "He's always been here, tending the rose bush, watching over me." She cleared her throat, continuing in a stronger voice. "But now he's telling me it's all right to move on with my life."

At first I didn't understand, until she nodded

towards the rose bush. Two blossoms were just beginning to open.

This year, the roses are red, Mom's favorite color.

- The End -

Trespassing Time
By Linda Madl

I knew I was going to see something special that June day in 2007 when I traveled to southwestern Kansas to interview Josh Trugood. But I had no idea how extraordinary, how gut wrenching, how life altering our meeting would be. That day I drove over the cattle guard onto Trugood ranch land and past the emphatic "No Trespassing" sign with a smug sense of victory and a complacent belief in an orderly, if impersonal, universe. Since that meeting, my view of reality has been forever altered.

As a historian I can no longer see history as a time line. Having witnessed what I did, I realize that time does not lie flat. It is not linear, stretching into infinity never to return. Time is far more complicated than a simple plane. Perhaps it's woven like fabric, yarns intertwined above then below each other. Perhaps time curls back on itself like a great raveling thread. Or is it a huge video loop interrupted by other loops? Or as the physicists theorize, are there worm holes in time? That's a rather disgusting image. But who is to say?

Let me tell you the Trugood story as it unfolded for me—then you decide.

Let's dispense with the boring stuff—my credentials. I'm an expert on the Santa Fe Trail. In 1987 Congress designated the old road a National Historic Trail, but still miles of it lie on private property. I've photographed the 186-year-old trail from Missouri along 800 miles across both the Mountain (long) and Jornada (short dry) route to Santa Fe, New Mexico. I know everything there is to know about the Cimarron River, the Staked Plains, the

Clayton Complex, Glorieta Pass, Bent's Fort, and Ratone Pass...I hear you yawning. So, you get the idea. I know all about the trail—except for the twenty miles that lie on the Trugood Rocking T Ranch.

For years Josiah Trugood and his family had refused to allow me, or anyone else for that matter, to personally see that section of the trail on his property. I suppose I don't blame him. The occasional writer/photographer, like myself, and the scholar and even the amateur history buff leaving open gates and dropping trash on the land are undoubtedly a nuisance to a rancher.

But most landowners along the route had indulged us trail lovers. Some are even dilettante experts themselves. They join us at meetings and festivals and fill their homes with maps and bits of Santa Fe artifacts—china shards, rusted buckles, partial wagon wheels.

However, the Trugoods were holdouts. The trail crossing their property was accessible from the air only. To be honest there appeared to be nothing exceptional along the route except a long stretch of wagon wheel ruts and a large campsite on a bluff overlooking a valley. But the point was, no one had photographed or walked along those ruts or explored that campsite since the 1940s.

I'm no genius, but I'm diligent. About ten years ago I began calling old man Trugood to make his acquaintance. I didn't expect miracles. Why would he grant my request when he'd refused so many others? Others, like Will Taber, my nemesis, had offered the old rancher money for a visit. All were refused. I prayed that one day my persistence and integrity would pay off.

But every time I brought our phone conversation around to asking to see the trail on the Rocking T, old Trugood would say "nope." I would thank him for his time and hang up. Then in six or nine months I'd phone again.

My tactic finally worked. Just last month Josh Trugood called me.

"When were you born, son?" he opened abruptly after identifying himself.

"1957," I told him, dragging my attention away from the article about buffalo hunters I was writing for a history magazine. I couldn't imagine why he was calling me now.

He made a sound that might have been a laugh or a grunt of displeasure. I wasn't sure which. I knew him to be the proverbial crusty old character who would think a fifty-year-old was a kid. "You still want to see that trail?" he demanded, though I'm certain he knew the answer to that.

"Yes, sir," I said, breathless with surprise and hope. "Any time. At your convenience."

"Well, it ain't convenient," he replied, his voice terse and gravelly. "But it's time. You be here at the ranch June 21 about 7 p.m., and I'll take you to see something the likes of which I'll bet you've never seen and will never see again."

"May I bring my camera?" I asked, thinking 7 p.m. was late, but I might be able to get some good early evening and sunset views. And I wanted to be clear on this point: I intended to take photographs. I didn't want any last minute change of heart on his part when I pulled out my camera and went to work.

Again he made that laugh or grunt sound. "Sure, bring your camera. That's why I called you. You're honest and you take good pictures."

He gave me directions which I scribbled down, though I knew exactly where his ranch was. All of us Santa Fe experts know. I hung up, whooped with victory, danced around my office until I knocked my bag of corn chips on the floor, and my wife came in to see what was going on. Then I began making preparations for the trip.

I called my editor at the academic publishing house that puts out my books to let him know of my victory. Not that he cared. He didn't understand how long and hard people, like me and Will Taber, have worked to get a glimpse of this section of the trail from the valleys and ridges the way the muleskinners and the wagon masters had seen it long ago.

Then I called Taber to see if he'd heard from old man Trugood. For all I knew the old rancher had invited a whole crew of us. But Taber hadn't heard from Trugood. It seemed I was the only one privileged to receive an invitation to the ranch. So you see why I was feeling so smug and victorious that June day as I cruised past that "No Trespassing" sign and up the drive to the hilltop ranch house.

I parked in the shade of a cottonwood tree and noted the shiny blue pickup truck sitting in front of the garage door. Trugood's? I wondered. Striding up to the front door, I admired the understated affluence of the red brick ranch house. It was clearly the second generation house on the place. The old two-story Victorian farmhouse that had probably sat on this site had been razed some ten or fifteen years earlier and replaced with the current sprawling brick residence.

The door opened before I rang the bell. I was greeted by a tall, slightly stooped man of about seventy-five, wearing cowboy boots, blue jeans and a Western shirt. He had thinning gray hair, alert blue eyes, and a long horsy face lined with age and years of working in the sun. Despite his years there was about him a vigor that I had expected. He'd always been a sharp old guy on the phone.

"Mr. Trugood?" I ventured.

"That's me," he said, shaking my hand with a firm, cordial grip. "Call me Josh and come in. I've been expecting you."

He ushered me into a large living room with a wood-beam ceiling, a wall of windows looking out over the grassland valley behind the house, and a fireplace. The fireplace got my attention. Above the mantel hung a massive Aztec calendar, a garishly painted one, like tourists sometimes bring back from Mexico. Only tourists usually bring back a version small enough to pack. This thing dominated the room like a billboard.

Trugood asked about my drive to the ranch. I answered his polite questions as I observed the pictures of conquistadors on the other walls. I also noted titles about the Aztecs, a tome of German folktales, and my own works about the trail on the bookshelves behind him. A show tune was playing on the CD player, something I should know, but didn't recognize immediately. What a curious collection of stuff for a Kansas rancher.

"You have a lovely home," I said, sincere, but curious about the handsome collection of pre-Columbian figures on the end tables and the mantel below the Aztec calendar.

At that moment a fortyish, slim, blonde woman walked into the room. She gave me a sullen frown. Her walk was filled with resentment. But as she neared me, I was astonished to glimpse fear in her eyes.

"My daughter, Trish Trugood Fredericks."

She made no move to offer her hand. "I want you to know I do not approve of this."

Mystified, I glanced at Trugood for a hint of what she was talking about.

"Ignore her," he said, waving a dismissive hand in her direction. "Ever since her mother died a few years back, she thinks she has the right to tell me how to live

115

my life."

"I do have that right, Dad. I'm the mother of your grandchildren. If you insist on going through with this ridiculous plan, don't expect me to take any part in it." She looked me up and down with distaste, as if I'd just slithered in under the door like a lizard. "I will not have anything to do with it," she repeated.

I decided I didn't like her. I was relieved when she turned on her heel and marched out of the room.

"Look," I began, a bit uneasy with her reference to "ridiculous thing." "I don't want to be a source of trouble…"

He shook his head and put a comforting hand on my shoulder. "Forget it. She'll come around. Have a seat. I want to ask you some questions before we go have a look at the trail."

Still puzzled, I sat facing the windows. Fence post shadows were growing long as the sun dropped to the horizon. I knew I was losing good light with every minute we lingered in the house, but I didn't want to offend by appearing impatient.

Trugood lowered himself into the chair across from me with his back to the glorious view. "What do you know about the Aztec calendar?"

Searching my brain for a connection to the Santa Fe Trail, I stammered, "Not much except that it was a solar and a ritual calendar observed by many Meso Americans in pre-Columbian times."

He nodded. "Basically the solar calendar was a 365-day year with eighteen months, each month with twenty days or four weeks of five days each. It was a secular calendar, if you will. The ritual calendar was a 260-day year based on the cycles of the moon. With it the priests forecasted lucky days for sowing crops, building houses, going to war, and so forth. The Aztecs viewed time in cycles, as circular, not linear like we do." He made a circle in the air with his right forefinger. A smile of pride played on his lips, as if his own grandchildren had invented this law of the universe.

"Right. I'd heard about that years ago on a trip to Mexico. What does that have to do with the Santa Fe Trail?"

About then the CD sound system began to play a melody I recognized from the musical *Brigadoon*. Years ago my daughter's high school had put on a production of the Lerner and Lowe play, and we'd heard those songs over and over.

Trugood smiled at the sound of the music and then continued. "Every fifty-two years the solar and the ritual calendar realign. For the Aztecs every fifty-two years is like the change of centuries for us. It's important that you understand that. Let's go on out to the trail now. I can see you're eager to get on with it. I'll tell you more when we get there."

Next thing I knew, he had me mounted on a four-wheel drive, all-terrain vehicle with my camera secure on a strap across my shoulder. I'd expected to do some horseback riding, and I knew how to manage a horse. But this mechanized cross-country stuff was new to me.

He gave me some quick instructions about first gear and the brakes. I thought I could get the hang of it. After all, kids do it all the time. Then he climbed onto his vehicle. We circled the yard once to be sure I was okay on the machine. We were about to start out toward the prairie when Trish ran out of the house, waving her arms in the air.

"Wait!" she shouted. "Wait! Dad? I changed my mind. I want to go."

Trugood regarded her for a moment. Something

passed between them in the silence. Some understanding between father and grown daughter. Something I didn't understand, but will perhaps one day.

"Get on," he said.

She threw a leg across the seat behind him, and we were off, roaring along a dirt track into the setting sun. Trugood's dust plume enveloped me, but I was too ecstatic to care. At last I was going to see the mysterious section of the trail that no one had seen for decades. I honestly didn't care what the old man had up his sleeve as long as I got my pictures as proof that I'd been there—the first one in sixty years. Eat your heart out, Will Taber.

The sun had dropped below the horizon by the time we reached the most important part of this section of the trail, the bluff-top campsite. I'd already taken some photos by then. I'd insisted on stopping to get shots of the first ruts we saw. They slewed across the prairie, parallel lines curving gently as they furrowed the grassland.

Trugood had stopped and let me snap away, that generous smile playing on his lips again. Trish watched me, her face full of a sadness that I didn't understand and at the moment wasn't concerned about.

As I worked, Trugood started up his strange questions.

"So, being an expert on the trail you know that Coronado crossed it at least once. Of course, that was three centuries before it became the trail we know."

I nodded but continued to work. The light was dying so quickly.

He went on. "How much do you know about Coronado and Padre Niza?"

"Not much," I conceded, deciding I had enough views of the ruts. "I'd like to get some shots of the campsite before it gets much darker."

"Sure. I'll tell you about the padre when we get

there," Trugood said and was off again with me happily choking on his dust.

The campsite wasn't really much to see. It was a level area atop a bluff with lots of grass for the stock and easy access to a spring-fed stream at the base of the incline. The location offered a good view of the surrounding ground including a wide valley to the west. No attackers, Native Americans or bandits, could surprise a wagon train camped on the site.

Again I went to work taking photos, determined to get as many shots as I could before it grew too dark. There were some nice long orange clouds on the horizon, and a full moon was rising in the east. I might get some good nighttime shots. As I snapped away Trugood started to talk again.

"I know you've heard this story," he began, leaning against his vehicle while I worked. Trish stood at his side and rested her head against his arm, much like I'd have expected from a child. "In 1539 Padre Niza organized an expedition north from Mexico to find the cities of gold that Cabeza de Vaca, another man, and their servant Esteban had learned of during their nine years lost in the wilderness. The three men had survived a shipwreck and wound their way back to Mexican civilization, carrying strange tales of rich cities and gold."

"Yeah, I remember something about that," I said still concentrating on getting the campsite from all angles. I changed memory cards in the camera, checked the battery reading, which was good, and kept snapping. "The Seven Cities of Cibola."

"Right. Attracted by the gold and the souls to convert, Padre Niza headed north with Esteban serving as a guide. To make a long story short, the padre and Esteban became separated. Esteban got himself into trouble with the Indians and was killed. When the padre arrived on the scene, there was nothing he could do for Esteban, and the Indians were too riled for him to remain in the area. However, he returned to Mexico and swore that he had seen the Seven Cities of Gold with his own eyes."

I stopped taking photos long enough to turn to Trugood. "Yeah, that's what brought Coronado to Kansas."

"Right, that next summer the conquistador headed north like the padre, but Coronado only found and conquered a few Zuni villages. He found no cities of gold. Since then scholars and history buffs have argued over why Padre Niza would have lied about seeing gold cities, if they hadn't been there. Why would a man of the cloth purposely fib or exaggerate?"

"For the notoriety and justification for making the trip," I offered. I confess to having become cynical in my mature years. I snapped another shot of the campsite.

"Maybe," Trugood said, clearly dissatisfied with that answer. "What if the padre truly saw something, then it disappeared?"

"Cities of gold that disappeared?" It was an odd enough thought to make me pause in my picture taking. "Like Brigadoon?" I asked, remembering the music on the CD player. "The Scottish village that only reappears every one hundred years?"

"There are other stories about disappearing cities," Trugood said, almost defensively. "Germelshausen for one. It was a German village that rose from a muddy swamp every century. It had had a curse laid on it.

"And you know the old padre wasn't the only one who placed gold in Kansas. There's an old 1750s map drawn by du Pratz that places a gold mine in southern Kansas on the Arkansas River."

"I've heard of it, but nobody takes it seriously." At this point I forgot about taking pictures. I had to pause for a moment to take it all in. "Are you suggesting that the Seven Cities of Gold appear and disappear every century like Brigadoon or Germitz—whatever?"

"I'm more than suggesting." Digging into his jeans pocket, he pulled out a small object and held it up for me to see. "Here, have a look at this."

The object I took from him weighed heavily in my hand. Upon closer inspection I could see that it, like the pottery objects in his house, was pre-Columbian. Except this particular object, a small seated man with a square face and big ears, was intricately worked in gold.

"Yep, real gold," he said without me asking. "Solid gold. None of this 18 karat stuff you see in the jewelry stores. This is the real thing through and through."

"Where...?" I barely managed to utter.

He smiled. "That's why we're here. You'll see tonight."

The wind had shifted with the setting of the sun. The warmth of the day had vanished. I shivered.

"Do I have your full attention?" he asked.

I let my camera swing against my side from its strap. "I'm listening."

Trish's frown deepened, if that was possible. She crossed her arms beneath her breasts, turned her back on us, and walked away, gazing back toward the ranch house. Trugood ignored her.

"In 1955 I was a young married man with a baby on the way," Trugood began. "Trish's older sister. I'd just inherited this place from my dad, and I was determined to make good. A bit of family pride, wanting to be able to pass the place on to my children, and I had mouths to feed. I worked hard. I spent long hours in the saddle."

He paused and kicked the tire of the all-terrain vehicle. "We rode horses in those days. Anyway, at sunset I rode up to the bluff here to get a good view of the valley. I'd been rounding up mavericks. I was moving the herd to the east side of the ranch to graze. The sun had gone down but it was still light, June 21, summer solstice, and the longest daylight of the year. There was a full moon rising that night too. A mist was beginning to settle into the valley, but I thought I'd be able to see any livestock that might have escaped me and my cowboys. Then the dangest thing happened. As I watched and the darkness gathered, the mist began to turn yellow.

"I dismounted to study the scene. Lights began to glimmer through the mist. I wondered if I was really looking at a prairie fire and its smoke. But it sure didn't resemble any other fires I'd seen. Little by little buildings began to take shape. Wedding cake like. Tiered adobe structures like the pueblos of Santa Fe. You've seen those, haven't you?"

I nodded.

"At first I saw only one village, but then as I watched, more took shape. Eventually the whole valley was dotted with seven villages, each marked by small cooking fires and in the nearest one I could make out shadowy figures moving about. At times I could hear voices, the sound of women singing and of men laughing. In the mist the seven cities took on a golden glow, bright even with a shining moon in a clear night sky above. At the bottom of the bluff only the creek separated me from the villages.

"I saw a crossing made of stones across the moving water. I wondered if anyone had crossed the stones into the village before. As if to answer my question I saw a group of Indian-like warriors come out to the creek bank. They looked around. When they saw me, they were up the hill so fast I didn't have time to get mounted. They grabbed me by my arms and began to drag me back toward the village. Then a golden-skinned young woman and an old man came out of the mist and ran across the stones as if they trod them several times a day. The older man wore a headdress like a shaman's or a chief's."

I glanced down the hill at the stepping stones that formed an irregular but negotiable way across the creek bed.

"At the sight of me and my horse the old man became agitated, but he ordered the warriors not to harm me. At least that's what it seemed like. I couldn't understand a word of what they were babbling to each other. The woman, well, she was interested in me. And I admit I liked the looks of her all right."

"Dad!" Trish turned just enough to frown at her father.

"Now, girl, I've been faithful to my vows," Trugood said, "but Yana is a fine looking woman. I won't lie about it. No, sir. But to get on with it, we had no common language other than facial expressions and hand gestures. They invited me to return to the village with them. With the warriors there and all it seemed best to go along with them. So I hobbled my horse because they seemed to be afraid of him. Then I was escorted into the Seven Cities of Cibola."

"Are you pulling my leg?" I demanded, vaguely aware that my mouth had been hanging open as he told his tale.

Trugood held up his right hand. "God's truth. I swear."

I glanced at Trish for confirmation. She pursed her lips and shrugged.

"Ah, Trish girl has heard this story too many times to

count. She knows it's true."

"You saw the Seven Cities of Cibola?"

Trugood laughed. "If you're having trouble believing that, wait until you hear the rest of the story. I was there for twelve hours and in that time I learned some amazing things."

"About Padre Niza? And what about the golden streets?"

"Yep, and Esteban," Trugood said. "There is gold there. Lots of it. But they consider it ordinary. They make pretty things out of it like that figure you are holding, bowls, and lamps.

"They had recorded Esteban's crime in a kind of picture writing. To them the event had occurred only a couple of weeks earlier. You see, Esteban had raped one of their women, the fool. They welcomed him into the village and then he did something stupid like that. So they executed him in a pretty nasty fashion. They are a generous and hospitable people, but they have no tolerance for crime. They had heard about the men with four legs, the conquistadors. So when they saw Padre Niza arrive with his party in search of Esteban, the old shaman knew things weren't going to get better. He conjured up some kind of spell having to do with time. So the villages disappeared only to reappear every fifty-two years."

"And that's why when Coronado returned a year later, there was nothing here for him to see?" I finished.

"You've got it." He smiled at me. "I didn't understand all of this in that one day that I spent there. When I got back, I started doing research. Hell, I've spent my life researching the Aztecs and the Mayans, their calendars and their hieroglyphics. I've spent my life trying to come to terms with what I saw and experienced. I figured the villages have appeared eight times since Padre Niza's visit. I figure someone down through the last four centuries has glimpsed the Cities of Cibola. Ever think that's where the gold mine on du Pratz's map came from?"

I was beginning to understand. "And tonight it's been fifty-two years since 1955?"

"Yep, exactly fifty-two years from the day I walked into the cities and then walked out leaving behind the prettiest girl I ever saw and what looked like a darn nice way of life and the riches of all that gold." Trugood looked out over the valley again. The mist had begun to gather and rested heavily in the lowland.

"I've learned a lot in the years since then. First thing I did was put up no trespassing signs. I couldn't take the chance that some hunter or trail enthusiast would stumble upon the villages. I didn't fully understand the fifty-two year cycle then. After learning about the calendar and about Niza, I studied Coronado. I wanted to go back. I kicked myself for not bringing back more gold, something I could have cashed in. Lord, we needed money in those early years. But as the years went by, my regrets changed. You know you've got to grow up sometime. I began to appreciate the mystery and the notoriety of it. I even thought about talking to the tabloids. Wouldn't they love a story about the disappearing cities of gold? Wouldn't they love the solution to the mystery? In the last decade, I've begun to appreciate the old shaman's wisdom."

"What do you mean?" I asked.

"He protected his family and his people," Trugood said. "He saved them from this insane world we live in. When the cities appear tonight, I'm entering. And I won't return."

"Dad? Don't do this," Trish begged, touching his arm.

"I honestly don't believe that anything is going to appear. I don't know what you saw on that night fifty-two years ago. But you know we need you here."

It took a moment for the full impact of his statement to make sense to me. "You're going to go back like the fellow in Brigadoon?"

"I don't expect it to be that simple," Trugood said. "But the old shaman will understand who I am. Yana will just think I'm an old man. I don't care. I'll live whatever life I have left with them. In their peace. Where gold is just another pretty thing. There's nothing here for me any more."

Trish turned away again so that I couldn't see her face. It was all making sense to me now, and I began to feel sympathy for her.

"I'm seventy-nine years old," he went on. "It's time to do what I wished I'd done fifty-two years ago. Trish will report me missing to the police. They'll search for me and find nothing. After five years, she and her sisters will petition the courts to declare me dead, and then they can probate the will and divide up the life insurance. There's no fraud involved. I'll be a goner as far as this world is concerned anyway you look at it."

I glanced at her again.

She met my enquiring gaze. "This is not what I want," she vowed.

"But why did you invite me here?" I asked Trugood.

"I wanted you to know about the Seven Cities of Cibola," he said. "I wanted someone who loves this land and the trail like I do to know the truth. You can write about it if you want. Publish the photos. No one will believe you, but it will become part of the record. Maybe fifty-two years from now one of you will come out here to see the cities return. If I'm alive, I'll come out to greet you."

The words "are you crazy" were on my lips as I glanced over his shoulder into the valley. Above the gathering mist the stars were starting to glimmer around us. Golden fire-flies were taking flight, bejeweling the prairie grass.

Trugood and Trish turned, following my gaze. As the twilight faded the tiered adobe villages began to take form just as he'd described them. I could see the cooking fires and hear the voices of women and children. Even the barking of dogs reached us. Between each of the villages appeared a patchwork of what I figured were garden plots. Suddenly the dry creek bed at the foot of the hill was full of rushing water.

The scene was one of domestic order and peace.

Trish clutched her father's arm. "Dad, you don't know anything about these people. They may have traditions and practices that you won't—that could be harmful to you."

She'd dropped her skepticism quickly enough. And I knew she was thinking of Esteban's fate and about the historic records that indicate the Mayans and Aztecs practiced human sacrifice. How could Trugood know that the place was as idyllic as it appeared?

"I'll take the chance, girl," he said with a smile of confidence on his lips. "You getting your pictures, son?"

"Uh, yeah." I groped for my camera and started taking shots, but I had no idea what I was getting. I didn't want to waste time or battery power to check. No doubt this mirage, or whatever we were witnessing, was not going to last long. Or so I thought at the moment.

Trugood turned to Trish and gave her a sound, fatherly kiss. "You know what to do. I showed you where all the paperwork is. Everything is in order. Give the kids a kiss for me. I love all of you. Never doubt it. This is something I've got to do."

With that he started down the hill toward the stepping stones in the creek. I followed for a few steps and kept snapping pictures. The villages had taken on a solid form, looking nearly as real as one could expect anything to look on a misty summer evening.

As we watched, a group of men, warriors with spears, appeared on the opposite bank. Then we saw a man with a headdress, the shaman probably, and a slender, beautiful woman joined them. She smiled at Trugood, revealing a lush mouth and large dark eyes.

Trugood paused, looked back at us and waved; then he started across the stepping stones toward the villages. He took the stones slowly but steadily, never wavering. In the center of the stream, he paused and looked back again. Trish sobbed, and then she gasped. At first I thought it was because she hoped that he would change his mind. Then I saw what took her breath away.

A younger man was gazing back at us, a younger Trugood with thicker and darker hair, with less of a stoop to his shoulders, with a face less marked by time. He waved. We returned the gesture.

Then he turned and completed his journey into the ghostly cities of Cibola. What we could see of his greeting from the shaman and Yana was cordial. He walked with them into the nearest village and disappeared around the corner of an adobe structure.

Neither of us said anything.

We watched the cities until dawn. When the sun brightened over the prairie, the villages began to fade, their gold winking out in the growing light. I never saw the likes before, and I've never seen the likes since.

When I got home and started viewing the photos I'd taken I was disappointed to find that the views of the villages recorded nothing but strange orbs, not unlike the fireflies. Not a ghost of the structures showed up in the pictures. I had some great shots of the ruts and of the campsite that I had taken earlier. Even one of the sunset that evening was good enough for a magazine to purchase for a cover. I had nothing to prove that the Seven Cities of Cibola lay in that valley below the campsite.

I published an article on the mysterious section of the trail, but gained little satisfaction from scooping Will Taber. I couldn't tell the real story.

I've started a study of Padre Niza, and I've taken up healthy eating. No more corn chips. Who knows, maybe I can live another fifty-two years. Maybe by then I will have figured out how to prove that the cities of gold exist—somewhere, on some plane.

Since that night Trish Trugood Fredericks has never been in touch with me. I got the feeling that she felt, wrongly of course, that I was to blame for her father's desertion. Nevertheless, she reported him missing, and he was never found. I've heard that she and her sisters live comfortably and privately behind the "No Trespassing" sign at the gate to the Rocking T Ranch.

- The End -

Author's Note:
The Rocking T Ranch and the mysterious section of the Santa Fe Trail are purely a figment of this author's imagination. However, history does record that Padre Niza, guided by Esteban, swore he saw the Seven Cities of Cibola, but Coronado never found them.

Whisper on the Wind
By Barbara J. Baldwin

ayne was sullen, looking out the window at green pastures and cornfields, feeling as though he were being taken away to jail. Mrs. Brownstone, the latest in a long line of social workers, kept telling him he would love his new home, that the family was very nice and wanted a boy very much.

"Probably just want free labor," he muttered under his breath, but otherwise ignored her.

"Now, Wayne, you are going to try this time, aren't you?"

Why bother, he thought. He'd been in ten foster homes in the last eleven years. What difference did it make if he ran away from this one, too?

All too soon they pulled up in front of a huge white house with a porch on both the first and second stories. Wayne eyed the top porch immediately and figured he could shinny down the end post and get back to his friends in town.

Wayne didn't open his door. Finally, the social worker walked around the car and opened it for him, taking him firmly by the arm and pulling him out.

The family stood on the porch, waiting for them. There was a man and a woman and a really old man with stooped shoulders who leaned on a cane. Wayne decided he wouldn't give them names. He hummed to himself when the woman spoke to them and the man put out his hand. No names, just faces. He didn't want to know anything about them because when they sent him back, he didn't want to miss them.

The social worker left then, setting his small bag of

belongings on the bottom step of the porch. The man put a hand on his shoulder. Wayne stiffened, not prepared for the strength he felt in that hand, nor the warmth. He stared at the cloud of dust as the car disappeared. He knew how to get back; he had memorized the turns and the street signs. With sagging shoulders, he turned and followed the man and the woman into the house. The old man sat in a swing on the porch and stared off into space.

Late that night, Wayne climbed out the window of the room they had given him, crept across the porch, and slid down the rail. There was no moon, and it was dark and creepy in the country. He was used to the streetlights in town glaring in his eyes at night.

That's OK; I'm not afraid of the dark, he told himself. He hitched his bag higher in his arms, clutching it tightly as he began walking away from the large white house.

He made it to the end of the lane before it started to rain. It wasn't a sprinkle, but more like buckets of icy water dumped right on his head. He ran to the side of the road, tripped and fell, skinning his elbows on the gravel. By the time he found his bag, the raindrops felt like needles stabbing him in the back. He made a dash for the barn beside the road.

The huge door squeaked as he pulled it open. An owl hooted somewhere in the darkness. The barn smelled dusty but the inside was dry and a lot warmer than outside. Shivering, Wayne pulled his tee shirt off and dropped it on the floor. He dug into his backpack and found another that was a little damp but better than sopping wet.

He'd leave when morning came, he told himself as he felt his way along the wall of the barn. He didn't want to stay here. The man and woman had no children of their own so there were no kids to hang out with. The really old man was grumpy and couldn't see hardly at all, poking everything with his cane. He'd even poked Wayne on the foot when he got up from the table.

Summer was coming and Wayne wanted to be able to hang with friends he had from school. He didn't want to live in the country, didn't want to listen to the old man talk about how things used to be when he was young like he'd done all through supper. Wayne didn't want to milk cows and pitch hay and feed chickens or anything else the man or woman thought he should learn how to do if he lived on a farm. Of course, he wasn't sure they did that here, but figured he wasn't going to stick around long enough to find out.

His eyes adjusted to the barn's dim interior and he found a ladder. Maybe there was a hayloft he could sleep in, and then sneak away in the morning. He had read a story once about a boy who slept in a cave on an island and floated down the river on a raft. At the time he thought it would be great fun, but as he listened to the thunder outside and saw lightning flash, he decided a hayloft was much better.

* * *

Wayne heard noises and opened his eyes, trying to remember where he was. His back was scratchy, and he felt a tickle in his nose that meant he was going to sneeze. He pinched his nose. Sunlight streamed through the wooden slats of the barn. It was time to go. He released his nose and silently crept toward the edge of the loft. Before he could stop it, his nose tickled again and he sneezed.

"Didn't get very far, did you?" The voice was loud and came from below. Wayne peered down from the edge of the loft. He knew it was the grumpy old man who couldn't even see—how did he know where Wayne was?

"Wow." The word escaped even though Wayne hadn't wanted anyone to know he was there. Directly below him was an old airplane—or at least part of an old airplane. There was no propeller on the front and one wing leaned up against the far side of a horse stall. Some of the tail-pieces hung at odd angles.

Wayne had done a report on Charles Lindbergh for school last fall. Oh, how he had wished he could fly. He would take off and all the kids would stand on the ground cheering him on. Better yet, he would fly far, far away and never come back. Never have to hear those kids taunt him about his clothes, never have to see the teacher's pitying glances when he had no one come to open house to see his work. Yeah, he thought, as he climbed down the ladder. He would fly away and be famous like Charles Lindbergh.

"Is this your plane?" he asked the old man who was scooping grain into a bucket.

"Nope."

"But it's in your barn."

"Yep."

"Then who does it belong to?"

The old man stopped what he was doing and turned toward him.

"Might tell you a story 'bout that plane if you carry this bucket of grain for me."

Wayne hesitated. He wanted to leave—run away somewhere. He looked longingly at the airplane. Maybe he could stay—just today—and help enough to find out about the plane.

He picked up the bucket.

"Thought maybe you weren't going to stay," the old man said.

"Maybe I will and maybe I won't," Wayne said. He

wasn't going to give anything away.

The old man made him do chores for most of the day. Then it was time for supper and he never did tell the story.

"Tomorrow," was all he said.

"Tomorrow, Wayne has school," the woman said, clearing the table.

That made Wayne think about his friends. At least he got to go to the same school, even if he had to ride the bus now.

"Homework," he muttered under his breath, remembering the books in his backpack.

The man heard him. "You'd better get to it then," he said, but nobody said anything about him trying to run away.

Wayne looked out his bedroom window at the barn. There was a light out there, he knew now, because the old man had turned it on this morning. He could go out there and do his homework.

He carefully scooted a sawhorse over to the big plane, climbed up and looked around. There were cobwebs and dust and bits of straw scattered across the seat and floor. Something had eaten the corner of one seat. Probably mice. He was just big enough to swing his leg over the side and step into the plane onto what was left of the seat. Something blew across his face. He swatted at it, thinking it was one of the many cobwebs that crisscrossed the open space.

Carefully, he straddled the stick as he sat down. After he had done his book report on Charles Lindbergh, he had read another book on planes because he had liked the idea of flying, and he loved to read. This cockpit had three gauges, although the glass was broken out of two of them. He couldn't remember what they were for, but knew they were important to the pilot. Maybe he'd ask the old man when he told the story tomorrow.

Sighing, he opened his math book and tried to concentrate on the long division problems. He wasn't good at math; he hated numbers.

He stared at the problem: eight hundred sixty-five divided by twenty. He knew he had to start by putting twenty into eighty-six.

Four.

He looked around. It sounded like the word came from beside him, but there was no one there. He looked back at the problem. Subtract and have six; bring down the five. Twenty into sixty-five…

Three.

This time he knew he hadn't said anything. He hadn't even written down the sixty-five before the answer came to him.

He moved his eyes around the barn, looking for—what?

He tried two more problems, hard ones this time, and he heard the answer in his head before he could lift his pencil off his paper. Something was going on.

He closed his math book and opened another book to study the states and capitols that all fifth graders had to learn when they studied American history. When he closed his eyes and tried to see the name for the capitol of Iowa, nothing happened. He liked social studies and he hated math. So why did the answers come to him when he was doing math?

"Wayne, are you out here?" The man that was married to the woman came into the barn. Wayne tried to hide, afraid the man would get angry if he found him in the plane.

"I used to come out here when I visited Grandpa

George as a kid," he said, popping his head over the edge of the cockpit and smiling down at Wayne. Wayne scowled. The man wouldn't have been able to see him if the wheels of the plane hadn't been flat.

The man looked the plane up and down. "Sometimes I swore she talked to me."

"She?"

The man smiled. "This is an old Curtiss JN-4HT from about the 1920s, called a Jenny. It was used to train pilots. Most planes of that era were called *she*." He gave the plane a pat. "Fact of the matter is, playing around here was what made me decide to become a pilot."

Despite himself, Wayne asked eagerly, "You're a pilot?"

"Yeah. Spent twenty-three years in the Air Force flying jets that went a lot faster than this. But I knew when I retired I wanted to come back to the Midwest and help Grandpa George farm."

Wayne couldn't figure why anyone would farm if they could fly.

"Time for bed. The bus comes early in the morning."

Chet—Wayne had decided to allow him a name—turned the light off behind them.

Wayne looked back as Chet pulled the barn doors closed. He wanted to ask him if the plane did math problems, but he didn't.

"I've been thinking about restoring that old plane. Do you want to help?"

"Yeah!" Wayne exclaimed, unable to keep his usual surly demeanor.

"That would mean you have to stick around, you know."

Wayne thought about the voice he heard when he sat in the cockpit. Something spooky was going on and it scared him a little. But the pull of the plane was stronger.

Two days later his teacher returned his math homework with a big red mark at the bottom. She had circled five words that weren't part of his math homework at all.

"Altitude, oil pressure, air speed." Those were the gauges on the airplane. But how had the words gotten on his paper?

* * *

It was almost the end of the school year and Wayne had to study for a big test. He took his books out to the barn after supper. When he turned the light on, his eyes went to an old wooden box sitting along the wall by the airplane. He didn't remember it being there before. It had a flip-over latch but no lock. He opened it. The hinges squeaked in the strange silence of the barn.

"Wow!" Inside was a leather aviator's helmet, like the one Charles Lindbergh wore. He took it out and put it on, sliding it back on his head when it flopped over his eyes. "Cool." He pulled a long white scarf out of the box and wrapped it around his neck, then found a pair of goggles and put them on.

The goggles were scratched and dirty, making it hard to see, but Wayne climbed into the cockpit, forgetting all about the test he had tomorrow. He positioned the stick between his legs, looked intently at the broken gauges on the panel and decided to take his plane for a spin.

"I'm Charles Lindbergh and I'm going to fly across the ocean solo," he exclaimed before making a long, whirring sound.

"Charles Lindbergh? That your name, boy?" The voice came out of nowhere.

Wayne gulped, sliding the goggles onto his forehead so he could see who was talking. It didn't sound like the old man or Chet, and he couldn't see anyone else in the barn.

"Dang nab it." The curse came from the front of the plane. Cautiously, Wayne climbed out of the Jenny, peeking past the broken wing. He could see a man—well, part of a man because his head was hidden by the engine cowl.

"Grab a crescent wrench." The voice came from inside the engine area.

Wayne looked around, saw the toolbox on the floor by the man's feet and reached for a tool.

"That's not a crescent, that's a ratchet. Crescent's got an open end."

Looking again, Wayne quickly picked up the correct one.

The man was dressed funny, with dark pants stuffed into knee-high boots. His shirt was white, and he had the sleeves rolled up to his forearms. He looked older than the boys at the Home, so Wayne figured he had to be over twenty-one.

"What do you want me to do with this?" Wayne asked, holding up the wrench.

"Fix the plane. You want to fly it, don't you?" the man asked.

"Yeah!" Wayne exclaimed, and then looked thoughtful. "How come you're here now? Chet said it's been here a long time, and he wanted to fly but it never got fixed when he was a kid."

"Some things have to wait for their time."

"Wayne, bedtime." The words floated into the barn through the open door. Wayne spun around to reply. When he looked back, the man was gone.

* * *

"You want to be my assistant?" the strangely dressed

man asked the next day when Wayne raced into the barn after school.

Wayne had hoped the stranger would be there again, giving him something to look forward to.

"Can I?" he asked.

The man put his hands on his knees, bending until he was eye level with Wayne.

"Yeah, all barnstormers had a kid assistant. You've been guarding the plane already and cleaning her up, so you might as well help get her going again. Heck, sometimes they even slept under the plane out in the field to keep it safe during the night."

"Cool," Wayne said.

"But you have to know a wrench from a screwdriver," the man said.

"I do. I just can't do math."

"If I can fly fifty miles on a gallon of gas, how far do I get on three gallons?" The man asked.

"One hundred fifty miles," Wayne answered without thinking.

"What about five gallons of gas?"

Wayne scrunched up his eyes in thought. "Two hundred fifty miles."

"There you go. You can do math."

"OK, but what's the capitol of Vermont?" Wayne countered.

"Never was any good at geography." The man shook his head. "Get a crescent wrench."

"But you know math."

"Yeah, because I have to know how many miles I can fly on how much gas with a head wind or tail wind. Now that's what you need to know, boy."

"Computers can do all that," Wayne replied.

"What are computers?" The man frowned.

Wayne looked again at the strangely dressed man. How come he'd never heard of a computer? "Where are you from?" he asked.

"Around."

"Do you know the man who owned this plane?"

"Yeah, I knew him," the man said.

Wayne thought his voice sounded kind of funny. "Who are you really?" he asked then, as the man climbed into the cockpit and looked at the broken glass on the gauges.

"My name's Buzz. Who are you? Can't keep calling you 'boy.'"

"Wayne."

"Hey, that's my name," the man said as he hopped out of the plane, looking as though he floated down to the ground.

"You just said your name was Buzz," Wayne said, confused.

The man shrugged. "Real name's Wayne but when you fly around to these little towns trying to make a buck, you gotta have an exciting name."

Wayne looked at him in awe. "You really fly?"

Buzz nodded before lying down and scooting under the plane. "Yep. I'm the best darn barnstormer this side of the Mississippi."

Wayne knew the man was lying then because there weren't any more barnstormers. Not since the 1920s. Even so, Wayne was curious. Something about Buzz made him want to learn more.

Before he could ask, Buzz slid back out from under the plane, hopped up—sort of floated up—and dusted off the back of his pants. "See, that's my girl." He thumbed over his shoulder toward the plane. "My Jenny. She and I traveled all over the countryside doing loops and dives and taking passengers for rides to pay for our gas and food."

Wayne could feel his mouth drop open. If the barnstormers flew in 1920 and this was 2005, that meant the man was—he scrunched his mouth as he did the subtraction in his head.

The man looked at him and grinned. "Yep. I would be about a hundred and nine if I hadn't crashed my plane in the field just north of here." He walked towards the front of the plane. "So do you want to be my helper or not?" He turned back around but Wayne was already hightailing it to the house.

* * *

Wayne told himself he wasn't scared of a ghost, but he still didn't venture back out to the barn for over a week. He asked Chet if he had found anyone to work on the plane.

"No. In fact, I just got the manual in the mail and thought we'd start work on it as soon as school is out," Chet said.

Wayne walked out to the porch where the old man was sitting on the swing. He sat down on the step and waited.

And waited. The only sound in the silence of the night was the squeak of the wooden swing. Finally, Wayne couldn't stand it any longer.

"Where did that plane come from?" he blurted out.

The old man raised a gray brow, apparently not at all surprised at the question. "Guess I never did tell you that story, did I?"

Wayne shook his head.

"What story, Grandpa George?" Chet asked as he joined them.

"You heard about it when you were young," the old

man said to Chet. "You used to play out there like you were winning the war, but I guess you've forgotten over time."

Chet nodded. "I do remember you telling me about a barnstormer, but you're right—I've forgotten the details."

The old man's eyes got a faraway look as he began telling the story. "My pa was farming this land back in the twenties. After the war, I guess there was a lot of Jennies because the government didn't think flying was ever going to amount to anything."

Wayne thought of the huge planes that left white trails across the sky every day. He shook his head, not being able to imagine a time without planes.

"I was only about four or five at the time. One day we were eating dinner when suddenly it sounded like the tractor was running right over the top of the house. We left our meat and potatoes right on our plates and all ran straight out into the yard. I thought it was a huge bird, but the wings didn't flap. My pa said it was one of those aeroplanes that he'd heard about on the radio news." He nodded, chuckling. "That's how we called them back then."

He continued. "Well, we hopped into our old pickup and followed the plane out to our field, watching as the pilot sat her down real smooth and gentle and rolled to a stop right in front of us."

Grandpa George shook his head. "Never saw nothing like it. The man flying the plane said he'd give my pa a ride if he could use the field to take off and land. By then most of the town was out here lining the road and gawking at this strange sight."

Grandpa George stopped, but Wayne knew it wasn't the end of the story. It couldn't be—the plane was still in the barn and someone was hanging around.

"Then what?"

"Called himself a barnstormer. From what I gather, they were trained as pilots for the war and didn't want to go back to regular jobs, so they started flying circuses and shows. Most were reckless, daring and foolhardy and died young." Again, he shook his head like he couldn't figure why someone would be that way.

"Anyway, the man flew people in his plane, charging them five whole dollars a ride. He gave old Joe Blake a ride for bringing a can of gas and oil out for him. Then at the end of the day he took off."

"Then how'd you get the plane?"

"'Bout the time he got to the end of the field and pulled up, he turned the plane and was coming back over to buzz us real low. That's where they got their names— barnstormers—from flying so low over barns and fields. While we watched, the motor quit and it glided a while but then the wind caught the wing and it dipped to the ground and snapped, tossing the plane over and over. Buzz—that was his name—well, we dragged him out and took care of him, but he was busted up pretty bad." The old man shook his head sadly. "After a few days he died."

A chill snaked down Wayne's spine. He shivered as he thought about the man in the barn. He opened his mouth to tell Chet and Grandpa George, but then closed it again. If they thought he was lying, they might send him back to the group home. That had happened at one of the foster homes he'd been in, and for once, he didn't want to go.

* * *

"Hey, what are you doing tossing all that paper in here?"

Wayne turned around to find Buzz in the seat behind him. He hadn't seen him when he came into the barn. He

143

frowned. Having a ghost around could be confusing. He never knew when he'd suddenly be there and start talking. After the old man's story, it had taken Wayne a while before he started going to the barn again. He finally decided that even if Buzz was a ghost, he didn't seem scary. In fact, he was more like a friend, and Wayne was kind of short on those lately.

"I have to write a poem or find one about something I like to do," Wayne said as he crumpled another piece of paper. "Poetry. Boys don't write poetry."

"Why not? Have you ever see a rainbow after a storm, or wheat, all golden, waving in a field on a summer day? There's poetry all around."

"Yeah, well that doesn't mean I have to like it."

"Fine. You ready to start work instead?" Buzz asked, pointing to a pile of wire lying on the floor by the cockpit.

"Can't 'til I get this done."

"Well then, write this down. I call it 'God's Patchwork Quilt.'" Buzz closed his eyes, speaking soft and slow as though remembering something from long ago. "The earth lay beneath me, in unending squares. Multi-shades of green and brown, all nicely straight…"

Wayne wrote, tongue pressed into his cheek as he concentrated on spelling the words right. Then he spent the rest of the evening stringing wire through the cockpit as Buzz instructed, carefully attaching it to the control stick.

"Tomorrow," Buzz said, "we'll connect the rudder to the controls."

The next day when Wayne got home from school, Buzz was again sitting in the plane. "How was school?"

"You got me in trouble." Wayne scowled.

"Hey, I did your math. I can't help it if I'm no good at geography."

"That's not what I'm talking about. They laughed at me when I told them I got that poem from you."

"I suppose you told them I was a barnstormer?"

"Well, you are."

"Was. Most people would laugh if you told them you were talking to a ghost."

"You don't act like a ghost." Buzz looked and acted pretty much like a real person and Wayne tended to forget he wasn't.

"Then why are you the only person who sees me?"

Wayne had to think about that, and couldn't come up with an answer. But he decided it really didn't matter because school was out, and he could spend all his time helping fix the plane.

* * *

Wayne and Chet started working on the plane in June.

"She's not in as bad of shape as I first thought," Chet said as he inspected the wiring and crawled around inside and under the plane.

Wayne wanted to explain that Buzz and he had already been working on it, but he wasn't sure what to say. Besides, as Buzz said one day while Wayne painted the newly repaired wing, "Who would believe you had a ghost helping you, anyway?"

The day finally came when they rolled the plane out of the barn into the late afternoon sun. Chet had registered it and the newly painted N number could be seen both on the fuselage and under the wings. The breeze sang through the flying wires that crisscrossed the upper and lower wings.

"Ah, listen to her sing." Buzz's voice held a hint of pride.

Wayne jumped, not having seen the ghost come out of the barn. He looked over at Chet and Grandpa George but neither appeared to notice the barnstormer.

Chet was hooking the towrope to the plane and then attaching it to the small riding mower so they could slowly taxi it across the dirt road to the hayfield. The first cutting had been raked and baled, and the huge rolls stood like sentinels along the tree line, leaving the field clear. Though rough, Chet thought they could take off and land.

"Just like the barnstormers did it," Wayne whispered, excitement making him tingle from his head clear down to his toes.

Once Grandpa George moved the mower out of the way and was standing by the woman, Judy, Chet turned to Wayne.

"You ready?" Chet asked as he put on his sunglasses.

Wayne grinned. "You bet!" He wrapped the white silk scarf around his neck and pulled the goggles down over the helmet. Judy had taken the goggles into town to have the glass replaced and Wayne peered out of clear lenses. Butterflies had already taken flight in his stomach as Chet lifted him up so he could climb into the front seat.

Chet climbed into the rear seat. The engine roared to life; the propeller whirred. A sharp wind immediately whipped across Wayne's face. Wayne thought he had never been so excited as Chet took the controls and slowly turned the plane to face the long length of the field. He couldn't see the field because the plane tilted back on the tail skid, but all around him was blue sky.

He felt the control stick move between his legs and spread his knees apart so as not to hinder its movement. Chet had control from the rear seat and Wayne knew not to touch the stick.

"Here we go!" Chet yelled over the roar of the engine as they sped down the hayfield, faster and faster. Suddenly they were up in the air, the bouncy jar of the field giving way to a feeling of weightlessness.

"Yippee!" Wayne hollered, leaning towards the side as Chet gradually banked the plane to circle the field. He could see Judy and Grandpa George down below and waved. They looked like little toy soldiers.

Suddenly the plane began to roll until the wings were perpendicular to the ground. Wayne's stomach dropped as the ground tilted wildly below him.

"Hey, don't do that!" Chet yelled at him, but Wayne wasn't doing anything except holding on tight.

Before he could say anything, the plane flipped again, and Wayne was hanging upside down by his shoulder harness.

"Wayne, let go of the stick!" Chet yelled.

"Man, this is great!" A voice seemed to come from directly beside Wayne. "Watch this." As quick as a blink the plane righted and began to climb.

"Come on baby, you can do it." Wayne recognized Buzz's voice now, coaxing the plane higher and higher and all Wayne could do was hang on tight to the sides.

The engine sputtered and died. As gracefully as an eagle, she turned on one wing and began spiraling down toward the ground.

"Oh, my God." Wayne heard Chet choke behind him. He couldn't speak, but it wasn't from fright. He knew who was flying the plane and he trusted Buzz. Wayne grinned into the wind as the world spun dizzily around him.

As quickly as the plane stalled, the motor sputtered to life again, pulling smoothly out of the spin and zipping across the treetops.

"That was great!" Wayne yelled.

"Yeah," muttered Chet, but he didn't sound very happy.

Too soon for Wayne, they touched down, bounced a few times, and rolled to a stop. Chet cut the engine.

"What on earth?" Judy raced to the side of the plane. "Were you trying to scare me to death?" She looked frightened.

Wayne stood in his seat, one leg over the side. He glanced at Chet who first looked angry, then confused.

"I didn't do it," Wayne replied. The words had been his pat answer for so many years that they popped out of his mouth automatically. But this time he wasn't lying.

Chet frowned. "I know. I saw your hands clutching the sides." He helped Wayne jump to the ground. "I don't know what happened."

"It was Buzz, the man who owned the plane," Wayne said without thinking as he helped Chet hook the tow bar to the plane.

Chet stopped, looked at him for a moment. Then he laughed, reaching down to ruffle his hair. "Yeah, right. A ghost flew the plane. I think more likely we got some wires crossed."

Wayne went to sleep that night with an exhilarating feeling of freedom, a huge boost to his self-esteem. He had done something none of his friends or the kids at school had done. He'd been a copilot. He dreamed again about flying the Jenny away from all his troubles.

Because it was wheat harvest time, Wayne didn't get to fly again for long weeks. He divided his time riding the combine with Chet, riding the wheat truck into town with Grandpa George, and helping Judy carry meals out to the harvesting crew.

The time or two he went out to the barn to wash and polish the plane, he found it very quiet. Buzz was nowhere around. One late afternoon, Wayne watched from the tire swing as the huge green combine rolled slowly into the farmyard. Chet climbed down from the cab.

"Ready for a ride?" he asked.

"I'm tired of the combine."

Chet grinned at him. "Go figure. Would you rather take the plane?"

Wayne was out of the tire swing in an instant, racing for the barn.

"Get her ready while I wash up."

The field was just as rough as it had been the first time they had taxied across it, but soon they were soaring above the trees and circling the house. Chet maneuvered the stick, making the plane go up and down slowly, like a baby roller coaster. Wayne wanted big climbs, and loops and rolls. But today none of that happened.

The sun was setting as they started to circle back toward the hayfield. The engine coughed and sputtered once, like it had a hiccup. Then Wayne heard Chet yelling. He couldn't understand what Chet was saying. He wiggled around in his seat to try to see over the back.

"The oil line to the pressure gauge broke! I can't see!" Chet yelled, frantically wiping engine oil off his sunglasses. He took them off with one hand, and Wayne could see where the glasses had kept most of the oil out of his eyes, but he still had them squeezed shut. "Wayne, you hear me, son?"

Wayne nodded, his stomach in such a tight knot he thought he would throw up.

"I can't hear you," Chet hollered over the engine noise.

Wayne noticed he still had a hand on the control stick, but the plane was tipping from side to side. Wayne clutched the sides of the cockpit, scared they were going to crash to the ground. The other day had been fun when they did rolls in the air. Today was not fun at all.

"I'm here," Wayne whispered, then yelled, "I'm here. What are we going to do? Can you see?"

Chet shook his head. "Oil in my eyes. You're going to have to land us, son."

Wayne's stomach fell to the ground faster than the plane in a nosedive. "I can't!"

"Don't have much choice. The oil's clouded my vision. I can't see much of anything. Now turn around and do as I tell you."

"I can't," Wayne whimpered, even as he turned in his seat and looked out over the side of the plane. The farm looked a long ways down. "I never meant to be bad," he whispered, more to himself than to anyone else. "All I ever wanted was for someone to love me. Now I'm going to die and nobody will even care."

"You're not going to die, kid," came a soft voice, not shouting as Chet was doing from the back seat. "You wanted to be a barnstormer like Charles Lindbergh, didn't you?"

"Buzz? Where are you?" Wayne's heart was pounding a hundred miles an hour and he didn't feel like he could breathe. Knowing Buzz was there somehow made him feel better, but not much.

"Put your hands on the control stick," Buzz said, his voice sounding as though it came from right beside Wayne. Or even inside his head.

"You fly it; it's your plane." Wayne refused to touch the stick, which was bobbing and weaving between his legs like a snake in a basket. He rubbed his hands on his pants legs.

"I can't. I'm a ghost, remember," the voice reminded him.

"No, you're not. You flew last time. We did rolls and dives and..." Wayne's voice died as the plane dipped with the wind.

"Take the stick and I'll help."

Almost as if his hands had a will of their own, Wayne clutched the stick, jerking it toward himself. Immediately, the plane started to climb, bouncing Wayne's head back against the backrest.

"Whoa, not so fast." Buzz's voice, still soft and slow, spoke over the roar of the engine. "She'll respond better if you're gentle with her."

Wayne watched as his hand pushed against the stick, bringing them back level. He then tried to take his hands off the stick but an invisible force kept them curved around the control.

Without consciously thinking about it, he turned the plane gradually so they were headed back over the field.

"I can't land the plane, kid," Buzz said. "You're right, I did fly her last time, but remember all those hours you spent working on her? Do you ever remember seeing me pick up a wrench, or a paintbrush?"

Wayne felt pressure on his hands as the stick gently moved forward and the plane began to nose down toward the ground. He tried to concentrate on what he was doing but Buzz's question vibrated against the wires in the wings. He couldn't remember Buzz actually doing anything.

"I can fly her—we're as one in the air—but when she's earthbound, I'm just a ghost, haunting the place I died and wishing I could have my life back. On the ground, I can't feel the smooth satin of her wing or fix the broken glass on her gauges. That's why you came to the farm. You were destined to belong with her. And now, you have to land her."

Wayne sucked in a breath, seeing the hayfield in the distance coming closer and closer.

"I can do this," he whispered, knowing it was the only way he and Chet would make it.

"Wayne, where are we? I can tell you leveled her off, but are we approaching the field?" Chet yelled at him from the rear seat.

"I can do this!" he shouted loudly so Chet could hear. "We're coming in over the trees and I'm bringing her down." Even though he knew it wasn't him, he clutched the stick tightly as the plane dropped lower and lower.

"You won't be able to see the ground but you'll feel the wheels hit. Just keep your eyes on the tree line and run parallel to them until she rolls to a stop." Buzz spoke beside him. "Remember from your math what parallel means?"

Wayne nodded frantically because he could see the trees off to the side of the plane now and knew they were only a few feet off the ground.

"Steady now, steady," Buzz murmured.

With a jar, the wheels hit and bounced. The stick jerked in Wayne's hands.

"Keep the stick tight or you'll flip!" The words echoed in his head. He clutched the controls tighter, trying not to move it left or right, knowing from the breeze washing over his hands that Buzz was no longer flying the plane.

Chet had cut the engine the minute the wheels touched the ground, but since the Jenny had no brakes, they had to roll to a stop.

Wayne immediately jumped up and turned in his seat to where Chet was unbuckling his harness. He reached his small hands over and helped him straddle the rim of the cockpit before jumping to the ground. Then Wayne turned on his stomach and slid over the side.

"Can you see now?" Wayne anxiously asked.

Chet shook his head. "Still got an oil slick in my eyes. Better get me to the house so Judy can drive me to the doctor." Chet put his hand on Wayne's shoulder as they carefully walked across the hayfield.

Wayne felt Chet squeeze his shoulder.

"You did great up there, son. I'm proud of you. I couldn't have landed that plane without crashing, just like the first pilot did."

Wayne knew he couldn't take all the credit, and only hoped Chet wouldn't get mad. "It was Buzz, the man who owned the plane. He did it."

Chet stopped, pulling Wayne around to face him. "You're trying to tell me that a ghost flew the plane?"

Wayne couldn't tell by Chet's voice if he was mad or not. He swallowed hard. "Yes, sir."

"Is he here now?"

Wayne looked all around the field, but couldn't see Buzz anywhere. He wondered how hard it would be for Chet to believe what he couldn't see.

"No, I don't see him anymore."

"Hmm," was all Chet said as they started walking again. "Maybe he figured his job was done."

"What do you mean?" Wayne asked.

Chet shrugged. "Well, I'm not saying that there really was a barnstormer here, you understand, but if he was, just maybe he was repaying a debt from when my great-grandfather tried to save him."

* * *

Wayne never did see Buzz again after that. In the years that followed, he and Chet flew the plane often, and when Wayne turned sixteen, he soloed in the Jenny. It was then that he would swear he heard the barnstormer laugh as he looped high above the ground and coaxed a little more speed from her as he soared straight up into the sky.

- The End -

Fireball Faye
By Jerri Garretson

They always said Faye was a fireball, a gal with plenty of spunk and wit. Faye wasn't scared of anything and she didn't take nothing off of nobody. Proud she was, tall and straight, but full of life. If there was fun around, Faye was part of it. Like as not, if adventure was afoot, she started it. Faye liked nothing better than a good time, and to her, a good time meant something doing with fire. Fireworks, bonfires, or at the least a fire on the hearth or a shelf full of candles.

Even on the hottest, brightest summer day there was a mess of candles burning on her mantelpiece. Folks found her downright fascinating. The gossip was, Faye wanted a husband but they all knew no one was going to marry the likes of her. No man around those parts wanted a wife like that, her playing with fire and so independent and all.

It was on one of those roasting days in August, when things were crackling dry and everyone was praying for a downpour to cool things off that Faye might have been lighting her candles with that long red taper she liked to use, and something startled her. Could be it was a mouse. Could be it was a thunderclap, but whatever it was, her little house was soon going up in flames.

Folks speculated that she dropped that candle and before she knew it, flames were spreading up her long crimson skirt and across her hand-crocheted tablecloth. There was nothing anyone could do, seeing how it was so bone dry and all. Faye's house went up like sawdust and she went with it. They say folks heard her screaming, but mercifully it didn't last long.

Odd thing was, it was that very night that someone swore he saw Faye sashaying down Main Street heading straight for the ashes of her house. He claimed she floated right on over the ruins and danced in the light of the moon. By the time he fetched the fellas from the saloon, though, no one saw anything but moonbeams.

Folks didn't believe his story at first, leastways not until a passle more of them had seen her. At her funeral, the whole town was standing in the cemetery atop the hill, when here came Faye, all decked out in her best dress, fine as day. She swept right past them and looked down on her own coffin. Then she pointed one of those long, slim fingers at it and shot a lick of flame that singed the top of it, leaving a long black scar that sure enough did look like the word, "Faye." People gasped and ran. Women fainted. The next thing they knew, she had disappeared again.

Warnt long before Faye took to rebuilding her house by night. By harvest time, she had a cozy little place again; tiny, but neat as a pin. At first, no one would see her at work. They'd just notice a bit more done on the house each morning. But once the house was done, they'd see her now and then, looking out the glassless windows or prancing down the street.

For months, everyone was too plain scared to talk to her and they all just cleared out of her way if they chanced upon her on the street, but after awhile, strange as it might seem, they got right used to Faye's ghost. She seemed so lively and solid-looking, showing up in broad daylight and all.

Things went back to pretty much the way they was before the fire, excepting that now Faye seemed to have the power of fire and could hold a flame in each hand upon occasion. Excepting that no townfolks would let

Faye in to their houses. They watched her carefully if she showed up indoors, like down at the dry goods store.

Mamas did warn their children not to be like Faye; no playing with fire, mind you. Fire was the death of her, and sure as shootin', someday it was bound to be the death of goodness knows who else if they ever let her in. There were rumors Faye carried fire in her body, but no one saw Faye start any more fires.

'Twas the Fourth of July celebration that made Faye famous outside her little town on the Plains. It started out with a big parade. Faye decked herself out in spangles and carried a torch, looking like a glittering and glamorous version of Miss Liberty. Had all the townsfolk staring at her, especially one fella named Willie Jones, newly come to town.

That boy just couldn't take his eyes off her. Followed her all the way down the street to the park. And don't you think she didn't notice, neither. Faye kept on smiling at him and nodding, and encouraging him along the way. Wasn't hardly a person along that street that didn't notice how smitten he was. You'd a thought somebody would have warned him, but he wouldn't have listened anyway. You think some stranger would have believed that woman was a ghost, flirting with him in broad daylight?

Faye did love attention, just about as much as she still loved fun, so when Willie took her arm at the end of the parade and promenaded her over to the ice cream social, she went along gladly, torch and all. She took that torch and stuck it in the ground, still so ladylike, and helped Willie to a heaping dish of vanilly ice cream.

"Yes, Willie," she said, "ice cream is one of the great pleasures in life, but fire, now that's where the greatest beauty lies. Dangerous beauty, like me." She laughed. "Are you ready to play with fire, Willie?" she asked.

"'Cause if you're with me, that's what you'll be doing."

Willie looked quizzical. Being new in town, how could he know Faye's reputation for loving fire? No way he could see she was a ghost, neither. Sure didn't look or act like one. No woman he'd ever known teased him about playing with fire. It was downright enticing. Sitting in that park, under the summer trees, eating a dish of ice cream, Willie didn't know one thing about Faye, except that he was bewitched. Except that sitting beside him was one gorgeous creature and he meant to keep her by his side.

"Miss Faye," he said. "Would you do me the honor of accompanying me to the barn dance tonight?"

"Why, Mr. Willie Jones, I do believe I'd enjoy dancing with you, as long as we don't miss the fireworks." She smiled one of her dazzling smiles, which lit a few fireworks in Willie's soul.

Faye flirted with Willie, and a few others on the side, all afternoon. Then she gracefully disappeared for awhile, saying she wanted to dress up for the dance. Willie couldn't imagine Faye looking any better than she already did, and that spangled dress was fancy enough for him, but Faye wasn't waiting for his okay to do anything. Off she flounced, torch and all, down the street and out of sight, calling back over her shoulder, "See you at the dance, Willie boy."

Willie could hardly wait for the dance but figured he'd best get himself gussied up as well. No good would come of him showing up dressed less than his best.

'Long about eight o'clock, folks were gathering down at the big livery barn when up sashayed Faye in a bright red dress, shining like satin, decked out in ribbons and lace. Her long auburn curls were piled fetchingly on her head, held in place by more ribbons and bows. In each hand, she held a flame. Just a small flame, mind you, but there they were, leaping and glowing and beautiful. Faye smiled her dazzling smile and curtseyed to the crowd.

"Look," the townspeople whispered. "She's got that fire in both hands." They backed off a bit. No use getting too close. No telling what was going to happen.

Faye stood near the door, waiting for Willie Jones, who came down the street in his Sunday best, hair all slicked down, looking like a bridegroom ready to say his vows. His eyes were riveted on Faye. He couldn't believe that vision in red was waiting just for him in front of the whole town. He walked a little taller, breathed a little deeper, but he didn't listen to that little voice inside that was saying, "Watch out Willie. You're playing with fire." He was so busy looking at that winsome face he never noticed Faye gently blowing those two little flames off her hands. They flickered right on down the street and lit up a passing tumbleweed.

Faye held out her arm and the two of them promenaded in to the dance. They were a fine looking pair, and boy could they dance! Burning up the floor, they were, whirling around like a prairie fire until pert near the whole town turned out to watch. Faye fairly glowed, like there was a fire lit within, and Willie Jones was plumb enchanted. He couldn't have taken his eyes off Miss Faye if he'd tried, but he wasn't interested in trying.

'Long about 9:45 it was time to head outside to see the fireworks. All the folks emptied out of the livery barn, hearing another band playing over at the park. They danced their way down the street, Willie and Faye leading the way, Willie so enamored he didn't even think it strange when Faye seemed to glow even brighter.

She waltzed her way right up to the fence. Eyes shining, she turned to the crowd and said, "Y'all watch now. Fourth of July is my favorite night of the year. Fire in the sky! This year I'll be a part of it. You, Willie Jones, you decide where you belong." No one knew what that meant, but sure enough, they were going to pay attention.

As the first of the fountains and Roman candles began to light up the night sky, the crowd oohing and ah-ing, Faye, red satin dress and all, slipped under the fence and climbed on top of a picnic table. She held both arms up to the sky. Mr. Willie Jones held back only a second or two. Then he thought as how he ought to bring her on back to safety behind the fence and went after her.

Miss Faye wasn't letting no one, not even Willie Jones, stop the show. When he tried to pull her back to safety, she pulled him up on the table instead. Just like she had at the ice cream social, she laughed. "I thought you were ready to play with fire, Willie," she said. "'Cause if you're with me, that's what you'll be doing."

The crowd gasped when Faye held up her arms to the sky once again and flames appeared in both hands. The flames stretched higher and higher, 'til Faye looked like a red satin torch burning so brightly in the night that the fireworks were no match for her. The band quit playing. No one spoke. The whole town was riveted to the spot, silent, watching Faye light up the night.

Showers of sparks flew from the flames. Great balls of fire soared into the sky. Red, orange, yellow. Green, blue and purple cascades of glowing fire spewed from Faye's outstretched hands. Then the fire began to spread, down her arms, down her dress, until she was consumed in a great fountain of light. But she did not burn.

Willie, however, commenced to scream. Whatever kind of sprite she was, he could now see she was not human, but he was powerless to run away. He was held there by his own fascination, getting hotter, starting to singe.

Faye's glowing eyes smiled on him. "Willie," she said, "you chose to play with prairie fire and now you're mine forever."

The crowd murmured. Mesmerized, scared and spellbound, they watched Faye's dress, with all its ribbons and bows, turn from red to white. A wedding dress; yes, that's what it was. She clasped Willie to her and they both turned to flame. That flame soared up from the picnic table and into the sky, taking off like a giant blazing arrow. Folks could just make out the hint of a wedding dress, disappearing fast in the fire. Farther and farther it flew, past the summer moon, until it looked like a falling star coming down to rest on the prairie again.

Folks say Faye and Willie are still out there on the prairie, dancing up a firestorm, their bodies pure flame now. Sometimes at night you can see them prance down the creek beds or up on the range land. If you see the fireball up close, you might just make out the hint of a woman in a white wedding dress and a man dressed like a bridegroom.

Travelers crossing the prairie tell strange stories about fireballs that roll and dance across their paths and almost seem to speak to them. Prairie fire sprites. Fire ghosts. Faye and Willie are lighting up the night together for all time, especially every Fourth of July.

- The End -

Author's Note:
Prairie fires are still started by lightning, and set by farmers and ranchers to clear the land of old vegetation in the early spring. Throughout the Great Plains and prairie states, there are also stories of mysterious lights, or orbs, that travel along roads, down creek beds, over

marshes and across the land. Sometimes they seem to be globes of fire.

In the case of marshes, glowing methane gas may come from decaying plants, but many of the other prairie lights are harder to explain. Some people believe the orbs are ghosts. Some folklore traditions speak of fire sprites.

Fireball Faye's story was inspired by these phenomena.

What's a Ghost to Do?

By Sheri L. McGathy

"Order. Order. We must have order." Cyrus T. Marshfire, Supreme Specter for the Dearly Departed, folded his arms over his rotund belly and waited for the room to grow quiet. "That's better." A tendril of transparent gossamer tickled his nose. He brushed it away as he scowled toward the front row. "Rupert, pull yourself together. We've serious business to discuss."

Rupert muttered, "I can't. I've tried." He shrugged, sending stray wisps of gray-white ectoplasm wafting in the air like octopus limbs.

"I see." Cyrus tapped a black fingernail against his pale blue lips. "Things must be getting desperate in your haunting zone." He poked a stray bit of ectoplasm back into Rupert's chest. "You've been out there too long. You'll need to be retired, at least for now. Maybe we can find you a nice plot near Death Valley. Would you like that?"

Rupert sighed. "Thank you. I wasn't sure I could hold out much longer."

The Supreme Specter nodded to one of two pairs of hands lying on the floor near his feet. "Clerk, see to it."

Two of the hands pulled themselves forward by their fingertips and grasped Rupert about the ankle. One tug and both Rupert and the hands sank below the floor.

"Let's all wish him a speedy recovery." Cyrus cleared his throat and glanced around the room before saying, "Now, to business. I'm glad to see so many of you here, especially those of you who've spent an extended amount of time in the hot zones." He folded his arms behind his back and began to pace, his steps falling several inches short of the straw-strewn floorboards. "I know it's a hard jump through the ether to get here—those radio waves make it difficult for all but the strongest amongst us. But rest assured, this farm's in the middle of Zone 7—Prairie sector—a subsection of Kansas Territory. It's a safe zone. Most of you should feel a surge of energy—if not immediately, then very soon."

A combination of moans, wails, and rattles forced the Supreme Specter to pause yet again. He tucked his thumbs into his waistcoat pockets, causing the corners to sag downward and spill bits of dirt to the floor. A large brown spider eased its delicate legs through one of the frayed buttonholes and escaped up a rotted coat sleeve.

Once the room quieted, Cyrus continued, "Refresh yourselves while you can. We'll all be returning to the hot zones soon enough. Now, I'd like to hear some reports."

The room exploded in a riot of sound as each ghost tried to out-shout the other in their eagerness to give their reports. One of the representatives of the Fae—a banshee—rose into the air above a small trio of gray ladies standing along the far wall near the horse stalls and proceeded to circle the room, her high-pitched wail trailing behind her.

"Now, now. Everyone will get a chance to speak. Raise your hand and I'll call on you when it's your turn."

A pitiful moan managed to rise above the clamor, followed quickly by a tug on the Supreme Specter's pants leg. "Hmm? Clerk, what are—"

One of the hands lifted a bony finger toward the center of the gathering.

"Ah, I see. Sorry." Cyrus slapped his forehead with enough force to make his eyes bulge. "Disembodied head, you bob up and down when you want a turn to speak." He wiggled a finger at the rafters overhead.

"Now, Banshee. If you'll come down from there, I'll let you start."

The Banshee floated downward amidst a cloud of her own pale locks. When she reached the ground, she gathered the silken tresses about her and wore them like a shimmering mantle of moonlight. Turning to face the others, she wrung her hands and screeched, "The living do not see the Fae when the bewitched boxes are pressed to their ears; they do not hear the death calls. I wailed in their faces, I did. Wailed loud enough to turn their skin white, I did." She tangled her fingers in her hair and cried, "Yet my call went unheeded, my presence unseen, death passed unremarked." She tossed back her head and let loose a soulful moan. "Whatever shall we do?"

"Sir Monty?" The Supreme Specter scanned the room. "Is this true?"

A tall ghost attired in a gleaming suit of silver armor suddenly appeared above the heads of the others, his form outlined by pulsing white light. Removing his plumed helmet, he bowed to Cyrus, sending an arc of light cascading across the room. "As many of you know, I am a castle ghost. I am in charge of all of Zone 2, the Green Isles Sector. 'Tis a grand position, to be sure. I have haunted there a long time. I have frightened both young and old...many I have frightened to their demise—"

"Aye," chimed in a monk in a drab brown robe with a braided rope cinched tight at his waist. "He scared me so badly, I dropped dead during an exorcism."

The castle ghost joined in the laughter ringing throughout the room, then shook his head and said, "I know my job, 'tis why I haunt the old castles...the fleshies expect a good scare when they are within. All that history, you know." He lowered himself to the floor and laid a glowing hand on the shoulder of a young woman with skin made all the paler by her dress of purest black. "My Lady Lasandra 'twas our main attraction. The living always thrilled to see a weeping woman roam the halls in the dark, wee hours, with naught but a candle to light her way."

He sighed. "But now, what my Lady Banshee has stated, 'tis true. Both Fae and spirit alike are ignored. I too have stood before a group of fleshies within my ancestral home. I did then give my best performance, only to have them walk past me as if I did not exist." He narrowed his eyes. "I am no weak and feeble wraith; I have great energies at my command, yet it did not matter. The strange boxes placed against their ears weakened me and forced me to fade, though I did not wish to go."

A low murmur rippled through the crowd, silenced only when a dark figure separated from the deeper shadows along the wall and stretched long over the floor. When the opaque nothingness floated before one of the ghostly orb lights, a bulky silhouette of a bear played across the far wall. His voice was low, and more a growl as the Shadow Ghost said, "These things distract the minds of the living. They force us into obscurity even as they erase the ability to believe. So complete is this distraction that now only a few fleshies hold the power to see."

"They are everywhere." A Grim Reaper stood and waved his scythe over the heads of his fellow ghosts. "I would gladly retire. I have walked many a hall and darkened road in search of those to haunt, but there is no peace for us now. These boxes are everywhere. We cannot rest easy, even within our graves." He shrugged, sending fine filaments of gray ectoplasm wafting off his shoulders. He turned his cowl-covered face to the Supreme Specter. "I ask you now, what is a ghost to do?"

"Now, calm down." Cyrus rubbed his fingers along

his chin. "We just have to figure out—"

A young man dropped down from the rafters, a noose tightly knotted around his swollen neck. His body turned in small, tight spirals as he said, "They don't see us; they don't hear us. All they do is talk to the little box near their ear. If they don't believe, won't we cease to exist?" He clapped his hands to his ears and cried, "What's a ghost to do?"

A ghost holding his head in the crook of his arm stood and pushed the hanging ghost aside. "Even in the Loch Zones, where the water should hold sway, there are these distractions." He lifted his head above his shoulders and turned slowly, his unwavering stare touching each of them before he added, "Used to be only a few boxes, the waves they produced nothing more than a minor annoyance." He closed his eyes and moaned. "There was a time when I was able to row ashore with the fog, my ghostly lantern in hand and my head perched on the bow. The sight sent all but the bravest of heart running."

He shrugged his headless shoulders. "Now, there are too many of them. All day long, talking and ringing and ringing and talking. I can't go for a float without passing through one of the waves." His form shimmered. "I can't even produce enough energy these days for the tourist cameras." He tucked his head back in the crook of his arm and sniffed. "Imagine, my fine form now reduced to a ball of hazy light on film, and the fine tradition of the death boat vanishing from lore. What's a ghost to do?"

The Supreme Specter sighed. "That's the question on all our minds, and that's why we have gathered here this day. An age-old tradition is being threatened. We can't haunt if we can't manifest a decent form." He pointed to a small group of ghosts sitting in the hayloft. "You four are newly dead. Do you understand the things we face? Is there no way to defeat them?"

"Maybe if we change our frequencies. We'd have to experiment; there might be some of us forced out of phase, but—"

Just then, the barn door swung open and a slender girl of perhaps thirteen walked in, her ear pressed to one of the small boxes. "My granddad is so old-fashioned, he doesn't even own a TV! If it weren't for my cell phone, I swear I'd go crazy out here."

"The enemy has found us," the Banshee wailed before disappearing through the ceiling.

One of the younger ghosts flew down from the hayloft and positioned himself before the fleshie, his form little more than a feeble ball of fine mist. She walked right through him. "Wow," she mumbled into the box. "He really said that about me? That just gives me chills."

The young ghost moaned and exploded into a thousand shafts of light.

A wailing woman dropped to her knees and covered her ears with her hands. "Is there no place to hide?"

The Supreme Specter offered her his hand. "Yes, yes, there is. Come with—" Before he could finish, she faded from view, leaving behind the faint echo of her cries.

Thick bands of radio waves crisscrossed the air, threatening to push Cyrus out of phase. He had little time left. "Listen to me," he wailed as he soared around the room. "All's not lost; we can beat this. All we need is a few days in a free zone to think this out." As he reached out to catch a panicked ghost, bits of his own ectoplasm oozed down his legs to drip on the fleshie's head as she walked past. She didn't seem to notice.

"Follow me," Cyrus shouted. "We'll regroup in Nebraska."

As the Supreme Specter drifted skyward, he heard the girl say into the talking box, "I tell you, I can't wait to get back home. It's boring here. Nothing exciting ever happens in Kansas!"

- The End -

One Night at Whistling Woman Creek
By Linda Madl

The minute Jake Wilson saw his wife press her lips together in determination as she poured coffee for their guest, he was sorry he'd invited the old cavalry scout to supper. He'd issued the invite to Virgil because he'd thought it would please Martie. She loved having guests. Shoot, he liked having company too. Opportunities to socialize on the prairie were darn few. But, dang it all, he could tell from the line of her mouth that she was going to bring up that infernal nightmare—in front of a man they hardly knew, no less—and tonight of all nights. The night before he and their son Tommy left for town, leaving her alone on the homestead.

"You've been around these parts for a long time, Virgil." Martie held a hot pad against the enameled pot lid as she filled the old scout's coffee cup with her thick steaming brew. Then she began to refill Jake's cup. "Weren't you part of the search party that went looking for that missing woman at Rock Ridge a few years ago?"

Out of annoyance, Jake kicked the table leg and dropped his spoon. Cold coffee splattered onto Martie's prized table cloth. She always treated company—drifter or parson—like royalty: white cloth, napkins, china cups and all. But she was too intent on her question to notice the coffee stain.

"That was a long time ago, Martie," Jake said, hoping to discourage her from pursuing the subject. At least she'd waited until Tommy had gone to bed before she brought up the cursed dream. "Virgil has probably forgotten all about Rock Ridge."

"I remember that search right well." Virgil poured a

generous amount of cream into his coffee. His faded blue eyes turned down at the corners, sad like a hound dog's. Gray stubble covered his chin, and his brow bore a hat line where tanned skin met freckled pink. His Indian scouting days were long behind him, but he still did odd jobs for homesteaders and told tales for his supper. "'Twas about three years ago," he added. "The mister came home from town to find the house deserted and his missus gone."

"I believe Hanson was the name." Martie poured coffee for herself. "I was wondering, did they ever find her?"

"Nope," Virgil replied without looking at either of them. "Only thing we found was one of her shoes."

Outside, the September wind blew, rattling the windowpanes and sending the windmill into a clattering frenzy. Inside, the well-polished kerosene lamp cast a golden glow on the table cleared of the supper dishes. Only the coffee cups, sugar bowl, creamer, and bare pie tin remained.

"A shoe?" Martie returned the coffee pot to the cook stove and then settled into her chair. "All the livestock was safe. But Mrs. Hanson was gone."

"Yep, that's how it was." Virgil still studied his coffee cup. "What made you think of that?"

Martie shook her head. "I dreamed about the Hansons a few nights ago." She was lying, but Jake said nothing. The damned nightmare had started over a year ago. She'd dreamed it infrequently at first, but now it troubled her several nights a week. He hated the whimpering sounds she made in her sleep when it came to her. He hated his powerlessness to stop it. She'd lost weight and become distracted and spiritless, except when she talked about it. He was sick of hearing about that dang thing.

"Sounds like the weather is changing," Jake said, desperate now to change the topic. Tomorrow he and Tommy were leaving on an overnight trip to town. Martie didn't need to be thinking about missing women. "What do you think it'll be like tomorrow, Virgil?"

"Fine." Virgil placed his spoon on the saucer, but spoke as if his thoughts were elsewhere. "You'll have clear weather for journeying tomorrow."

"Jake thinks I'm being foolish about that dream," Martie said without looking at him, but Jake saw a blush stain her cheeks. "I never met that poor Hanson woman, but since I had that dream, I can't forget her," she added. "I understand some say she ran away. Others thought Indians kidnapped her."

Jake cursed inwardly. "Hasn't been any Indian trouble around here for years. Ain't that right, Virgil?"

The old scout shook his head. "I don't put no stock in that Injun story. The Injuns around here ain't never been much for kidnapping. All the livestock was left behind. The milk cow, beef cattle, and all the horses. Injuns would take the livestock. The horses at least. Same with outlaws, and if the missus had run away, there'd have been a horse missing. She wouldn't strike out on foot."

Martie leaned across the table. "Then what do you think happened to her?"

"Maybe she run off with some drummer," Jake volunteered, his annoyance erupting at last. "That's not so mysterious."

"Nonsense, we don't get any salesmen calling out here," Martie snapped. "There sure weren't any traipsing from homestead to homestead three years ago."

"Well, there are other things that might have happened," Virgil said, glancing at Jake uneasily.

"We don't need any wild tales around here tonight,

Virgil," Jake said, inclining his head, to give the old man a signal to shut up. Martie didn't need to hear the other stories that had come to his ears from time to time of homesteader's wives who'd disappeared or gone mad.

"Oh, pooh." Martie shot Jake a withering look, the kind of headstrong expression she used to give him when they were first married, before they homesteaded on the prairie. Obviously, she intended to wheedle the story out of the man. "I want to know what you think, Virgil," Martie persisted with a smile. "It's the least you can do to indulge me after I served you a meal."

Virgil considered her for a moment, leaned back in his chair, and then began searching his pockets for something. "Do you mind if I smoke my pipe while I talk?"

"Go ahead." Martie slid a saucer across the table to the old man as he set about cleaning and filling his pipe.

Another lie, Jake thought with a frown. Martie never allowed tobacco in the house.

"Years ago when I was an army scout," Virgil began, "I met some fellas who'd scouted up north for the army. One of their number went missing, a well-seasoned man who knew how to take care of hisself. His disappearance seemed mighty strange to his compadres. No one could account for it. That's the first time I heard about this Injun superstition. About a creature or some called it a spirit that lived in the woods. Some folks said it lived in the treetops. There're big old trees up there, forty to fifty feet tall, the likes of which we never see around here. This thing is of great size, and it can travel as fast as the wind through the treetops.

"It's a force left over from the darkness of long ago, according to the legend. Left over from the darkness before creation. A wilderness spirit. It howls above the trees and brings a great stench with it when it comes."

"A stench?" Martie's eyes grew wide. "What kind of stench?"

"Like death." The old scout tamped tobacco in the pipe bowl with his thumb. "And like life. Like a place full of growing mold and decaying carcasses. Least that's what they say. I never smelled it myself, mind you."

"Go on." Martie prompted once more.

Jake ground his teeth but remained silent.

"It only comes during the new moon when the woods are the darkest and it cain't be seen," Virgil added. "It takes the shape of a moose when it wants to be seen. And it takes great pleasure in seducing those who stray into its wilderness. It ensnares its victims. Somehow it makes them one of its own kind. Here's the strangest part of the story. It does something to their feet. Something painful. Then it forces them to run. It pulls them into the treetops and drags them away. Drives them crazy."

"But why?" Martie asked, looking pale and unnerved.

"Revenge on those who invade its virgin forest some say." Virgil struck a match on the seat of his chair and lit his pipe. "Or maybe taking payment for the bounty of the land men steal away. Others say it feeds on the victims' fear. Craves men's terror. And believe me I've seen grown men's faces turn chalk white at the mention of the Wendigo."

"Never heard of it," Jake said, determined to belittle the story. "If it's a wilderness beast, what does it have to do with the Hansons?"

"It's not a beast exactly but a spirit, a shapeshifter, as the Injuns describe it." Virgil talked around the clay pipe he'd clamped between his teeth. Smoke curled over his head as thin and vague in the air as the yarn he was spinning. "If there are such things, it's a primal spirit that lives in the vast woods protecting its isolation. Why wouldn't there be a likewise thing on the prairie?"

"Spirit hidden on the prairie?" Jake said to his wife. "Hogwash. Injun hocus pocus. There's nothing hiding in the cottonwoods down by the crick. You know that, Martie."

"I never said there was," Martie snapped. Then ignoring her husband's obvious logic, she asked, "What do the Indians around here say?"

"To be honest, missus I haven't heard any prairie Wendigo legend, if that's what you mean," Virgil said. "But have you ever noticed how the Injuns all stay together? You don't see them go off by themselves unless they're on some vision quest. That don't happen often. No, the Plains Injuns, they all stay together, and I suspect there's a reason for that. I remember in the early days there were frontiersmen, able men, mind you, who went out there on the prairie and never were seen again, just like in the woods. It was like the miles and miles of tall grass just swallowed them up."

"Like Mrs. Hanson," Martie muttered.

Virgil puffed on his pipe and nodded.

There'd been others—missing wives—Jake had heard of at least one other poor woman from years past. The fellas who loitered in front of the general store had talked about her when the Hanson thing happened. But he'd never told Martie. He hadn't wanted to worry her. He hadn't wanted to worry himself. Abruptly he stood up and tossed his napkin on the table. "I think that's enough storytelling for tonight."

The old scout shoved back his chair and rose slowly. He thanked Martie for the meal, shook Jake's hand, and took his leave. He would sleep the night in the barn and be on his way to a new job early in the morning. That was their agreement. Jake was damned glad to see him go.

He bolted the door behind the old man and turned to Martie, who was already washing up the dishes.

Martha Ann Simmons Wilson had been a pretty woman when they'd first settled by the spring-fed creek that they'd never named. They'd disagreed about what to call it from the beginning. Martie wanted something romantic like Cheshire Springs. What did Cheshire have to do with anything? He wanted to call it Spring Creek.

There'd been a bloom in her cheeks in those days, and she'd been strong and fearless, ladylike and elegant. Homesteading had been hard on them both. They'd lost two children in the six years they'd been here. A little boy and a girl buried on the hill behind the house. Now Martie was too thin and her skin was lined and dry. When she spoke, the rich, bubbly confidence he'd so loved in her voice was gone, replaced by a muttering that he was coming to hate.

"Why'd you bring up the nightmare in front of company?" Jake asked.

"Because I thought Virgil might know something helpful." Then she asked, without looking up from the dishpan, "You'll just be gone one night, won't you Jake? You'll get Tommy settled with the Connells and come straight home, won't you?"

"You're not going to let that old man's story get you spooked, are you?" Suddenly he felt guilty and resentful all at once about leaving her alone. "Someone has to stay with the livestock; you know that, Martie. Somebody has to be here to milk the cow twice a day. The dogs will take care of any varmints that might trouble you. The shotgun is loaded and ready behind the door if you need it. There's nothing to worry about. Shoot, you've stayed here alone before."

"No, Tommy was with me," she said as she continued

with the dishwashing.

"The boy needs more schooling to be able to go to the agricultural college like we want him too, right?" Jake said, trying to reassure himself and her that they were doing the right thing.

Pressing her lips together, she gave a jerky nod. "I want Tommy to go to school. It's the best thing. But, darn it, Jake, I feel like this place is taking everything dear from me."

"I know it feels like that," Jake said, relieved that at least she wasn't going to argue about their plans. "I'm going to miss Tommy, too. When you say goodbye to him in the morning, don't bring up the Hansons or the dream. Don't make parting hard for the boy."

"You know I wouldn't do that."

The anger in her voice made Jake glance at her in surprise. Indignation darkened her eyes, like his old Martie, like the spirited girl he'd courted and wed. Without another word, she went back to washing the supper dishes. Whatever else was on her mind about Tommy's leaving and about staying alone she left unsaid. Her silence eased his conscience. He didn't need any reminding about how hard prairie homesteading was for a woman.

* * *

At dawn, after a dreamless night, Martie put on a cheerful face, just as she had promised, kissed her son goodbye, and waved to the wagon bearing him and her husband out of sight. Then she went back into the house, sat down at the table, and wept—only a little.

She was entitled to a few tears, she told herself as she wiped her cheeks dry. Tommy was her first-born, and when he wasn't in the field with his father, he was her helper and her companion. Now he was gone. He was excited about going to school, and she was glad of that. Still, oh my, she was going to miss him.

She sobbed. The hiccupping sound echoed throughout the modest three-room frame house they'd managed to build after two years of living in the soddy. She frowned, annoyed with her self pity.

"The day is slipping by, Martha Ann," she said aloud, comforted by the normal sound of her voice. She went to her dresser for a clean handkerchief, blew her nose, found her bonnet, and went out to face the chores.

There were eggs to gather and chickens to feed. She skimmed the milk. Tommy had milked the cow for her before he left. She set the milk and cream in the spring house to cool. Then she fed the horses and checked their water before she walked to the garden. It needed to be cleaned of spent plants.

Thanks to the work, the hours slipped by.

But part of her was always listening for the soft noise—a sound she'd first heard in the dream. Since then she'd heard it outside on the windiest days when Jake and Tommy were in the field and she was alone. A whistling sound—melodic, illusive, seductive—chilling.

Now and again as she labored, she stopped, straightened and turned toward the western prairie to listen— ears straining for that sound.

But she heard nothing out of the ordinary. The wind sighed through the golden prairie grass that would turn red by November. From the unnamed creek she heard the shiny cottonwood leaves rustle. The windmill clattered, the noise rising and falling at the whim of the ever-present breeze. The chickens clucked around the henhouse and the workhorses whinnied idly in the corral. From faraway she heard the sweet, plaintive song of a meadowlark.

Nothing from a nightmare. Nothing from an old

Indian scout's tall tale of treetop monsters. Nothing to fear, she told herself, ignoring the cold anticipation pooling in her stomach, a sensation she'd begun to experience since she'd started having the terrible dream.

She walked from the garden to the hillside apple orchard they'd managed to establish above the creek. Next to the orchard lay the small fenced cemetery where their children were buried. Her gaze rested briefly on the small headstones, but she didn't allow her thoughts to linger there. She'd cleaned off the plots only yesterday. Her babies were at peace in their little graves. She took comfort in that.

She set about picking up fruit that had fallen since she and Tommy had apple-picked the week before. She worked steadily, her apron becoming heavy with fruit. The dogs followed with pink tongues lolling, ears perked, and tails wagging. While they were at her side, she had no reason to fear snakes or feel alone.

Then she heard it.

She'd just bent to pick up another apple when the soft sighing whistle reached her.

She froze. Turning her head slightly to listen more intently, she held her breath, praying that she was mistaken. The soft deep whistle came again.

Martie straightened slowly. Icy anticipation returned. Forgetting about her apron full of apples, she faced south, the direction the sound came from. Fruit tumbled to the ground.

Queenie's tail went stiff. The dog thrust its nose into the breeze, where the sound came from, and woofed tentatively. Rex, too, put his nose to the wind, probing for a scent.

Martie followed the dogs' gaze southward. Nothing stretched out before her but prairie and sky. The sound came again, drawing the dogs toward the southern edge of the orchard.

The sun had sunk low, nearly resting on the horizon, its brightness weakened by a thin layer of clouds that had appeared after noon. It was going to be dark soon. She hadn't realized it was so late already.

Chilled, Martie rubbed her arms and whistled softly to bring the dogs back to her—whistled to herself. Whistling against the coming darkness—and her fear.

After a moment of silence the dogs lost interest in the deserted prairie. They returned.

She took a step toward the house and stumbled on the apples she'd dropped. How silly of her to drop the fruit. She bent to pick up the apples.

Just as she did, she heard the crackle of footsteps in the dry grass from behind her.

She whirled around to see who was there.

No one.

She stared in disbelief. The sound had been unmistakable.

As she stared, she heard another footstep.

All she could see was innocent prairie grass waving in the wind. The stalks brushed against each other, rustling, unlike the sharp sound of dry grass crushed underfoot.

Alarmed, she caught her breath and retreated several steps.

There was nothing in the orchard but her and the dogs. Yet she could have sworn she'd heard a footstep. What was worse, she felt someone was watching her.

Raw fear began to crawl into her bones.

Suddenly an irresistible itch on the bottom of her foot distracted her. She rubbed the sole of her shoe against the toe of her other foot. She sighed. Ah, that was better. Something must have gotten into her shoe.

She glanced around the orchard one more time. Whatever she thought she had sensed seemed gone. She was alone with the dogs. Was she imagining things?

She whistled to the dogs again, more softly this time, and decided to forget about the apples. It was time to shut up the chickens, milk the cow again, and go in for the night. Everything was fine. Just fine.

The last of dusk was still filtering through the west windows as Martie lit the lamp on the table. She had pulled off her shoes, stoked up the fire, heated water on the cook stove, washed up quickly, and decided to spend the evening shoeless. Going around the house in her stocking feet was unusual for her. But she decided to pamper herself with the small pleasure. She also decided to indulge herself in an evening of reading.

Supper finished, she settled herself at the table and opened her favorite novel, *Alice's Adventures in Wonderland*, and with a smile she began to read the familiar words. She'd read the book at least once a year since they'd homesteaded on the creek. Twice she'd read it aloud to Tommy. Repeated readings failed to steal away the pleasure of the story.

The story seemed different each time she read it. Perhaps that was because she had changed a little herself every time she opened the book. She'd been young and hopeful that first time, and she'd had little fear of the prairie. Then they'd lost the children. There'd been bad crop years. Blizzards that killed the livestock.

Her hopes had withered. Her energy and optimism had been replaced with fear and prayers. She prayed that they could hang on, breaking the virgin sod, putting in crops, and raising the livestock, earning enough to give Tommy an education and keep the roof over their heads. There'd never been a discussion about quitting the place, about giving up. Everything they owned was invested in this ground.

She was soon lost in the story of Alice. In the glow of the lamp, she was blissfully oblivious to the gathering darkness and the rising and falling of the wind.

As she was turning the page to the opening of chapter five, the whinnying of the horses caught her ear. Rex barked. Then all was quiet again. She raised her head to listen for a moment. Nothing more reached her. Probably just a possum or a raccoon searching for fruit in the orchard. She returned to her reading.

The rising wind made the windmill clatter louder. Lord, how she hated the sound of that windmill in a high wind. For a moment she thought she heard a sigh, like a low whistle, like the sound in the orchard. It passed over the house, rattling the stovepipe, subtly vibrating the roof above and the floor beneath her feet. Then it was gone.

Goose bumps prickled down her arms. Just the wind, she told herself.

The dogs began barking again. This time both Queenie and Rex issued vicious barks.

Martie turned to the door without getting up. There wasn't a prairie critter that Queenie or Rex couldn't deal with. Even coyotes usually kept their distance.

She realized she hadn't heard any coyotes all evening. They were always restless this time of the year. Fall was when they came together, forming packs for the winter, fighting among themselves and teasing the farm dogs with their howling and yipping.

Maybe she should go have a look. Yet, a reluctance to leave the safety of the lamplight kept her in her chair.

"Don't be silly, Martha Ann," she said aloud, placing the bookmark in the book but not closing it. "Just go out on the porch and see if you can tell what is stirring up the dogs."

Put that way, it sounded so simple. She rose from the table, lit a lantern, found the shotgun behind the door, and carried the light and the firearm out onto the porch.

The wind grabbed at her skirt, but she ignored it. There was no moon, no stars, only the soft darkness of a cloud-covered night. The dogs barked on. She could just see their stiff tails on the edge of the lantern light. They faced the southwest barking for all they were worth.

Bossy gave a nervous low. Martie glanced toward the barn to see the horses circling in the corral, the wind lifting dust from their hooves—like smoke coming off their feet.

She was immediately aware that her stocking feet itched something awful. She rubbed one foot on top of the other for relief. All of a sudden the sense of being watched overwhelmed her.

"Anybody out there?" she called. A drifter might make the dogs bark like that. "Make yourself known, sir. I'll call off the dogs."

Nothing. Rex and Queenie persisted with their barking.

"Queenie, come on in, girl," Martie cajoled, feeling the need for company. The dog came to her. Queenie wasn't a house dog, but knew how to behave indoors. Rex, the outdoor dog, fell silent, but refused to come when called.

Martie hung the lantern on the porch. The light might discourage whatever was troubling Rex. She brought Queenie into the house and was soon settled at the table again, the shotgun lying on the chair next to her. Queenie lay down on the braided rug and began to chew on her front paws.

Just as Martie was about to resume reading, she noticed that the room was too warm, though the fire in the stove was dying. Her feet were hot. Without thinking, she peeled off her stockings, wiggling her toes against the fibers of the rug.

She balled up her stockings and threw them into a chair. Then Virgil's words about the Wendigo came to her.

It does something to their feet. Something painful and then it drags them through the forest.

She gave a snort of disbelief. She was being silly, letting Virgil's story carry her away.

A sudden gust of wind rattled the stove damper. The lamp on the porch went out. The table lamp flickered but remained lit.

The low whistling moan hummed through the house again. Queenie raised her head and looked toward the door. Outside Rex began to bark once more.

Fear blossomed in Martie's belly.

The whistle consumed the house. Just like in her nightmare. Terrorized, she pressed her hands over her ears and squeezed her eyes shut. But she could still hear the sound, could feel it to the core of her body.

A dark sweetness, a tempting melody—a siren's chorus? The deepest inflections reverberated through the floorboards like the tones of a cathedral's pipe organ she'd heard once. Then the sound rose, the pitch lightened, until it sang like the music of an Indian flute. Finally it shrilled into a whistle, like a steamboat's whistle, shattering to the ears.

Out in the darkness, Rex yowled. Then abruptly, he stopped.

The whistling ceased.

Queenie, who'd leaped to her feet the moment Rex began to howl, stood with her gaze fixed on the door.

Uncovering her ears, Martie raised her head, listening for Rex. Silence.

"It's all right, Queenie," she said, without conviction.

"He's just chasing something, saving his breath for the run."

Queenie whined and remained at the door.

Fear fixed Martie to her chair. She was not going outside again, nor was she letting the dog out. She picked up the shotgun, but she was certain the firearm was of little use against whatever was out there.

The burning sensation renewed in her bare feet. She rubbed them together. How much cooler it would be on the porch—to step onto the earth.

Oh, to feel the grass between her toes.

The shuddering moan coursed through the house again.

The lamplight shimmered as though it was about to have the life sucked out of it. She closed her eyes against the seduction of the reverberating sound. Against the allure of relief.

How cool the grass would feel beneath her feet, with the wind tangling her skirts and freeing her hair.

She opened her eyes. But what would truly happen if she went out there?

The moan rattled the windowpanes this time, the pitch rising again from a melodic hum to a whistle. Then it wavered into a painful scream-like quality. The wail stretched out longer than any human voice could possibly sustain.

Martie began to whimper. She couldn't help herself.

Abrupt silence.

Wind hit the walls of the house like a blast from a passing freight train. Cold invisible fingers raced under the door and swooped down the stovepipe, pulling at her skirts and dousing the table lamp. Only the flickering stove fire lit the room.

Blinded by the darkness, she smelled it—the stench.

Sweet, sickly, rank, and fetid. Like something rotten. Panic sucked the breath from her lungs.

At the door, Queenie began to whimper.

All but paralyzed with fear, Martie turned toward the dog. Queenie's tail was tucked between her legs. Flat-eared, the dog slunk away from the door.

Strangely, Martie was filled with the urge to go outside, into the cool night air. Unable to defy the longing, she stood up, her hands flat on the table. Her head knew it wasn't safe to go. But her feet burned so painfully that she had to find relief. She hobbled toward the door.

The dog cowered under the table.

This was wrong. She knew it was wrong, but she couldn't help herself. She had to do something to stop the burning. The doorknob was cold to the touch. Nevertheless, she turned it slowly, uncertainly.

The wind blasted the door open. The door nearly struck Martie in the face. The wooden panel slammed her back against the wall, imprisoning her there.

The moan shuddered into the house. Invaded the three rooms. Caught at everything: tablecloth, curtains, Martie's hair, cupboard doors, and Queenie.

Martie's feet throbbed. She was mad with burning now, crazed with the need to make it cease. She had no will of her own. Her feet demanded to carry her out into the night's soothing coolness. But the door imprisoned her against the wall, the doorknob gouging into her abdomen.

Queenie yelped. Martie glanced at the dog. The poor animal under the table struggled against invisible forces. It braced its legs against the unseen power and whined. Resistance seemed useless.

Powerless, Martie watched indiscernible fingers drag Queenie toward the open door.

The dog's claws ripped at the braided rug and then scratched frantically across the wood floor. Halfway toward the door she lost control of her body functions.

Martie could only stare in helplessness as the hound was hauled out the door. She listened to the yelping dog being pulled across the porch.

Then Queenie's protests ceased—so did the wind.

In the silence, Martie realized the burning had gone from her feet. The pressure of the door had vanished. She pushed it closed. Still, she stood with her back against the wood, afraid to look out the window.

But she could breathe again, if only in short shallow gasps. Her mind grappled with what she'd just seen. Something invisible had dragged a large dog away. What about the other animals, the livestock?

In the quiet she could hear the frantic circling of the horses in the corral and the soft lowing of Bossy, the milk cow.

Would the whistling wind return? Would she be next? Was this what had taken the Hanson woman? Had it dragged her, stumbling helplessly across the prairie—forced to run though she was exhausted? Run and run and run?

Was this the Wendigo? What did it want? How could she survive where others hadn't?

There had to be a way. She'd given up too much to allow this thing to make her into a victim. She had not let the prairie beat her before. She would not let it beat her now. She threw open the door and went out into the night, terrified, but determined to win.

* * *

The next afternoon when Jake drove into the homestead yard, the first thing he saw was an empty corral and an opened barn door. He was baffled. And where were the dogs?

He glanced toward the house. To his relief, Martie was sitting on the porch steps with her bare feet sticking out from beneath her skirts. Her hair hung in lank strands around her face as if it hadn't been combed yet today. Strange. Her locks were streaked with gray that he didn't remember noticing before he left. Her feet appeared to be either dirty or bruised and blistered. He was unsure which.

Martie had never been one to go about with untidy hair and bare feet, nor had she ever been the sort of woman who did a lot of porch sitting. She was a hard worker who liked everything tidy and proper. But today she wiggled her bare toes and waved to him, smiling as if she were happy, which she hadn't been for a long time. Smiling as if the corral wasn't deserted.

"Dammit, Martie, what happened?" Jake demanded, satisfied that she was all right.

"They went off in that direction." Martie fluttered her hand toward the north.

The lack of concern in her manner infuriated him. At the same time he was struck by the careless youthfulness of her countenance. Demanding more of her at the moment seemed a waste of time. The horses were gone, the dogs, and the cow. Even the henhouse was silent.

Hastily, he saddled a wagon horse and rode off, tracking the livestock across the prairie. At first, the trail of trampled grass was easy to follow. At one point in a dusty hollow, he thought he saw small barefoot prints among those of the animals, small like those of a woman. Martie's? But that would be impossible. Martie wouldn't have followed them, kept up with them as they bolted across the prairie. He rode on.

He found nothing more. Nothing that made any sense.

Oddly, in another dusty ravine, the hoof prints took on twisted shapes. He thought he caught the whiff of rotten egg in the air. Thinking he might be close to finding something, some evidence of what had happened, he pressed on. The trail led uphill along a ridge—then vanished abruptly over the bluff edge.

Vanished into thin air.

Jake halted his horse and, without dismounting, peered down at the thirty-foot drop. There was nothing below. Nothing. No dead or injured animals. No footprints. Only silence—accompanied by the strange feeling that he wasn't alone.

A chill crawled down his backbone. He straightened in the saddle and glanced over his shoulder. Vacant prairie stretched out beyond him. Still, he could not dismiss the sense that he was being watched. How could that be?

Feeling a bit foolish, but certain there was nothing more he could do, he turned his horse toward home.

By the time he returned, Martie had climbed into the wagon, which now had no horses hitched to it. She sat there with her hands in her lap as if she anticipated going somewhere. Her bonnet was on crooked and an expression of expectation livened her face.

She was whistling, a tuneless sound. Strange, Jake thought. Martie had never been a whistler except to summon the dogs. She smiled at him again. He could see now that it was not her old smile, but a simpleton's expression. An unnatural vacant light glimmered in her eyes.

"Did you find the livestock?" she asked, as if she knew he had not.

"No, nothing." He halted near the wagon, and remaining on horseback, studied her more closely. "What happened, Martie? Injuns? Rustlers?"

"Can we go to town now?" she asked, still smiling. "I put my bag in the back. I don't want to stay here tonight. We have nothing more to offer it."

"Offer what?" he asked, more confused than he'd been when he'd driven up and first seen her on the porch. "Martie, you aren't making any sense. For god sakes, what happened here last night?"

Martie's smile vanished but the unnatural light remained in her eyes. That chill crawled along Jake's spine again.

"It came last night, Jake, seeking its price for what we've taken," Martie said. "That's what my dream had been telling me. It was coming. It was just like Virgil described it. Taller than the treetops. Powerful as a cyclone. Lord, I'm so glad you took Tommy to town. I wouldn't have wanted to lose him, too."

"Martie, you're talking nonsense," Jake began, dismissing the chill in favor of the more familiar impatience.

"Not nonsense." Martie's vacant smile returned. "Virgil was right, you know. It exacts a price. The Wendigo or the spirit of the prairie or whatever it is. It exacts a price for what we take. Last night we paid, Jake."

He opened his mouth to argue with her. Then, seeing there was nothing useful to say, he closed it. This woman was only a shade of his Martie, of the pretty, vital girl he'd married, of the woman who'd worked side by side with him to build their homestead. They'd paid all right.

"Can we go now?" Martie started to whistle again.

Jake glanced around at the homestead once more. The sense of being watched had returned. It was not as strong as it had been out on the bluff, but something was out there studying them.

Without another word, Jake hitched the horses to the wagon. His hands shook as he fumbled with the harness buckles, but he tried not to think about what might be out there, what might have driven off all that was dear to him. When the harnesses were secured, he turned the wagon toward town, and put as much distance between the place and them as he could, as fast as he dared. When they arrived in town, they rented a house.

Jake found a job at the livery stable. Martie became known for her excellent apple pies, her serenely vacant smile, and her tuneless whistle.

The Wilson homestead fell into ruin, and the land was bought up, becoming part of a large cattle operation. The small spring-fed stream that Martie and Jake could never agree on a name for became known as Whistling Woman Creek.

- The End -

Author's Note:
When I was about nine years old, I saw a black-and-white TV production of Algernon Blackwood's famous short story, "Wendigo." Poor though the production was, even to my unsophisticated eyes (it was done on a sound stage without the benefit of special effects), the show scared the bejeebers out of me. I always wondered if there was a spirit such as the Wendigo to protect the forest, why wouldn't there be a spirit to protect the prairie? Perhaps there is. Why else did so many hardy pioneer women go mad when left alone on the windswept prairie?

Dreams of the Dead
By Barbara J. Baldwin

ightning flashed as I stood mesmerized at the window. The radio crackled in the background, intermittent spurts of a voice warning that the storm was turning in on itself and residents needed to beware. I lit a candle in case the electricity failed as it often did during these summer storms. Stepping onto the deck of the lake house, I noticed a sudden drop in temperature as the wind whipped through the wood railing, swinging the hammock wildly and causing a patio chair to crash into the table. The waves splashed against the rock front of the dam not far from where I stood. Constant pressure against my back felt as though some unknown force was pushing me. Where did it want me to go?

Suddenly I had the same unsettled feeling—off to the side somewhere, just out of reach—that had often plagued me lately. I would concentrate and nothing happened. I would try not concentrating, hoping it would float into range where I could see it, try to capture it with words, but it was like I was dreaming while awake. Something I couldn't get my hands on was there, poking, probing, and making me angry. Like the dream you remember ever so briefly upon waking, but before you can speak it out loud, it disappears as though never there in the first place. Maybe I was trying too hard. Maybe if I just let loose and opened my mind...What exactly was I looking for?

Words lingered—*come with me—dream—dream— over here.* What did they mean?

My stomach ached, knotted so tight I thought I would get sick. I closed the door on the rain, hoping to shut out the rumbling in my brain, but it only got louder. The feeling of impending disaster was unlike anything I had ever experienced.

I lay down on the couch and shut my eyes, trying to relax and let the calmness come, the peace I needed. But it wasn't there tonight. Maybe it was the storm. Maybe it was my own uneasy feeling that something was about to happen and I couldn't stop it.

* * *

"You finally decided to find out what the rumors are all about?" The old man spoke from the edge of the road.

"I haven't lived here long," I replied, confused. I looked around at the unfamiliar landscape, thinking I must be dreaming. "I didn't know there were rumors."

He turned without another word and walked away down the road. I couldn't see where the road went. It just stretched before me. I started walking behind him, wondering why I could be so trusting and feel no fear.

We walked past houses and yards, and trees that for some reason weren't blooming even though it was summer. The limestone of the houses had a greenish appearance, as though moss or lichen had grown on the sides. Faint light glowed from the windows, but I saw no people.

I couldn't see enough of the road to know where we were going. It was the strangest feeling, walking on a road to nowhere, yet the road just kept going and my feet just keep walking.

Eventually the road turned and I saw the cemetery.

"See, they had dreams." The man waved his hand towards the tombstones, but I didn't understand what he was talking about.

I blinked, trying to make sense of the scene as I looked through the gloom. At first I thought they were tall stems of grass, swaying in the breeze, but there was no breeze that I could feel. Just an oppressive weight bearing down on me. It was difficult to breathe.

I looked harder and realized that people were there, in the cemetery, but they weren't real people. Where eyes should have been, only hollow sockets remained. Their thin, shapeless bodies swayed back and forth like river grass in a gentle current. Stems—translucent and gray—floated around them, waving like arms. Beckoning me.

My heart pounded hard and my ears rang. I had no choice except to move towards them, letting them wrap me in their embrace. Long, reedy stems wound around me, tangling my legs and hugging my arms to my sides. *We had dreams, too. Why?* The words gurgled eerily as though spoken from a great distance, or underwater. I struggled, my lungs burning, gasping for breath and choking.

"Are you crazy? Come inside," my husband yelled from the doorway, just arriving home from a business trip.

I coughed, spitting out water as I looked around in a daze. I was on our deck in the middle of a thunderstorm. I had no idea how I had gotten there and why I would be foolish enough to stand in a torrential downpour with lightning cutting hot, yellow slashes across the sky. The broomstick skirt I wore was soaked and wrapped so tightly around my legs I could hardly walk. The sleeves of the jacket over my shoulders were knotted, pinning my arms to my sides. I stumbled towards the door, shivering from the rain and the sudden drop in temperature.

Why? The wind whistled the word under the eaves.

I jerked my head around, searching, but the lake was hidden behind the curtain of rain.

* * *

The dreams became worse. At least I called them dreams, for I had no other way of categorizing them. What would you call the vivid impressions of old limestone houses, tall trees with barren branches, even dirt roads meandering past fields and going nowhere? Places I had never been before; a ghostlike town I had never visited.

In the dreams, I ended up at a cemetery, staring at strange markings on tombstones that I couldn't quite make out. And always—that whistling, whispering sound echoing inside my head, murmuring over and over again. *Why?*

I would wake up drenched, choking on my own spit, wrestling against the invisible web that tangled around my limbs and held me immobile. One night my husband found me on the deck, staring out at the lake. I was soaked to the bone and shivering, but the deck was dry and the stars were out.

"They're out there," I said, sucking great gulps of air into my lungs, feeling as though I had been holding my breath.

"Who's out where?" he asked.

I shook my head and shrugged. "I don't know. But they're living out there just as sure as you and I are living here."

My husband scoffed. "Are you coming back to bed?" He walked inside, ignoring what I had said.

I looked once more at the lake where a glimmer of light rippled across the surface. I quickly scanned the sky for the moon but there was none. My eyes caught the light ripple again and then it was gone.

They went to bed for the night. But I had no idea why I thought that.

* * *

The dreams became so troubling that I called in sick to work and spent days on the computer, then at the library, looking up everything I could find about the lake. Even though records indicated the dam would prevent damaging floods, controversy surrounded the building of it, like it had in so many places on the Plains. The government paid the people more than enough money to relocate, but families were angry, knowing their homes would become the bottom of the lake bed.

One article noted that the dam hadn't been completed quickly enough because in 1932, four days of storms had dumped over eighteen inches of water on the area, causing the worst recorded flood along the lower Missouri River.

There were other articles on the flood but I only skimmed them as I printed them off until one headline jumped off the microfiche page at me: "Remains Moved from St. John's Cemetery at Enrube—Last Step Before Lake Is Formed." I quickly scanned the article, jotting notes about the new location of the remains of the people once buried at St. John's.

The Green Meadows Cemetery, as it had been renamed in 1939 when all the bodies from St. John's were moved there, actually sat on a rather high hill in another county. I drove up the dirt road and parked near a broken-down gate. The place was untidy and overgrown. Granite markers tilted at odd angles. Some lay flat on the ground, as though they had hurriedly been tossed around with no real care.

I squatted down by one stone, brushing the weeds aside and trying to read the name that was almost weathered away. The neglect made me wonder if Herman Kratts really lay under this stone bearing his name.

Not here. You know where. The words fluttered across my mind as my fingers touched the letters. I watched, stunned, as my shaking fingers moved of their own volition, tracing first the M, then the K. Moisture seeped from the granite, beads of water running in tiny rivulets down the coarse surface. I clutched my hand into a fist, my fingers icy cold as I pulled away from the gravestone.

I went to the shoreline that afternoon, staring out over the turbulent water. Another storm was brewing. The waves crashed on the shore, whitecaps crested and rolled, the water rushing up over my feet. I took a step and then another.

Come with me—over here.

Something…I closed my eyes, trying to locate that just-out-of-reach entity. I took a deep breath, feeling myself falling, deeper and deeper.

They welcomed me, their thin, reedy arms floating open to slide along my face. There were others today, two more who floated in my dreamland like the others—weightless, ghostlike, with wide, sightless eyes. They didn't seem to mind that they were here in this gloomy town where the sun barely filtered through the murkiness.

Mark, Kane. The words echoed silently inside my mind. In the dreams no one ever talked and yet I knew what they were saying. The names weren't familiar, their faces not ones I had seen before. *M and K,* but that thought didn't stay with me long enough to understand.

We took them because our own dreams were taken away.

I didn't know whom they were talking about. I opened my mouth to ask and began choking.

* * *

"Why would she try to drown herself?"

The voice came from a great distance. I tried hard to concentrate on the words but they sounded all jumbled together. My lungs burned; my arms felt weighted down. I opened my eyes but the glare of white light proved too bright. When I tried to shield my eyes, bindings cut into my wrists and blocked the movement, much like the arms that had earlier caressed me. Then it had been in welcome. Now it was restraint.

My husband said boaters found me in the lake as they tried to reach shore before the storm. He kept asking me why I was there, and I kept telling him I didn't know. If I confessed to hearing beckoning voices, would they think I was crazy and never let me out? Did I want them to? Would the dream call to me again and take me within its arms so deep that I could never resurface?

By the second day they had removed the restraints, but I remained behind locked doors. The doctor came by once a day. The psychologist stopped at least twice, fascinated with my story, which I told reluctantly. Of course it was unsubstantiated. The lake had covered the town of Enrube and the surrounding acres for most of the last seventy years.

I had been there, I insisted. I saw people. I walked past the houses.

Nobody actually *lived* down there, for God's sake, the psychologist stated. Finally I agreed with him, because I knew it was the only way I would ever be released.

That night, alone in my room, I read the newspaper. There had been a double drowning at the lake the day they found me. The bodies hadn't been recovered. Pictures of the two young men were eerily familiar but what caused my breath to catch were the names—Mark Jones and Kane Norris. *Mark and Kane—M and K*. The words screamed in my brain. I finally understood.

* * *

The movers had loaded the last box. As I walked off the deck towards the car, I handed the keys to the realtor. In my hands, I held the newspaper clippings and photocopies.

My husband reluctantly walked with me down to the lake shore. Could I do this? Would it put an end to what the doctors had called nightmares, but which still plagued my nights, still caused my husband to lose sleep as he watched over me to make sure I stayed in the house?

I knew there were people down there, entities that somehow continued even though they were dead. They wanted me, lured me down there to be with them. I had almost gone. I don't know why. I'll probably never understand, just as my husband really couldn't accept what happened even when I told him the story. But he was willing to see this through to the end, just as I knew I had to.

The day was calm and mild for early October. When we reached the shore there was barely a ripple across the surface of the lake. I knew I wouldn't be able to see the lights under the water from here and perhaps that was best.

I opened the newspaper article and looked at the pictures of Mark and Kane. I wished them peace as I shredded the paper and let the breeze lift the pieces from my fingers. They floated out across the water.

Then I slowly unfolded the photocopy of the newspaper article from July 13, 1939. I reread the story about two young women from the old town of Enrube who had accidentally drowned when the temporary earthen dam was blasted open to redirect the river and create the lake where I stood.

"Perhaps they are happy, now that they have Mark and Kane," I whispered. I cried for them as I tore up the article and, as before, let the breeze carry it away.

Our dreams were taken...and so we took them.

- The End -

Lost in the Fog
By Jerri Garretson

Maria was overjoyed when Seth McClintock came back to Pennsylvania from Fort Larned and proposed to her. He was a good man and she'd waited for him, thinking he'd be ready to settle down when he came home.

She married him without hesitation, but she soon realized that he would never get over his hankering for the wide open spaces he'd grown to love as a soldier stationed in Kansas. After he received the letter from that Hiram Williams fellow who'd stayed there when he got out of the army, telling Seth about the Starnes place and how he could get it so cheap, there was no end to his talk of going West again. They could own far more land than they could ever hope to have in Pennsylvania.

Maria liked being near her family and couldn't see much advantage in leaving her loved ones and most of her belongings behind. She didn't share her bridegroom's yearning for his own piece of land but she finally gave in to get some peace. She knew life on the prairie would be hard and lonely, but she loved Seth. She'd be a good wife and make the best of it.

After the long days of traveling on stifling trains, she was tired and grimy when they pulled into Larned and unloaded their satchels and trunks. No matter how bleak and small the town looked, she had to start looking at it as home. It wasn't as though they would be homesteading. Lands around Larned had been claimed and settled. She hoped that Seth was right when he insisted they would prosper now that the railroad ran all the way to Colorado. More folks were moving out West every day.

While Seth made the arrangements at the bank, Maria looked over the stores and dusty streets. People seemed friendly enough but when she told them they were buying the Starnes place, they would draw a breath and look away.

"Well, now, that's right nice," one woman said, twisting her handkerchief nervously, eyes darting around to see if anyone was listening. It didn't sound as though she thought anything of the kind. "Just you be careful out there, you hear?"

By the time Maria screwed up her courage to ask why, the woman was gone, hurrying down the street as though she had an important engagement.

Back at the hotel, a tall, neatly-dressed woman caught her arm as she came through the door. "Mrs. McClintock, might I have a word with you?"

Surprised, Maria nodded. The woman guided her to a small sitting room and offered her a chair.

"Mrs. McClintock, we haven't been introduced, but I'm Abigail Jacobs, the school teacher," the woman said. "Please just call me Abigail." She looked quickly toward the door, then perched stiffly on the edge of a chair. Before Maria had a chance to answer she went on. Her cultured voice was low, almost a whisper, but it carried a sense of urgency.

"Folks here were glad someone was coming out to buy the Starnes' place, it standing empty and all, but now that you're here, well, we're worried."

"Please," said Maria. "Tell me why. Everyone in town seems frightened."

"I might just as well come right out with it," the woman said. "The place is cursed."

"Surely you don't really believe that," protested Maria.

There was a long moment of silence, as though

Abigail was trying to decide how to convince her. "I'd never known a place to be haunted by the spirits of the dead, but the Starnes' place is. They say Carrie Starnes was an innocent girl who lost her mind on the lonely prairie, out there living with no one but James, her husband, and Ethan, his brother, but not all of us believe it.

"We buried them out there on a small rise by the river, under that little grove of trees, because the preacher wouldn't allow them in the church cemetery. Said after what they did, they couldn't be buried in sacred ground. Said they were damned souls. They're buried, but folks have seen ghosts out there."

Maria didn't believe in spirits, but the woman's account was unnerving. "What did they do that was so evil, Abigail?" she asked.

"Murder."

The word hung in the air like an ugly thing. Maria was stunned into silence. Abigail glanced nervously at the door, as though she expected someone to dash in and stop her from telling more.

"What happened? Who was murdered? Why won't people just tell us the truth?" Maria finally asked.

"They're scared. Scared the Starnes won't stay on their own land. The Starnes are doomed to haunt until they find someone to take their places."

"How would anyone know something like that?" asked Maria. Her stomach was churning.

"Carrie came into town last fall, the week before the murders. Her mind was not well. She wandered around town claiming that soon after they came out to homestead—her and the two brothers—she started hearing voices. Sometimes she saw shapes when the fog came off the river. The brothers never saw a thing. Least that was what they said.

"Carrie was angry because Ethan complained to James that she was losing her mind. She said the spirits were making all the trouble, that they said someone had to die to take their places so they could finally be free.

"No one knew what to make of her strange behavior and wild talk. James came to town to get her. She made a scene and said she wasn't going back there, that if she did, they would all die. She raved and screamed like a madwoman. James finally had to get her drunk so she'd go back with him. He apologized to everyone in town for her behavior, and most folks felt right sorry for him."

She took a deep breath and let it out slowly. Maria noticed how tightly Abigail clasped her hands.

"It wasn't more than a week later they were all dead. Near as we could tell, James must have found Ethan fighting with Carrie and shot him, but Ethan managed to shoot back and killed them both before he died. Carrie had a knife clutched in her hand when they found her. Ethan had knife wounds on his hands and arms. The townsfolk all thought Ethan had been sweet on Carrie, and maybe he tried to force himself on her. They thought she was just defending herself with the knife, but I'm not so sure."

"But what else would account for it?" Maria asked, eyes wide. By now she was trembling slightly. That poor girl.

"Some say maybe Carrie was attacking Ethan with the knife and he was just defending himself. If you'd have seen her that day…"

Her voice trailed off. Abigail stared out the window for a long moment.

"Isaac Brown went out there to take care of the animals, the four horses, and he got caught in a storm. Had to stay the night in the house. He said he was lucky to escape with his life. He heard voices on and off all night long. He swore there was a man and a woman arguing down by the river. Later, the woman's voice kept saying, low and breathy, 'Come out, Isaac.' He couldn't see much, but later when the storm stopped and the fog started crawling up from the river, he was sure he could see the shape of a woman in the mist."

"Anyone could imagine ghosts where three murders took place," said Maria, trying to reassure herself. It couldn't be true.

"Just be careful, Mrs. McClintock," Abigail warned. "You couldn't get me to stay one night out there. The evening I rode by at sundown was enough for me."

"Are you trying to tell me you've seen the ghosts, too?" Maria asked.

"I don't know what it was...but I saw and heard something. Scared my horse so badly it nearly upset the buggy. Jasper took off like a shot. I didn't have time to investigate, but I wouldn't have wanted to."

She reached out and patted Maria's hand. "You've come such a long way to find a new home. Maybe it would be just as well to wait a little longer and find another place."

"Seth has already bought the place, Abigail, and from what you say, I don't think he could find someone else to buy it now. We'll be all right. We don't believe in spirits." Her brave little speech sounded at least partly convincing, but Maria was having a hard time maintaining her composure. Whether she believed in spirits or not, what would she do if she thought she saw one?

Abigail stood up. "You may not believe in them, but most folks here do, even those that didn't before."

For long minutes after Abigail left, Maria sat alone in the little sitting room. It was a hot summer day, but she was so shaken by what she had heard that she felt herself trembling, shivering as though a cold draft were seeping in and wrapping itself around her.

Seth found her still sitting there. "Maria, you're so pale! Are you ill?" he asked, taking her hands in concern.

"Why didn't you tell me?" she asked. It came out more an accusation than a question.

Seth shook his head. "Tell you what?" He looked genuinely puzzled.

"About the murders. The ghosts. The curse." Saying it made it more real. Tears spilled down her cheeks.

Seth pulled out his handkerchief and dabbed at her eyes. "I thought I told you that's why the land was so cheap, even with the house on it. Too many people out here are superstitious. Who scared you? You don't put any stock in that foolishness, do you? You know I'd never put you in danger."

He was so sure, so strong. She had never believed in departed spirits haunting a place. Abigail's tale had just unnerved her. If there was something strange out on the Starnes place, there must be a natural explanation. She let herself gradually relax as Seth stroked her hair.

* * *

The house was a surprise. Instead of the one-room cabin Maria expected, there was a well-built, three-room home with real glass windows. It stood on a slight rise near a bend in the river. There was a tiny front porch with a rocking chair on it. Sitting there, you could look way out past the river to the far horizon, even see where the Santa Fe Trail stretched out across the plain. Maria was relieved that she couldn't make out the wooden grave markers under the clump of trees, those crude wooden slabs with just a name and the year of death painted on them. She promised herself to put wildflowers on their graves. Did anyone mourn for the dead Starnes?

The largest room had a stone fireplace. The two smaller rooms were bedrooms. They'd have a place for the babies that would bring laughter into the sad house.

The Starnes' furnishings were still there, untouched since the funeral. It all came with the property. Maria wondered how long it would take them to save the money to replace those things. She didn't want to be reminded every minute of the day of the three poor souls that lived there before.

At first Maria was sure that Abigail and all the others who believed the place was haunted were dead wrong, or at the very least, any spirits that might have been there had gone on to the hereafter. The sunny days and balmy summer nights brought no horrors with them. Seth so clearly loved the land that Maria was glad they had come. When no frightening incidents happened, people no longer gave them nervous looks when they went into town. They relaxed, forgetting their fears.

* * *

It was on a cool evening in September when Maria first heard the voices. She was on the porch darning socks by the light of the kerosene lamp she'd set on the little table Seth had made for her. It sounded as though a man and woman were talking down by the river, their voices barely carrying to where Maria sat. She stilled the soft squeak of the rocker to listen. She could only make out a word here and there, not enough to make sense of it.

Don't you touch her...not yet...leave me alone, you dirty cur!

She could see nothing. She sat paralyzed, straining to hear the sounds. Was this how it started for Carrie? Was she going mad, too?

The sounds faded away as Seth trudged back from

the barn. Maybe they hadn't been there at all. It was easy to imagine things in the twilight. Her tense muscles gradually relaxed. She didn't say anything to Seth.

Two nights later, while she stitched the seam of a shirt for Seth and he sat whittling by the fireplace, she heard footsteps on the porch and a soft voice, barely a whisper above the sound of Seth's knife against the wood. *Maria ...Maria...*A woman's voice, right outside the door, soft as a whisper. Was it really murmuring her name, or was it just the sighing of the wind? Did they have a visitor?

Maria rose from her chair and opened the door. Nothing. No one. Only the still prairie night. For once, there was no wind, but a blanket of fog was spreading out from the river. Tendrils of it moved between the cotton-wood trees where the Starnes were buried and reached toward the house. She felt a cold finger trace down her arm. She drew back, heart pounding. Something brushed past her into the house.

"Seth," she whimpered.

He looked up from his carving. "What's wrong?"

"Did you hear anything? Did you hear footsteps on the porch?"

"No," he said, his eyes narrowing. "Did you?"

Maria nodded. "And a voice outside the door." She looked out again. The fog was curling around the house, circling it like something alive that would swallow it up. "There's a fog bank rising from the river. Something came here with it."

She looked around. There was nothing she could see. But she could feel it, oppressive and suffocating, like a cloud of evil that enveloped the room. She rubbed her arms, feeling suddenly chilled. She couldn't speak. She couldn't breathe. She stood there as though turned to stone, afraid to move, afraid to see or hear.

Don't you touch her, you crazy witch!

The man's voice moved past her. She nearly fainted.

Seth moved easily, naturally, and closed the door. Didn't he see the wisps of fog that swirled into the room and scuttled into the corners before they could be shut out? Didn't he hear the voices?

He put a hand on her forehead. "Maria, are you ill?"

Was she? She collapsed in his arms.

Seth brought her tea and honey, stroked her hair and held her hand. What had really happened? She felt safer now, with Seth so close. She still sensed evil in the house but it wasn't some impersonal cloud any longer. She knew there was someone watching her—from the doorway of the bedroom. From over Seth's shoulder. From the window. Waiting.

For what?

She tried to explain to Seth what had happened, what she heard and felt and saw, but the more she talked, the crazier it sounded. Like someone whose mind was disturbed.

Seth had seen and heard nothing.

He told her that she must have been hallucinating. Something she had eaten must have made her ill. Or perhaps it was because she was in a family way. If Maria had been her old self, she would've snorted at that one. No one she'd known began seeing and hearing things just because she was pregnant!

She begged him to leave the place, move into town.

That brought a stern response. "Stop acting like a frightened child. This is nonsense. You just let that schoolmarm scare you. I've a mind to tell her what I think of her," he said. "Get a hold of yourself! I don't want people spreading rumors that my wife is going mad like Carrie Starnes."

"But Seth, there is something evil here," she whispered.

She could barely say the words.

"Then where is it?" he demanded. "Show me."

She couldn't.

* * *

She stared first at the window, then at the ceiling all night, afraid to sleep. A picture formed in her mind of a thick, cold cloud of fog covering her face, smothering her. She huddled against Seth for warmth and comfort, scarcely daring to breathe.

With the morning sun, the oppression lifted. Sunlight streamed across the prairie and in through the windows, burning away all the fog, erasing the ominous events of the night.

Had they really happened?

She watched Seth walk whistling to the barn, could see in his every step how much he loved the open land. She closed her eyes and prayed, "Dear Lord, save us from the spirits of the dead, and save me from becoming a madwoman."

The only evidence she had that what she experienced was real were Abigail's stories. Was she—were all the townsfolk that believed in the ghosts—just spooked by Carrie's ravings and the Starnes' deaths?

In the warm light of day, it was easier to tell herself that if she just acted normal and refused to acknowledge their presence, if she just ignored them, maybe they would go away.

It was not to be.

The weather was strange as fall crept in. More and more the nights brought fog crawling up from the river. Maria tried not to look at it, but in the end, she would be drawn to the window. She began to see wispy figures in the mist. They always rose from the grove of trees where the Starnes were buried. Their vaporous shapes streamed slowly toward the house.

And then they would seep into the walls.

Maria could feel their presence in every room. Sometimes she glimpsed a calico skirt brushing past, or caught the fleeting sight of a black leather boot. Nothing more. But she knew they were there, in her house. The Starnes' house, she corrected herself.

She soon learned not to tell Seth. He didn't see a thing and grew frustrated and impatient with her attempts to convince him. He feared she was losing her mind to the incessant prairie wind as other pioneer women had and seemed to think that showing his temper and stomping around the house would bring her to her senses. He refused to take her into town anymore, stating that he didn't want her fevered mind influenced by gossips like Abigail. He insisted he was only trying to protect her from the frightening gossip.

Seeing the ghosts wasn't the worst. No matter how many times she reassured herself, appealed to the Lord with fervent prayers, or even begged the ghosts to leave, the apparitions returned. It was the faint, whispering voices that truly scared her. They were growing louder. Maria began to make out more words. Over and over, she heard the woman's voice, yearning, pleading, and threatening all at once...*you'll come to me...time...It isn't time...*

Time for what?

She came to believe the ghosts were always there but she could only perceive them when the night was just right. Somehow, the wraiths grew stronger in the mistiness, as though the fog gave them substance.

Their presence was unsettling partly because Maria knew they were ghosts, and partly because she knew their story, knew where their graves lay and why. Out there in the grove were the three graves, each with a simple wooden marker that was weathering and rotting away. Maria never went there anymore. At first, she'd placed flowers by the markers, feeling sad about the tragic tale and the lonely graves out on the prairie with no one to tend them. What had really happened between James, Ethan and Carrie? Had Ethan really accused her of being crazy? And hadn't she acted crazy that last day she went into town? Had Ethan really attacked her, or tried to force himself on her? Or did Carrie attack him?

Well, Carrie could have been interred in sacred ground if she'd truly been blameless in the murders, but folks allowed as how a woman should be laid to rest beside her husband, no matter what he had done. Maria had once stared a long time at Carrie Starnes' grave marker, traced the painted letters and numbers with her finger. To come out here to start a new life and end up beneath the sod, only twenty years old. No babies, no more sunshine. Maybe that was all Carrie really wanted, to share in Seth and Maria's lives.

But then why did Maria have such a sense of doom? Why was she so frightened?

The first anniversary of the Starnes' deaths was coming. She'd found out the date the last time Seth allowed her to go to town with him, the time he got so upset with Abigail that he wouldn't take her back again.

Abigail had accosted her in the dry goods store.

"Are you all right, Mrs. McClintock?" she asked, her eyes searching Maria's drawn face.

Maria had looked away. Abigail might have been her one source of help, but if Seth had found her talking with the schoolteacher, she would have been in for a harsh scolding.

"Something's wrong," Abigail said. "You look so

pale. Not the eager young woman I met last summer."

"It's just the baby," Maria lied.

Abigail expressed both delight and concern, hoped all would go well when the baby came. "But it's something more, isn't it?" she asked.

Just then Seth entered the store. There was no time to tell Abigail anything, even if she'd wanted to.

Abigail gracefully swept past Maria. On her way out the door she whispered, "Be careful. It's been almost a year since they died. Last October 31st."

Maria gave a little start. All Hallows Eve. The night when the spirits of the dead came back to haunt the living.

Except that the Starnes were already there.

* * *

The next evening, she felt the fog wrap itself around the house. She heard the words as if from a great distance, although the ghost was in the kitchen beside her, *Soon! It won't be long now.*

Carrie's ghost. She knew it must be Carrie.

Later that evening, as she sat by the fire, trying not to let Seth see how she was shaking, Carrie spoke close to her ear, softly, invitingly, *Come out. Come with me.*

Don't go out in the fog! Don't let him go out. Never go out in the fog. The man's voice was clear, urgent, warning her.

The voices ceased. Maria did not move.

When Seth hoisted himself out of his chair and said he'd go fetch some firewood, Maria persuaded him to stay in until the morrow.

From that day, the oppressive evil in the house seemed to trail after her like an invisible cloak. She sensed a rising menace from the unseen presence, but her husband never mentioned a thing. The ranch was thriving under his capable hands and he took pride in his growing herd of cattle.

Maria tried to keep a cheerful demeanor, to push the ominous presence from her thoughts and concentrate on putting up preserves, quilting and knitting socks. Each time the fog rolled off the river, she found a way to keep Seth by her side while she prayed that she could outwit or outwait the evil. She was certain now that it was Carrie—Carrie who whispered to her to come out. Was she still mad? What did she want with Maria?

Who was warning her? James? Ethan?

She saw Carrie's hazy figure outside the window at dusk. It stared at her with burning eyes. She put down her paring knife and stared back, defiant. What else was left to her? She felt her mind slowly slipping away.

On October 31st, Seth set off in the buckboard to lay in supplies for winter. Maria begged to go along, but Seth insisted that the long jouncing ride to Larned would not be wise for her, being in a family way. He expected to return the following day.

Maria didn't burden him with tales of the haunting presence. She knew he wouldn't believe her. Did she really think that one day without Seth was going to be different than another? If he stayed home, he'd still have to go soon. The weather was growing steadily colder. And he was right that if she went jolting over those ruts and rocks when she was already feeling poorly, she'd risk losing her baby. They'd already lost one before they came out West and Maria wanted so badly to hold a baby in her arms. She'd seen the apparitions for over a month and no harm had come to her. Surely one night, even Halloween night, without Seth would be all right.

The weather was clear the morning Seth took off, kissing her goodbye and patting the tasty lunch she'd packed for him. "Maybe if I make good time I can get back tonight," he said.

Maria's heart gave a leap of hope. Until that moment, she hadn't allowed herself to feel how much she dreaded the coming night alone with the ghosts.

She busied herself during the day with farm chores, cooked apple butter with the gratifying smell of apples and cinnamon filling the house, and settled down with fresh bread and a hunk of cheese for supper as the last rays of the sun reached across the land.

As it grew darker, the fog began to roll in from the river. Watching from the window, Maria saw the long, thin shapes form down by the trees. They stood out eerily against the dense fog, more clearly defined than she'd ever seen them before. They were struggling. Angry, indistinguishable words shrieked across the prairie. Maria could make out a phrase here and there over the sound of her pounding heart.

Carrie wailing, *they're alone...going after Seth ...first...it's time...*

The man howling, *not again, Carrie...I wasn't blind like James...let them be...*

It must be Ethan. Maria felt a small flicker of hope. He'd seen Carrie's madness in life. Would he protect the living from her now?

Carrie yanked herself free, lifted above the spreading fog and streamed toward Maria. As she came closer, her shape took on more distinct form. Hair floated around her dead white face. Her eyes burned darkly. And this time, she had a knife.

It's time...Seth...Seth...

Maria's heart nearly stopped. She couldn't breathe. What did Carrie want with Seth? He was safe in town at the hotel. Unless he really was on his way home. Terror for Seth choked her.

The door flew open and banged against the wall. Carrie stood in the doorway, cold tendrils of fog streaming from her. The air in the house turned to ice.

Maria screamed.

Get out of my house, Carrie shrieked.

Ethan swirled up the porch steps and dragged Carrie away. She lunged for Ethan with the knife. It passed through him.

That won't hurt me anymore, Carrie, he growled.

Carrie broke free and skimmed swiftly along the fog bank toward town. Toward Seth.

Ethan surged after her.

Maria let out a low moan. "Dear God, protect my Seth," she prayed, and sank to her knees.

* * *

It was late afternoon when Seth finished loading the wagon. He tucked his last purchase into his jacket pocket. He knew Maria would be delighted with the pretty gold locket he found for her. They'd have a picture of their baby taken and she could wear it over her heart.

He was glad he hadn't subjected her to the long, hard wagon ride, but he'd be even happier when he was home with her. He hadn't wanted to let on he was worried about leaving her alone. It wasn't because of those silly ghost stories, but Maria hadn't been feeling well lately. He couldn't imagine what he'd ever do without her.

Seth was heading for the hotel when Abigail accosted him. She actually grabbed his sleeve. "You didn't leave her out there, did you?" she asked, eyes wide, her voice filled with fear.

Seth brushed her fingers off his arm. "What are you talking about?" he asked. "It's only one night. She'll be fine."

"But it's a year since the murders," Abigail pursued.

"They'll be there."

"Who will be there?" he asked, thinking to himself that here was another woman crazed by life on the plains.

"The ghosts," she said, her voice insistent. "She's in danger. Don't you know the story?"

"Of course I know it," he said, irritation creeping into his voice. "That's why I got the land so cheap. Superstitious folk said the place was cursed. I don't put stock in evil spirits and I've never seen any on my land. I'm sick and tired of hearing malicious tales that get my wife upset. I've got half a mind to pull up the grave markers and burn 'em."

Abigail drew in her breath sharply and put her hands on her heart. "Go home, Mr. McClintock. Your wife needs you."

He strode past, pretending to ignore her, but a nagging worry grew at the back of his mind. He didn't think Maria was in danger from any Starnes ghosts, but what might a woman do who claimed to hear voices and see things that weren't there? She didn't talk about it much anymore, but he'd seen that haunted look on her face almost nightly.

Finally, after a long moment of contemplation, he got back on the buckboard to head for home. Starting now, he wouldn't reach the house until late.

Night fell quickly. As he tried to follow the trail in the dark, the fog began to roll up from the river. It wasn't long before he was driving through a thick curtain of mist and he no longer could tell where he was going. He pressed on for awhile, but he wasn't sure he was going in the right direction and the horses were acting skittish. Finally, he admitted to himself that he was lost, or at least lost as long as the fog surrounded him. By the time the sun came up and burned it off, he'd probably discover he knew where he was. He had little choice but to tie up the horses and bed down for the night.

Toward morning, Seth woke up gasping. Hands gripped his neck and a weight pressed on his chest. Struggling to breathe, he flailed his arms, trying to find a way to throw off his unseen opponent. His hands passed through empty but bone-chillingly cold air. His lungs burned.

He caught a murky glimpse of burning eyes and a glint of metal. With the strength of utter desperation, he dodged the knife but the viselike grip held him. His breath was failing and he knew death was coming when suddenly he was wrested free by a second unseen force. It dragged him from the wagon and dropped him at the foot of a tree. Before he passed out he saw churning turmoil in the dim fog, vaguely human shapes grappling violently, and heard an unearthly woman's voice scream, *you won't save her!*

When Seth regained consciousness just before the sun came up, an overwhelming sense of terror flooded him. In the dim light, he could see his overturned wagon. All his goods were scattered. The horses were gone. His neck was bruised and his chest hurt. He scrambled to his feet and ran blindly.

Seth didn't get far. He stumbled on a rock and fell into a creek. The cold water brought him to his senses. The ghosts were gone. He struggled his way to the opposite side, hauled himself onto the muddy bank and collapsed just as the first rays of sunlight reached out from the horizon.

It was still misty, though the dense fog was lifting. He could scarcely see across the prairie but he thought a dot in the distance might be the house. My God, what had he left Maria with? Cold fear panicked him. He splashed back across the creek and took off running.

When he got to the house, he found the door ripped

off its hinges. Maria was not inside. His heart was pounding. He called to her, but there was no answer.

He bolted for the barn, berating himself for doubting her, hoping he would find her safe. She was not there.

Light crept over the land. The last of the fog swirled around him as he called Maria's name again and again. When he stopped walking and listened, hoping for any sound from his wife, a man's low voice said distinctly, *Over here.*

Seth could see no one, but the voice came from the direction of the graves. Fearing what he would find, he made his way to the rise by the river and fell to his knees, sobbing. Maria lay on Carrie Starne's grave with a knife-wound in her chest, her face as white as the fog.

Over her stood the transparent figure of a tall, thin man in overalls. He dropped a flower on Maria's chest.

I'm sorry I couldn't save you both, he said, and then he sank into Ethan Starnes' grave.

- The End -

Halloween at the Gates of Hell
By Linda Madl

The ghost awoke slowly, disturbed not so much by the call of Halloween or the loud music that the three young men had brought to the cemetery as by their dark, swirling vortex. He fumbled his way to consciousness, responding to their self-absorption and vanity, their arrogance and pettiness, like a sleeper to the smell of fresh brewed coffee, like a lover to his name on a beloved's lips.

He stretched cold, vaporous limbs into the far corners of the graveyard and yawned with a gaping, vacuous mouth. Welcoming their darkness, he turned toward the three young men. But the light of their fire assaulted him. Momentarily stunned, he shrank back into the shadows.

A bonfire was a rare thing in a cemetery, especially the Lutsville cemetery. Among the century-and-a-half old headstones was no place for mortals to linger after dark, let alone build a fire and commune around it.

But the youths, boys old enough to die in a war, but too young to understand a universe bigger than their egos, had built a roaring blaze and were perched on the tombstones around it, drinking beer. Music reverberated from their vehicle, feeding vibrations into the damp ground and pounding waves through the night air.

The violence of the melody annoyed but inspired the ghost. He pulled himself together and swirled upward to appraise better the extent of the opportunity the youths presented to him.

"So Darren, how did Steve describe what he and Bill saw when they broke into the schoolhouse?" the blond boy with spiked hair asked, crumpling an empty can in his fist and tossing it carelessly over his shoulder. Then he lifted the lid of the rectangular chest at his side and took out another can.

Darren, the long-haired boy wearing a plastic skull on a leather thong around his neck, took a beer out of the chest while his companion held it open. Black polish stained his fingernails, making his hands appear claw-like in the firelight.

Black lipstick marred the lips he spoke through. "Steve said this huuuge red mist, 'a bloody red mist' he called it, formed inside the schoolhouse and chased them outside."

Red mist? How unlike the old school teacher revenant, the ghost thought. They must have antagonized her.

In silent unison, the three youths turned to look uphill at the Lutsville schoolhouse jaggedly silhouetted against the moonlit sky. Clouds towered in the west while the waxing moon hung low in the east. Halloween wouldn't be a moonlit affair much longer. A cold west wind had sprung up, promising to tug the clouds across the starry firmament and shut out the heavens.

The ghost reveled in the perfection of it.

The blond continued, "Steve said it was like the mist knew what was on their minds. It appeared between them and the cloakroom, cutting them off from the door. It moved back and forth. They finally managed to sprint around it and get out."

"Ah, Steve is a coward," jeered the dark-haired boy with an earring, as they all turned back to the safety of the fire. "Ghosts don't understand what anyone is think-ing." "But what if they did understand?" the blond asked. "Wouldn't that be cool?"

"You mean a ghost could like, read our minds?" Darren asked.

"Yeah, like it would know what scares us most," the blond said.

"Suppose that ghost in the schoolhouse knew that Steve can't stand the sight of red ink, let alone anything that looked like blood."

"So the ghost made him think he saw a red mist," finished Darren. "A mist of blood."

"Naw, ol' Stevie is just a coward and it didn't take any mind reading for a ghost to know that," said the boy with the earring. "He was scared so bad after that break-in he wouldn't even come with us tonight."

The ghost knew the pleasure of a smile. How easy and uncomplicated was talk of courage for these young men. Deciding to explore their naive darkness more, to feed on it for a while—since they had brought it to him— he settled on the edge of the firelight, out of sight.

"Yeah, even this chance to meet a girl Satanist couldn't get ol' Stevie to Lutsville again," jeered the skull-wearing, long-haired Darren.

"Steve is only Goth because he thinks it is cool," said the blond youth who'd decorated his eyelids with black diamond verticals. He seemed unaware that the effect made him look more like a clown than anything Gothic.

"It is cool, man," said the earring boy. A gold stud in the center of his bottom lip glittered as he spoke. "But being Goth means more than dying your hair black and helping set up a website dedicated to the dark forces."

"You're freaking right, it is. It's about having the courage to express yourself, to show the world that you won't be defined by them, that you are going to be yourself, wear what you want, listen to the music you like, stay up all night if you want." The blond passionately waved his beer can in the air, slopping gold liquid on the ground.

Disappointed, the ghost shifted in the shadows. The blond's darkness was sincerely rebellious, but hardly rich enough to be worthy.

"So where do you think those Satanists come from who're supposed to celebrate the witches' Sabbath here?" asked Darren, glancing toward the road.

The ghost regarded the long-haired, skull-wearing youth carefully. His soul truly longed for the darkness, but had it the stamina to endure the ordeal?

"They'll be along," said the lip-pierced boy. "Probably around midnight. Shees, it's getting cold out here."

Uncertain about the pierced youth, the ghost rose up and hovered above the fire for a moment, assessing the three again. Then, as repelled by the flame's heat as the boys were by the chill wind, he surged away, gathering himself close into the shadow of the cedars once more.

"Look at the fire!" The clown boy pulled his black leather jacket close across his midriff against the chill. "It's like something is sucking the life out of it."

"We just need more wood," said Darren.

This time the threesome looked downhill toward the impenetrable scratchy shadows of the cedars. Not a one of them moved.

The pierced youth put the last dead branch on the fire. "We've got enough wood for now."

All nodded in ready agreement.

Just as the ghost settled against a weathered obelisk to continue his observation, he felt a tap on his shoulder. The touch sent him eddying into a ghostly curse. A spirit had materialized at his side. Duty called.

"Is this it?" the eager spirit soundlessly inquired. "Will the gate open for me tonight?"

"No," the ghost made known. Being gatekeeper, the

guardian of this portal into the mortal world, was an awesome responsibility. He did not know precisely when the responsibility had become his, nor did he know exactly how he'd come to be the gatekeeper. That was unimportant. He did know he was here because of his sensitivity and his innate timing. Ushering evil into the world was a delicate undertaking.

For not every mortal deserved a ghost. Not every ghost deserved to walk the earth. The conditions had to be complete. The host's vortex powerful enough. The darkness suitably profound. The wraith's dedication to evil sufficient.

"I think not yet, anyway," the ghost silently declared, unconcerned about the spirit's disappointment, but feeling mildly irritated that he might have been awakened for nothing.

The spirit groaned.

"What was that?" Skull-wearing Darren jumped up and stared into the darkness. "Did you hear a moan?"

"I didn't hear anything." The blond glanced around and laughed. "Hey, Darren, you're not going to get spooked on us like Stevie, are you?"

"No, but I heard something," Darren declared, looking around the fire-lit circle with bewilderment on his face. "We're not going to sit here until midnight waiting for them, are we?"

"Why not?" the blond taunted. "I'm willing to see if some goth-a-licious Satanist babes show up."

"Yeah, what else is there to do?" probed the pierced boy with derision. "There're only so many jack 'o lanterns to smash."

"We could go turn some flags upside down at the city hall," offered Darren, but he had settled back onto his tombstone and picked up his beer can. "Or we could go roll some trash cans along Main Street."

"Naw, the police have extra patrols out tonight," said the pierced youth.

"You afraid of getting in trouble with the sheriff again, Ed?" Darren asked, fingering the skull at the base of his throat. "You really don't like Merritt, do you?"

"It's just that my mom and dad believe everything he says," muttered Ed, the pierced lip growing full in a threatened pout. "Especially Dad."

But the ghost saw more than worry about his mother on Ed's mind. Love and resentment tangled there in his youthful psyche. Rebellion and vulnerability. Twisted a bit into more turmoil than the youth communicated with his spoken words. Still, was it enough? Being Goth with a few piercings hardly guaranteed enough darkness to be successfully evil. Quality wickedness required more than black makeup, bad music, dark fantasies, and whining.

Evil required a truly corruptible heart.

"Okay, then. Toss me another beer, Darren," said the blond, with a laugh and a leer. "Let's wait to see if these Satanists turn out to be hot chicks who practice naked rituals."

The ghost shifted restlessly in the shadows, wondering who these Satanists were. The ghost chuckled at the prospect. His slumber had never been disturbed by anything as delightfully bad as naked Satanists.

"There, I heard it again." Darren jumped up, spilling his beer this time. "That sound. But this time it was more like sobbing."

"Shut up, Darren," the blond snapped, turning toward the road. "All I hear is a car coming."

Hopeful, the other two turned away from the fire to watch headlights pierce the darkness. The vehicle turned the corner beyond the school and headed in their direction. Lutsville was a deserted farm town, an out-of-the-way place on the road to nowhere. No one just drove by Lutsville. Whoever was in the car was either lost or had business here.

Against the sky, the youths recognized the outline of a police vehicle.

"Shit, Darren, you didn't tell anybody we're coming out here, did you?" the blond demanded.

"Hell no, not me."

"Just be cool and let me handle this." Ed stood up, threw his beer into the darkness, and tugged nervously on his earring.

"Hello, boys." The car door slammed and a tall figure in law enforcement blue walked toward them. His badge flashed in the firelight.

The ghost rose at the approach of this new mortal, intrigued and appreciative of the potent disturbance the man brought with him.

"Hello, Sheriff Merritt," the threesome chorused.

"Not up to anything I wouldn't do, are you?" The lawman placed his fists on his hips and glanced around at the tombstones as he came to a halt at the firelight's edge. He was a big man who looked like a sheriff should: tall, lean, and sternly handsome. He walked with all the confidence and authority bestowed by his job and he cast a long shadow. It was apparent that he was proud of his position and made an honest effort to do the job well. "Not vandalizing anything, are you? I'd recommend showing proper respect for the dead on a night like this."

"We're just enjoying some fireside talk," Ed said, sticking his hands in the back pockets of his black jeans. Mayhem bubbled inside the boy, and the ghost was alert.

"Yeah, old man Cathart saw the fire and reported it," the sheriff said. He looked from Darren to the blond and then to Ed. "I promised him I'd come take a look. He keeps a pretty close eye on this place since the break-in last month. You three wouldn't know anything about that, would you?"

All three shook their heads.

"What was that, you say?"

"No sir, we don't know anything about any break-in," Darren said, with a wary glance at Ed. No one seemed inclined to mention Steve and Bill and the red mist. "We just like to hang out in the cemetery."

"On Halloween?" the sheriff asked.

"There's nothing to be afraid of," Ed said, obviously unable to keep a note of mutiny from his voice.

"I didn't say you were afraid, or should be." The sheriff appeared more amused than concerned. "You guys don't believe that story going around about naked Satanists, do you?"

Before any of the youths could stammer out an answer, headlights from a car swung around the corner. All four of them turned to watch the car slow at the top of the hill, as if the driver was surprised to see the sheriff's cruiser and Ed's battered black Escort in front of the schoolhouse. Then the vehicle sped up, passing the school and the cemetery in a cloud of dust. At the bottom of the hill, the red taillights disappeared around the curve to the bridge.

"That looked like your mom's car, Ed," the blond blurted.

"No, it didn't." Ed's words were clipped and defensive. "What would my mom be doing out here? It's just somebody who's lost."

What an interesting twist. The ghost undulated in delight. Goth-a-licious.

The fire flickered.

The sheriff looked pointedly at the flames. "Looks like you boys are about out of firewood." Then he gave each of them a long measured stare. "Why don't you put out the fire and clear out of here before you get yourselves into trouble?"

It was an order, not a question.

Working swiftly under the eye of the sheriff, the three youths doused the fire with the ice from the ice chest, scattered the embers, and carried the chest to their car. Ten minutes later they drove over the hill and out of sight.

"They're gone!" complained the spirit. "You let my chance at the world get away."

"Have patience," the ghost soothed. This was where his intuition would pay off, he hoped.

The sheriff lingered, glancing around the cemetery and then walking back up to his vehicle, where he called in to the dispatcher. The dash lights cast a grim, green glare on his face. He would be taking a few minutes break, he told her, and signed off. Then he switched off the lights and waited in the darkened vehicle.

It wasn't long before the car that had driven by earlier returned. It pulled in this time, turned out its lights, drove past the sheriff's vehicle, around the schoolhouse, and parked in the back. Without turning on his lights, the sheriff started the cruiser and followed the car, parking beside it out of sight of the road.

Undaunted by the loss of the young men and their darkness, the ghost swirled along the ground, allowing the October breeze to aid him and the spirit to drift nearer to the two vehicles.

A red-haired woman wearing tight blue jeans and a loose sweater climbed out of the car, ran around the sheriff's cruiser, and climbed in.

The ghost with the clinging spirit followed her.

"Was that Eddy's Escort?" she asked, breathless from running between the cars or from surprise; it was difficult to be sure which.

The sheriff didn't seem to care or to listen to her question. He grabbed her by the back of her neck, hauled her across the seat toward him, and kissed her, long and hard. She didn't protest.

When he released her, the sheriff chuckled. "Yep, it sure was your little Eddy's car. He was out here drinking beer and waiting with his buddies for those Satanists to show."

"Damn, I should have known he'd come around a place like this," the woman muttered, more to herself than her companion. "Did he recognize my car?"

"I don't think so," the sheriff lied.

The ghost closed his eyes and shrugged, like working his way into a favorite garment. How he savored lies. The sheriff desired the woman in tight jeans, and he would tell her anything to ensure her continued favor—her presence.

"How long do we have?" she asked, moving closer to the sheriff.

"Not long," he murmured. "I'm on break. Where's Ed's dad?"

"Big Ed is working the late shift, but he'll be home by 11:30," she said, just before planting her mouth on the sheriff again.

Over the next several minutes the mostly silent interior of the cruiser grew hot, and steamy. Hands fumbled with clothing, lips sought sensitive skin, and sighs labored, heavy with lust.

"Let's go." The spirit clutched at the ghost. "There's nothing here for me."

The ghost refused.

When the couple finally pulled apart, the sheriff seemed more frustrated than satisfied. He wanted this woman with more than just his loins.

Ah, frustration. Dissatisfaction, more than the mere physical kind. The kind that threatened the purity of the heart. Deep, lacerating discontentment and angry hopelessness, the kind that could move a man to do things he wouldn't ordinarily do. The ghost was jubilant.

"What's the matter?" the woman asked, pulling her sweater back into place.

"You know what's the matter," the sheriff said, leaning back against the seat, but without taking his arms from around her. "I hate this. I hate not having you. I hate pretending. I hate sneaking around like we should be ashamed. There must be a way for us to be together without all the mess—"

"You mean a nasty divorce," she said, staring out the windshield. "If we're lucky, that's all it will be. Big Ed is not a man to just let go. He'll drag your reputation and mine through the mud. He'll make life hell for Eddy."

"Like he doesn't now?"

She shook her head and began to cry.

"Don't, dammit," the sheriff ordered.

Ah, more frustration. Ecstatic, the ghost surged around and over the cruiser.

"Don't cry. I'll think of a way to fix it. I will," the sheriff vowed, his thoughts already full of men he knew, men who could make the world change. Mysterious disappearances. Unexplained deaths. Such things happened all the time.

"It's so cold in here," she said, crossing her arms over her breasts.

He released her long enough to start the engine and turned on the heater; then he held her in his arms until it was time to say goodbye.

After another lingering kiss, he watched her start her car and drive off, not turning on the headlights until she had reached the crest of the hill. Why shouldn't they have happiness together, like other people? Why should one bastard stand between them and a future together? He'd worked hard in the military and to earn his way through the police academy. He'd put everything into becoming a good law enforcement officer and to win the office of sheriff. Now, when possible happiness with a woman presented itself, why should all of his efforts be threatened by one human being?

The sheriff took a deep breath. What was he thinking? He forced murderous thoughts from his mind. He was a lawman. He did not plot people's deaths. He protected and served. He forced himself to check in with the dispatcher, but he only half heard the reports of Halloween mischief.

The murderous thoughts were back. It could look like a carjacking. A mugging gone bad when Big Ed drove away from the remote casino.

Why should he and she settle for brief glimpses of happiness when one less person, one less poor excuse for a human being in the world was all that kept them apart? He, the sheriff, would be the last person anyone would suspect of hiring a murderer.

There were those who would be glad to see Big Ed gone. The man was a bully. A braggart and a clod.

Still, the sheriff swallowed hard. He was thinking murder, for God's sake. Murder. No, there had to be another way.

The ghost sighed. The sheriff had a strong soul, yet his heart wavered. The ghost turned to the spirit. "This is it, my friend. This is your pass. Use him well. Guide this mortal. Give him what he needs to do what he wishes, and you will make your way successfully in the world."

The grateful spirit took a deep breath and nodded. "Yes, I will. I swear."

Then the ghost summoned his strength—his ordained power to initiate evil into the mortal world—but he refused the option of visibility. This was not the time to be seen. Once his power was in hand, he knocked on the cruiser window—for evil always asks for admittance.

At the sound of rapping on his cruiser door, the sheriff, who'd just finished checking in with his dispatcher, hesitated. He switched on all the cruiser's exterior lights, looked out the window, scanned across the hood to the other side, and studied his rear view mirrors. He saw nothing. Shrugging, he threw the cruiser into gear.

The ghost rapped again, forcefully this time. This mortal was too good to let get away. This mortal was too vulnerable to deny him.

The sheriff paused again, his foot on the brake pedal. Those kids wouldn't have circled around to come back and pull a stunt on him, would they? They wouldn't dare. He put the cruiser into park, opened the door, and walked around the car.

While he was peering underneath, the ghost motioned the spirit into the vehicle. The spirit flowed inside, coiled up in the back seat, and settled himself with a satisfied expression.

Outside the vehicle, the sheriff muttered, "Well, I'll be danged if I see anything."

He climbed into the cruiser, put it in gear, and turned toward town.

Suddenly, murder plans, so easily dismissed earlier, jumped back into his mind, growing more detailed and plausible by the minute. More satisfying and logical. It could be done very simply. He had all the necessary connections. He knew how to launder the payment. The benefits would be great.

It never occurred to him how strange it was that he, a proud, honest lawman, was plotting the death of another—for the best of reasons, of course.

Dust swirled up into the night as the cruiser reached the top of the hill. From the rear window, the spirit waved to the ghost. The gatekeeper of the Lutsville cemetery extended his limb above the dust and waved back. He turned back to the graveyard and his resting place, gratified that his duty was done—for this Halloween anyway.

- The End -

The Authors of Trespassing Time

Back: Jerri Garretson and Barbara Baldwin.
Front: Linda Madl and Sheri McGathy.

Photo by Peter W. Garretson

Barbara J. Baldwin
Barb was born in California, married in Iowa and now resides in Kansas. The years in between were lived in most of the southern states and three years in Japan because her father was an Air Force pilot and they moved on an average of every three years. That probably explains why she still loves to travel and explore new places and has each of her manuscripts set in a different locale.

She has written practically all her life, beginning with journals of family vacations. She is now published in poetry, short stories, essays, magazine articles, teacher resource materials, and full-length fiction. Of course, her writing is sandwiched in between playing a little golf, traveling, and a job with the 8th Judicial District Community Corrections, where she writes grants.

She also enjoys writing Christmas story cards for family and friends. When she tried to "retire" after five Christmases, her friends clamored for more, so she began an "encore" series which continues today.

Barb loves talking almost as much as she loves writing, and has been a teacher for grades K-8. While in education she made over 100 presentations at state and national conferences on material she had developed for the classroom. Later, during 14 years with public television, she was on air as a program moderator and during annual pledge drives. She has a BS in Education and an MA in Communication and has taught public speaking classes at the college level.

Samples of Barb's stories and her current books can be viewed at her website:

http://www.authorsden.com/barbarajbaldwin

Jerri Garretson

Jerri grew up in Manhattan, Kansas. After graduating from the University of Kansas, she traveled the world with her husband, an army attorney, for 24 years before returning to Manhattan when he retired from the military. They lived and worked in Germany, Japan, Hawaii, Puerto Rico, Kentucky, Illinois, and Virginia.

Jerri holds an M.Ed. in educational technology from the University of Hawaii, and is a reference librarian at Kansas State University's Hale Library. Previously, she was the head children's librarian at Manhattan Public Library and children's library services consultant for North Central Kansas Libraries System in Manhattan, Kansas. She was the first public affairs officer for the U.S. Army Corps of

Engineers Japan District at Camp Zama, Japan.

Her published writing includes newspaper and newsletter features and columns published in Germany, Japan, and the USA, and articles in national children's magazines such as Highlights for Children, Child Life and The Friend. Many of the articles are illustrated with her photographs. She is a member of S.C.B.W.I.

In 1997, she founded Ravenstone Press to fill a need she saw for more stories about Kansas, the Great Plains and the prairie. She is the author of six books, including the young adult mystery and ghost story, THE SECRET OF WHISPERING SPRINGS.

Visit the Ravenstone Press website at:
http://www.ravenstonepress.com

Linda Madl

Linda is a Manhattan, Kansas, writer who collects ghost stories. She first became interested in ghost lore when she was attending summer school in Exeter, England.

One evening she heard a broadcast of a radio host and an English lord waiting in the manor house for the appearance of the family ghost. She expected them to reveal the joke at any moment, but they were serious. Astonished, she listened closely as they told the story behind the haunting.

The ghost never appeared but the host and the lord were not dismayed. They would try again. For the first time, Madl realized that there were credible, sophisticated people who truly believed in ghosts. That summer she began collecting ghost story books: tomes of true ghost stories.

Over the years she has acquired more than 100 volumes of ghost tales from across the country and abroad. Two books are ghost stories from Fort Riley, Kansas, where she was a ghost tour guide for two years.

She is a member of the American Ghost Society. However, she is not a ghost investigator. Though she remains a skeptic, she wants to record Manhattan, Riley and Pottawatomie county area ghost lore for a book.

"I consider ghost stories and folklore part of our heritage and culture," she says. "Also, recording testimony from witnesses to the unexplained is an important part of observing supernatural phenomena."

Her work includes ten novels, eight novellas, several short stories, and nonfiction articles. The settings of her books are as varied as her travels. England, Scotland, the Rockies, and the Kansas River banks have all served as locales for her historical romances.

Her nonfiction work includes feature stories, book reviews, newsletters, and technical project profiles. She is active in professional and community organizations including the KS Writers, Inc., UFM Community Learning Center, and Novelists, Inc. Currently, she is at work on her eleventh novel.

Born and raised in Kansas, Madl is a graduate of Paola High School and Baker University. She resides with her husband, dog, and parakeet in Manhattan, Kansas. Family, friends, and travel fill her non-writing hours.

Find more information and a list of her book titles at http://www.lindamadl.com or you may contact her at linda@lindamadl.com.

Sheri L. McGathy

Sheri is married and has one grown son. She works in prepress in a graphic design department as a Graphic Arts Coordinator/Copy Editor.

Sheri is a member of The Kansas Writer's Association,

EPIC, and IFWA—Internet Fantasy Writers Association and the Coffee Shop Writers authors' group.

In addition to works within TRESPASSING TIME: Ghost Stories from the Prairie, published by Ravenstone Press, she is the author of the fantasy novels, WITHIN THE SHADOW OF STONE, ELFEN GOLD, and novellas "Thief of Dreams" from the anthology TWILIGHT CROSSINGS, "Where Lies Beauty" from the anthology TWILIGHT CROSSINGS II and "The Ancient One" from the anthology FROM WITHIN THE MIST, all published by Double Dragon Publishing.

Visit her website:
http://www.sherilmcgathy.com

Troy Taylor

Troy Taylor is the author of nearly three dozen books about ghosts and hauntings in America, including HAUNTED ILLINOIS, THE GHOST HUNTER'S GUIDEBOOK and many others. He is also the editor of GHOSTS OF THE PRAIRIE magazine, about the history, hauntings and unsolved mysteries of America. A number of his articles have been published here and in other ghost-related publications.

Taylor is the president of the "American Ghost Society," a network of ghost hunters, which boasts more than 600 active members in the United States and Canada. The group collects stories of ghost sightings and haunted houses and uses investigative techniques to track down evidence of the supernatural. In addition, he hosts a National Conference each year in conjunction with the group, which usually attracts several hundred ghost enthusiasts from around the country.

Along with writing about ghosts, Taylor is also a public speaker on the subject and has spoken to well over 1,000 private and public groups on a variety of paranormal subjects. He has appeared in literally dozens of newspaper and magazine articles about ghosts and hauntings. Taylor has been fortunate enough to be interviewed hundreds of times for radio and television broadcasts about the supernatural. He has also appeared in a number of documentary films, like AMERICA'S MOST HAUNTED, BEYOND HUMAN SENSES, GHOST WATERS, NIGHT VISITORS; television series including MYSTERIOUS WORLDS and MOSTLY TRUE STORIES; and in one feature film, THE ST. FRANCISVILLE EXPERIMENT.

Born and raised in Illinois, Taylor has long had an affinity for "things that go bump in the night" and published his first book, HAUNTED DECATUR, in 1995. For seven years, he was also the host of the popular, and award-winning, "Haunted Decatur" ghost tours of the city, for which he sometimes still appears as a guest host. He also hosted tours in Chicago, St. Louis, St. Charles, Missouri and the "History & Hauntings Tours" of Alton, Illinois. He is the co-founder of the "Bump in the Night Tour Co." with fellow ghost author Ursula Bielski.

Publisher's Cataloging
 Trespassing time: ghost stories from the prairie /
  p.   cm.
 Summary: sixteen eerie ghost stories by Barbara J. Baldwin, Jerri Garretson, Linda Madl and Sheri L. McGathy.

ISBN 0-9659712-6-0 pbk.

[1. Ghosts -- Fiction. 2. Ghost Stories, American 3. Prairie--Fiction. 4. Short Stories 5. Horror Stories.] I. Title.

[Fic] 2005
Library of Congress Control Number: 2004099714

Beyond Imagination
Afterword by Jerri Garretson

Whether one chooses to believe in ghosts or not is influenced by a complex interaction of culture, experience, imagination, and the desire to believe that death is not the end of a human life, or perhaps in some cases, the fear that it is not. Belief in and stories about ghosts seem to be a part of every culture, and those stories serve to explain experiences that often seem to have no other explanation.

People who believe they have experienced ghosts are convinced the spirits are real. Those who don't believe find "scientific" and "reasonable" ways to explain those experiences, though often there is no more proof for their explanations than there is for the experience itself. Hoaxes make it harder to distinguish the truth about ghosts, but disproving a hoax does not exclude the possibility that ghosts exist. Is belief in ghosts only superstition or gullibility? Or is it openness to an experience beyond our daily lives? A faith in the continuance of the soul after death?

Ghost theorists speculate that there are varying kinds of ghost experiences, from those that are truly the spirits of departed souls who have a mission to accomplish before letting go of the mortal realm to some form of "recording" of an event that somehow gets replayed over and over. Experiences with "real" ghosts are usually more fleeting than those described in the stories in this book, which are imaginary.

Why are we frightened of ghosts? They challenge the boundaries of our earthly reality. They threaten our sense of security and force us to look beyond imagination to a world we cannot know, a world that trespasses time.